MW01169055

SPACE COAST

By

Rocky Schneider

© 2002 by Rocky Schneider. All rights reserved.

No part of this book may be reproduced, stored in a retrieval system, or transmitted by any means, electronic, mechanical, photocopying, recording, or otherwise, without written permission from the author.

ISBN: 0-7596-8611-4

This book is printed on acid free paper.

1stBooks - rev. 04/25/02

CHAPTER ONE

The party was bubbling over out of the house on to the large wooden deck not more than twenty yards from the echoing surf of the Atlantic Ocean. A relaxed laid-back air usually permeated the oceanfront community. Beach attire draped many of the seaside inhabitants attending the party. Shorts, sandals, and palm-printed shirts were mandatory to be considered a member of the unconventional clique. Steve Wilcox had just arrived at the festivities. He sold insurance by night and surfed by day. His arm had completely healed from his recent Hammerhead shark attack a few months earlier while surfing. Steve's courage and willingness to assist his fellow man produced the mishap. He'd rescued a young girl from the large fish and was rewarded by receiving fifty-odd stitches at the hospital. The stretch of beach from Daytona down to Vero Beach, Florida, had recently become infamous as the number one shark attack area in the world. Steve's arm could give sore testimony to those statistics.

Someone shouted from the congested rows of people. "Hey, Steve. The arm looks good as new. I saw your picture in the paper. You're a bonafide hero. You out on the waves yet, dude?"

Steve answered, "Yeah, the arm's better than new. I was out shredding the walls last week. Did you see my brother Bobby around?"

The party goer responded, "No, I haven't seen him."

"O.K. Thanks."

Steve was being shuffled by the crowd into the center of the now swelling party. Seas of halter tops and tanned bodies initiated synchronized body movements to the hypnotic sounds of the Rolling Stones "Honky Tonk Woman."

John and Cindy, a couple of successful local artists and hosts of this party were laying out various dishes of seafood and other delicacies for the crowd's pleasure. Octopus casserole, deviled quail eggs, along with an armada of unidentifiable dishes that lined the extended tables against the wall. Cindy spying Steve yelled, "How's your arm, Steve?"

"Oh fine. It's practically healed."

"That's great," she said.

"How are you and John doing?"

"A little hectic, as you can see, but real good. I recently sold one of my paintings that was being exhibited at a national show."

"Wow! That's pretty cool. Congratulations," Steve shouted over the music. "You haven't seen Bobby have you? I was supposed to meet him and his girlfriend, Kim. She has a friend visiting from college for a couple of weeks."

"They're not here yet, but I ran into Kim and her roommate at the grocery store yesterday. We spoke about the party. Are Bobby and Kim trying to set you up with her friend or what?"

1

"Nah. I don't know about that," Steve answered.

"C'mon you dawg," Cindy said with a sly smile appearing across her face. "Hey, I've got to get this food out. Grab yourself a drink and mingle."

"I will, thanks."

John and Cindy were highly successful artists who had started out with nothing except some colored pencils and an old sketch pad. They contrasted sharply with most of the barely average middle class incomes on the barrier beach communities. Both of them are presently members of the small but growing BMW set. Aside from dolphins and manatees, the original inhabitants in town arrived here in the 50s and 60s during the large space program buildups at Cape Canaveral. Today's native residents, like their parents, work as engineers, NASA employees, or are military personnel at Patrick Air Force Base, which is responsible for security around the Cape.

Incomes in this area are modest and until a few years ago, the only ones making any substantial money were doctors and topless bar owners. However, more and more northern snowbirds are purchasing upscale winter homes on the beach. They allow for a welcomed infusion of substantial capital into the area. Your average person in this neck of the woods disseminated from all parts of the country. It's a white middle class beach community supported by NASA, its contractors, and the military base. If either of these groups were to ever pull the plug, there would be nothing left here except surfers, fisherman, and the standard level of Florida elderly retirees. All in all, if you're not attempting to accumulate a million dollar fortune, the barrier island community of Brevard County provides a pleasant quality of life.

Steve Wilcox was raised with that quality of life instilled in him. His dad owns a small orange grove right off Route US1 on the mainland. Its only a stone's throw over the Indian River directly across from the beach. His family always lived well due to the farm's success. Unlike his brother Bobby, Steve chose to leave the family business and try his hand as an insurance agent on the beach. Maybe it was the surfing or the laid-back atmosphere which drew him away from the farm. Whatever the attraction was, the lifestyle fit his personality like a glove. In any event, he was sorely missed on the citrus farm.

The pounding music flushed Steve out of the crowd and onto the large wooden deck outside the house. Finding a vacant spot along the ornately carved railing, he received a gust of strong westerly wind against his back. Winds from the west blowing toward the ocean holds up the waves, creating better surfing conditions. If the winds held overnight, there would be a good chance for some promising walls tomorrow. Steve was anxious to return to his surfing form a few months previous to the unfortunate shark bite that put him out of commission.

A tap came from behind. Turning around, Steve saw his brother Bobby. "Hey, bro. How's it doing?"

"All right," answered Steve. Trailing behind Bobby was his girlfriend Kim and her roommate.

Kim smiled, "This is my roomie from college, Carol Cole."

Caught a bit off guard, Steve nodded. Carol was extremely pretty and shapely. This black girl looked more like Vanessa Williams than Vanessa.

She spoke softly in a reserved manner, "How do you do?"

"Glad to meet you, Carol," responded Steve, who quickly regained his composure and controlled facial expression. Carol's beauty stood out like a perfect blue diamond in a drawer full of common clear gems.

From the begining she appeared to be attracted to Steve, who gave the impression it was more than mutual. If these two were separate bank accounts, the translation of their body language pointed toward a co-mingling of funds. Steve, gazing directly at Carol, asked, "Can I get anyone a drink?"

Bobby cut in, "We're going over, so I'll grab two more beers." He nudged Kim to follow him. They cut through the crowd stranding Steve and Carol in an awkward proximity to one another. Carol spied the recently-healed arm. "Is that the result of your run-in with the Hammerhead?"

"Yes. I guess my brother filled you in. It really wasn't life-threatening because the shark was only an eight footer."

"That would terrify me."

"There's no denying, I was pretty scared."

Carol inquired if Steve was on the board when attacked.

"Yeah, he grabbed my arm that was hanging over the side. I was just real unlucky. I was trying to reach a swimmer in trouble."

"So you're a hero."

"Nah, you would have done the same."

"Was the swimmer O.K.?"

"Yeah. She came on my board and was fine. Have you ever surfed, Carol?"

"No, I wouldn't know where to begin. It does look like fun."

Oh, it's a piece of cake. You'd love it. I'll teach you if you'd like."

"There won't be any big hungry fish around, will there?"

"Nah, we'll stay in the shallows."

"All right."

"Cool. Bobby mentioned you might be going to the beach tomorrow."

Bobby and Kim reappeared through the thickening masses of revelers balancing four beers. Kim, fanning herself with her free hand, asked, "Who wants to get out of this hot party and take a stroll on the beach?" Each person surveyed the complying nods of the others and the party of four filed down the stairway running off the side of the elevated deck. The overgrowth of grassy dunes almost completely camouflaged the narrow, sandy path they chose. Moonlight guided the group over the twenty yards of uneven trail to the flat, open ground at the ocean's edge.

3

The beach was nearly deserted. Not unlike many other sections of the country in recent years, a rash of condos had been built encroaching on the peaceful natural serenity. But tonight the tranquillity stretched up and down the desolate beach.

Swinging north, the party of four walked leisurely in the direction of Cocoa Beach and the Cape. Their distant lights were visible at about 10 to 15 miles away. The strange arrangement of lights illuminating the Kennedy Space Center's different areas was easily distinguishable from the town of Cocoa's.

"Is that the Cape?" Carol asked.

Kim answered, "Yes, that's where the shuttle goes up into Space."

"So you guys get to see quite a few launches?"

"Like clockwork," said Steve. "I think one's scheduled to go up while you're here."

"That would be great," Carol said, turning her attention as she walked out towards the sea. She glanced at Steve who was paralleling her strides. Pointing out over the water she asked, "What are those lights out there on the horizon?"

"Those are shrimp boats. My friend, Al, owns one. I used to work with him on his boat before I became an insurance agent."

"That must have been exciting, but I'd be afraid working out there at night."

"You're too busy with the nets and the catch to be afraid."

Bobby interrupted. "That's not totally true about not being afraid. Steve, tell her about some of the things you've encountered out there at night."

"What things?" Carol questioned, searching Steve's face for an answer.

Bobby spoke before Steve saying, "The guys on the boats like to pretend these incidents never occurred, so no one laughs at them."

"What incidents?" implored Carol.

Steve spoke hesitantly, "We all saw a number of, for lack of a better word, saucer-shaped lights entering and departing the water up into the sky and back."

"You're joking, right?" Carol asked.

"No, I'm dead serious. Their lights could be seen moving underwater. Another interesting thing was when these objects rose into the air, they would hover making absolutely no noise. I also noted these craft never hovered above the altitude of one hundred feet. It was as if they intentionally knew what height would avoid the radar waves produced by those large balls at Patrick Air Force Base right over there."

Carol became very intrigued by the sudden revelations Steve was relating. "How many of these things have you seen?"

"I personally have had four sightings, one being very close. It was a grayish metallic disc-shaped craft. Its metal shined when it crossed too close to the boat's halogen flood lights. Captain Al has caught some on videotape."

"Did you report it to anyone?" Carol wanted to know.

"No. That wouldn't do any good. But I have taken an avid interest in the subject since seeing is believing. You wouldn't believe the huge quantities of data supporting evidence that things are not as they seem.

Bobby stated matter-of-factly, "Cape Canaveral isn't the only reason this area is called the Space Coast!"

"Wow, that's really interesting. I've got an insatiable curiosity when it comes to UFOs."

"I don't care to know about those things myself," blurted Kim.

"If it's true I want to know," Bobby expressed in an more serious tone.

Carol asked Kim, "Aren't you a little curious to see the big picture unraveled?"

"No! I've got enough problems here on earth, thank you!"

Steve's head cocked towards Kim and he said, "Most people are too busy handling life's game of survival to notice out beyond our earthly cage and discover there's a big zoo out there. I feel this phenomena is way too important not to take the time to notice."

Kim did not respond but was quietly hashing over Steve's words.

As they all plodded along sinking into the wet sand, a small fire became visible down the beach. This small beacon was nestled up under a four foot-high walkway with wooden steps which give the public access to the water.

Bobby asked Steve, "Do you think that's Spaceman's fire?"

"Yep," came the immediate reply.

"I don't want to go over there," Kim announced.

"Who's Spaceman?" Carol inquired.

"He's an old surfer who lives on the beach," answered Kim. "This guy's a little strange and I would rather not talk to him."

"To say Spaceman is strange is a gross understatement," Bobby commented. "He's the ultimate cosmic enigma."

Steve continued, "Yeah, he surfs with us on occasion. Most people think he's crazy but if you like stories pertaining to UFOs and aliens, then you've come to the right corner of the Space Coast. If he likes you, maybe we'll get lucky and he'll relate a few tales from his mysterious past. When I first met him, I thought he was nuts, too. After listening to him ramble about his past experiences while we surfed, I'm not so sure. Due to the weird things I'd witnessed on the shrimp boat, I started actually listening closer to what he was saying. The information he told of was just too specific and accurate concerning people and places involved."

Bobby added, "He's either the greatest liar of all time, or the truth is he had access to super secret military installations at one time in the past."

Kim said, "I'd rather not stop. I think he's just a homeless crazy!"

"C'mon honey," groaned Bobby, "we don't even know if that's his fire."

"I'd really like to meet this guy," said Carol showing no fear.

"You would?" retorted a surprised Kim.

"Good. Let's check it out," urged Bobby, happy to have an ally in this debate. "It's only another half mile."

(Western Australia)

The general was called over to examine the display screens. Everyone in the facility had an Astro I Security Clearance. Special technical military personnel along with CIA and NSA people manned the control panels. This American deep space tracking station was located for security reasons underground in the most remote part of the western Australian desert. Any unwelcome visitors could be detected at distances of hundreds of miles by air or land. A military technician announced, "Sir, there it is. It's a confirm between Mars and Earth. The trajectory indicated a possibility the point of origin is Mars itself. Our satellite in Moon orbit picked it up first."

"I see it," replied the General nervously moving nearer the screen. "Was there any reply on our normal friendly beacons?"

"Negative, General Scully."

"Call our advisor in here on the double," ordered the general.

One of the CIA men jumped up leaving the room but reappeared momentarily with a barely four foot high thin shadowy figure. He stopped by the screens, stared at the general exhibiting no emotion, and then turned to examine the telemetry numbers. After a moment of studying the data, he touched a small device on his waist which emitted a dull glowing light. The anxiety-ridden general watched in anticipation and finally incapable of silence any longer questioned the odd little fellow.

"Well, what's your opinion? Are they friendlies or not?" he asked without much trust or confidence.

"One moment," was the annoyed reply. The short, frail figure stared up into empty space as if in a trance. It almost appeared the answer to the general's question was being transmitted into the stranger's head. The answer arrived as it had on numerous occasions previously containing a similar deadly determination. "This craft is hostile and should be terminated with the SDI particle beam weaponry satellites as quickly as possible."

"You're positive about this?" the general questioned.

"Correct," was the brief monotone answer from the shadowy silhouette.

"All right, get me a link up with Langley SDI Command Center," ordered the now-decisive commander. The small advisor had sealed the fate of the object streaking towards an earth orbit. General Scully secretly harbored heavy feelings of suspicion pertaining to the strange consultant's information. But like a good soldier, he followed his directives and chain of command. The advisor slinked off retiring to his separate living quarters adjoining the command control room.

"Sir, I have Langley on one."

6

"Hello, Admiral Dirk? This is General Scully. We've got a situation…"

(Virginia—Langley Field)

The secret facilities at Langley Field, Virginia, direct all of the U.S. satellites containing Star Wars weapons since they first became operational in the mid 80s. Despite what the public has been spoon fed, these quiet sentinels do not face inward at unfriendly nations, but rather outwards at a much more sophisticated and camouflaged enemy. Russian missiles were never its intended target.

Particle beam weapons work as coherent light with electromagnet properties. Tremendous energy is required to produce and control these beams. Small nuclear reactors powered them originally. Extremely powerful superconducting magnets are used to guide the particles in a narrow beam to its target. Once there, the electromagnetic quality of the beam allows it to penetrate any metal or barrier. Even non-terrestrial metals which are much stronger than those manufactured on Earth, due to their being created in zero gravity. Once it penetrates, the beam disrupts anything operating on electricity. Traveling at the speed of light, it is impossible to evade. It is pure genius. But not all our genius. Outside forces assisted for years in its development at Los Alamos and other national laboratories.

A senior scientist at Langley began briefing a colleague who recently received a transfer from another top secret facility in the program. Of course they both possessed ultra-security clearances.

"I see you came into the program in 1984 under Ted Eller's tutelage," observed the senior technician reviewing his subordinate's file.

"Yes," he answered.

"You were up at Area 51 for two years while Ellers was director. He achieved good progress on the back engineering of the alien reactors. That's excellent. And I see you worked a year at Oak Ridge calibrating the beam weapon's assembly."

"Are we going to have an opportunity to test fire the two new fusion-powered weapons platforms?" asked the subordinate.

"Yes, but it won't be a test." The senior scientist let the information sink in. "Our two newest particle beam weapons containing the matter/antimatter annihilation alien-style reactors are already in orbit. The last one went out of Vandenburgh Air Force Base last week. Of course, you know the element used for fuel we've salvaged off the recovered discs and alien craft amounts to a mere 500 lbs. Since it does not occur naturally on earth, you understand the importance of our efforts to reproduce it synthetically. The very judicious use of this long-lasting fuel is crucial.

"I'm sure you're also aware of the benefits to using the copies of the alien reactors in the two new satellites. No radiation, more compact, and less chance it will destroy the platform. The real benefit, though, will be more power and accuracy for the weapon. That's why we need a live test firing from orbit. Have you read your latest briefing booklet explaining the alien histories and various races to visit earth?"

"Yes, and it never ceases to totally amaze me. I've worked with some of them at S4 in Nevada."

"Believe me, we're not going to be watching any of that material on the Evening News with Peter Jennings," assured the chuckling senior scientist. He continued.

"The military boys, NSC and MJ are currently determining whether to intercept an incoming track. Our job is to make damn sure all the satellites are operating at 100% on demand. I'm anxious to see how the smaller, more powerful superconducting magnets enhance the disrupting particles of the beam when the target is encountered. This will be a most interesting field test."

"Yes it will," agreed the subordinate.

"Do you see that light on the screen up there?"

"Yes."

"Let's get to our stations. We are going to fire on the one target shortly."

(Washington, DC)

A wood-paneled conference room accessible with only the highest security clearance known to man lies one hundred feet below the Naval Observatory in Washington. This section of subterranean rooms is the domain of MJ12, or Majority 12 a.k.a. the Jason Scholars, set into motion almost fifty years ago by then President Truman and the CIA. The purpose: to deal with the clear and present danger. Aliens. Included in the group are directors of the CIA and FBI, Secretary of Defense, Chairman of the Joint Chiefs along with others needed in controlling the ongoing situation. An elite group whose directive was established to shield the public from what was determined to be the harmful truth. The truth to be hidden was quite simply outsiders from other parts of our universe not only were here but some groups have visited for a very long time.

Through massive debunking efforts like disinformation, ridicule and character assassination of anyone smart enough to understand aliens and UFOs are real, they try to secure secrecy for national security. These activities are guided by the goal of slowly desensitizing people to prepare us psychologically. The Jason Scholars oversee the crucial task of back engineering captured and recovered alien craft which has produced transistors, lasers, microchips, fiberoptics, night vision devices, just to mention a few. Right down to Velcro fasteners they used on their little silver spacesuits. The enormous impact on people when learning that there are highly evolved beings in our universe who've visited earth and even tinkered with mankind's evolution is what the MJ12 group has been entrusted to prevent. They are the policy makers for anything relating to the subject. The Brookings Institute study years ago concluded these revelations

8

made to the general public would be catastrophic to our civilization on every level. The slow release of these realities became the solution for MJ through desensitizing. Anyone believing the Pentagon and MJ cannot keep this secret, with its unlimited resources, is truly naive.

Communications occured with the visitors from the beginning at the highest levels of government. We actually allied ourselves with a very deceptive group. The deals cut and promises made to appease them, one group in particular, only grew in scope over the years. The big treaty was originally signed at Edward's Air Force Base in 1954 by President Eisenhower, who was the last chief executive to be totally in the loop. Congress and the American people were not consulted about the treaty. There was no time.

The technologies demonstrated at Edward's that day by the aliens were overwhelming. Eisenhower knew he needed to buy time so as to let us catch up in technology and ultimately survive. Our society's tremendous technological leaps in recent years is no accident. Well, thats the jist of the story and as they say on TV, believe it or not.

Meanwhile back at the Naval Observatory, an emergency meeting was called of all MJ members. The usual "Eyes Only" documents lay on the long oak table. All of the powerful members entered and were seated.

"Gentlemen, this meeting was called in response to a reported hostile craft approaching earth. It was identified by our advisors from Group 4. Two new SDI satellites will defend our territory to prevent any penetration by this intruder. Questions or comments? Yes, go ahead J2."

"Could you please repeat which group had ID'd the intruder, J1."

"Yes, it was Group 4 from the Orion Confederation. J6 you're recognized."

"Thank you, J1. The Group 4 advisors seem to prefer to shoot first and ask questions later. Do we really know who we are firing on? I propose a debate on this issue including many members' reservations about Group 4's motives. Please make that a matter of record."

"Thank you, J6. It will be taken up in one week at our next meeting. If there are no further comments, the action will stand. Langley is preparing to intercept this threat. Go ahead, J9."

"I believe J6 is correct. We've destroyed several other incoming signals on advisement of Group 4 in recent years. An assessment of their trustworthiness will be quite prudent and necessary a week from now."

"As you well know, we are not in a realistic position to dictate to them at this time." Members' faces grew pale. The realization of universal powerlessness was daunting; their earthly governmental powers equate to zero out there. J1 announced, "Our opinions matter to them as much as a primitive aboriginal tribe's witch doctor's opinions would matter to this body. But we will proceed anyway. Any objections to that menu next meeting?" asked J1.

"Noted."

"All agreed. Meeting adjourned, but remain on alert for another emergency meeting if it becomes necessary."

(Langley, Virginia)

The control room was abuzz at Langley. Two hundred and fifty nautical miles above the earth, the two new SDI satellites small retro rockets fired maneuvering them into position to intercept the rapidly approaching unknown craft. The new annihilation reactors of matter/antimatter stood ready to provide plenty of power. Another ten minutes and the target would be in optimal firing range for the first satellite. Also in orbit, fifteen hundred miles away, the second SDI weapon was prepared to back up the first if necessary.

The two project scientists supervised a half dozen military specialists operating the sensitive equipment relaying commands to the weapons aboard the satellite. A group of naval intelligence people, Admiral Dirk, and a few plain-clothes individuals stood by anxiously awaiting the outcome from the live test firing of the newly incorporated alien-influenced technologies.

"Two minutes," shouted the technician.

The senior physicists in charge was checking over initial statistics when he said, "The laser range finders are prepared to lock on."

"Thirty seconds."

Another technician shouted, "Both reactors are full power."

The admiral and others leaned in to observe the action. The countdown was commencing. "Five, four, three, two, one…"

After a couple of seconds, the technician started fidgeting and reported, "We're not getting any activation on #1. It's not firing!"

The senior physicist pulled the technician out from in front of the monitor mumbling, "Let me see that. I can't understand this. It should have energized."

Observing the distressing events, Admiral Dirk asked, "Can we hit it with the backup satellite?"

The senior scientist stared at the screen, "The second satellite should have fired automatically. I'll override the controls and shoot manually."

The technician whose station had been commandeered added, "That target is traveling at unbelievable speeds."

"Here we go," answered the senior physicist. "It's energized and firing."

No one in the room said a word as the tracking screen began to reveal unwelcomed results. An apprehension from not achieving success permeated the facility.

"Did we get him?" questioned the Admiral.

A specialist on another screen answered, "The target is still there but moving in a much slower and highly erratic track."

"Was the target destroyed? Damn it, man," steamed the Admiral.

"Not totally, sir."

"How could we have two malfunctions?" asked Admiral Dirk.

The subordinate scientist quietly turned to his senior partner. "Do you think the light sensors on Particle Beam Mirror #2 were calibrated correctly?"

"I just don't know at this point," he responded. "I won't know until all the data is in. I know we incurred multiple malfunctions."

"That does us a lot of good now," the admiral snorted. "So this thing is still in one piece?"

"It appears that's the case, sir," the technician shyly responded.

"Admiral, the Pentagon in on the line."

"Admiral Dirk here. How are you Preston? Yes, we had a malfunction on both satellites. Yes, the bogey was hit by the second weapon. Yes sir, we're tracking it as we speak and it appears presently its point of impact will be somewhere off the east coast of central Florida. Very good, sir. Goodbye." The Admiral turned to his men, "Get me our surveillance stations. I want this damn thing's splashdown pinpointed!"

Satellite Beach, Florida

The moon was rising cautiously over the vast nocturnal ocean, illuminating a large expanse of water. It resembled a spotlight centering itself on a stage and awaiting the arrival of its star player. The deep black water on either side created a backdrop which sharply contrasted with the moon's bright light show. The view was surreal. This arena was empty save two lone fishing trawlers at the far corners of the dark horizon. They slowly strained their engines in an effort to reach the well illuminated center stage.

"It's so beautiful out there," said Carol, admiring the moonlit water.

"Yeah, we locals don't really appreciate the sea's uniqueness, being our homes are on the water," answered Steve.

"Would you care for the rest of my beer?" Carol asked.

"I could probably force it down," Steve said with a laugh.

"I should have brought more wine," Kim said.

Seeing his opportunity to tease her, Bobby said, "I think Spaceman might have some extra wine to give you."

"Ah...no thank you," came the quick reply.

"Hey, what's that light out there," Carol asked, pointing towards the water. "Someone must be shooting a flare."

"Look at that! It's getting brighter and brighter," stated Kim.

"That's weird. It's way too high to be a flare," Steve said. "It's coming down."

"God, what is that?" asked a concerned Kim.

"Take a look at the water," Carol observed. "The way the light's reflecting you'd think there were two moons in the sky."

"Yeah, but it's still getting brighter," Bobby said, allowing some alarm to creep into his voice.

"It's going to hit the water!" yelled Steve. "I bet it's at least ten miles out."

The object's illuminated tail revealed the irregular path taken into the darkened corners of the horizon. "That thing sure isn't traveling on a straight course," said Steve. "Did you guys see the zig zagging as if someone or something was struggling to regain control of the flight path?"

"I thought we were witnessing one of the military's Delta rocket launches from the Cape but upside-down in reverse," said Bobby. "That's really strange. I wonder if Captain Al's boat is out there tonight?"

"That thing came down a lot further out than the three mile distance the trawlers are fishing. But I'm sure he got a bird's eye view if he was out there," said Steve.

Everyone remained implanted in front of the grassy dunes for a while, staring out over the sets of crumbling waves when a resounding boom erupted from behind. The silent breeze-filled night air became violated with a tearing loud crack. Instinctively, all four observers ducked their heads expecting something big to crash down on top of them. Maybe only one hundred and fifty feet high in the air and streaking from the direction of Patrick Air Force Base were three F-18 fighter jets knifing across the beach on a bee line for the projected terminus the strange falling projectile had taken into the ocean. There was no mistaking the high performance acceleration of the F-18s' twin engines ripping across the atmosphere.

"Jeez, someone check my underwear. They caught me by surprise," sounded Bobby as the other three party revelers peered up from the sandy dune they had dove behind.

"Yeah, no kidding," said Kim shaking sand out of her halter top.

"Are they going out to investigate that light?" Carol asked.

Steve responded, "Probably. That's very unusual for these planes to be flying that low at high speed."

"Maybe it was a downed Air Force plane of some kind," Kim commented. "It was maneuvering from side to side."

"Nah. The speed it came in at and then pulled up tremendously before impacting the water gives it flight characteristics like I've never seen before," said Steve. "Also, the powerful odd light given off just doesn't fit the mold."

"Look. Here comes another plane," Carol shouted pointing up.

"It's a J-Star electronic surveillance plane. They usually protect the perimeter around the Cape, but it's flying awfully low," commented Steve. "Something's going on out there alright."

The big jet followed the path of the previous faster aircraft, heading out hugging the deck and sparing no power. The impact point must have been a minimum of ten miles out. Many lights could be seen circling that area in the distant sky. Soon the rotor noise of Black Hawk helicopters could be heard buzzing way out at sea. The planes and choppers searched in vain for about twenty minutes before disappearing even further out.

Speaking with a tone of humor in her voice, Carol asked, "Does this go on every night out here?"

"Nothing this weird," Bobby answered. "We only get shuttle launches and military rockets going up. I've never seen the likes of this thing."

"I've come across similar objects but that was when I worked on the shrimp boat," said Steve.

"Is there a possibility it was a satellite or something?" questioned Carol.

"I kind of doubt it," answered Bobby. "Nothing was in the newspaper for launch or recovery. They have a section devoted to launch activities. Whenever a Delta, Atlas, Titan, or shuttle is designated to take off, they always try to notify the civilian population living around the Cape."

The group could only wonder about the mysterious sighting they had witnessed as they began moving north along the beach toward the distant camp fire. They were all somewhat awed by the strange object which had fallen to earth right before their amazed eyes. The majority of witnesses to these events are steered away from the true reality by the powers that be. Their motives are tranquility for society by lying. Most people's minds simply can't correllate witnessing these events as connected to the outside.

Some of the members of the group falsely tried to rationalize the experience to achieve a feeble sense of security. It is only natural. For those entities which orignate beyond our known peramters of existence, it must be rationalized at this point in human history.

CHAPTER TWO

The small burning campfire was tucked under the short elevated boardwalk adjacent to the dunes and sea grapes. A rough cut character stood on his feet, straining to scan the cloudless skies. His ratty t-shirt and long gray beard gave quiet testimony to a person whom had fallen between the cracks. Whether he'd actually fallen or was pushed remained open to speculation. Spaceman dropped out of society as most people know it years ago. If ever an individual epitomized a loner who'd let his trust in mankind escape his soul, he was that person. His very mysterious past was a large contributor to the current confused situation he found himself enveloped in. Space tried to evade his memories by distancing himself from authority and organized society. Normally he had exhibited a soured, apathetic and disillusioned counter-culturalist personality like you would see displayed as a returning Vietnam vet living back in the real world. Tonight, however, there was an alert, more serious posture about him. The evening's events hadn't gone unnoticed by his fireside. Memories were stirred up in him that were far better forgotten.

In short, Spaceman's past was like having had a pit bull attack your ankle. You can look away and pretend it didn't happen but the agonizing pain never lets you forget that those voracious teeth once locked deep into your flesh, forever scarring you.

He hardly noticed the four visitors approaching his make-shift campfire. A trance-like state had gripped him.

"Spaceman," yelled Steve, snapping him back.

"Did you see it, man? Did you?"

"Yeah, we saw it," answered Bobby with a ringing confirmation in his voice.

"Man, they are here."

"Relax, take it easy. You don't know for sure what that was," said Bobby. Kim and Carol loitered in the background not knowing whether to proceed to the fire's warmth or not.

"I know Bobby, man," he uttered with a wild look in his eyes. "Did you see the zig zagging trajectory and the deceleration before it entered the water. And how about that blinding light show. No, that can be only one thing."

"What?" Carol asked bluntly.

"Oh, hey Spaceman, this is Carol Cole, Kim's friend from school," interrupted Steve as he tried to tone things down a bit.

Glancing at her for a second he muttered, "Cool, baby," out of the side of his mouth so as not to break his train of thought.

"Nice to meet you," she volleyed back. "So you think UFOs are real?" diligently trying to keep him talking on the subject.

Spaceman was quiet for a minute. After a moment of reflection, he began laughing loudly at some invisible irony. "Real, baby? Most people think I'm really out there. But take it from me, a man who was on the inside, when I tell you—if the general population knew the truth, they would never be able to handle it."

"Try me," Carol retorted, bravely staring eye to eye not losing her intense interest.

A slightly surprised look came over Spaceman's weathered face. He seemed impressed with her spunky determination and said, "Where is my etiquette? Why don't you all take a seat by the fire?" There were no chairs save a long wooded plank supported by beach rocks.

Everyone sat except Kim. "We've got to get back soon."

Bobby jumped in, "There's still a little time. Sit, honey."

"Man, I've got some killer weed if anyone's interested," offered Spaceman who had become more relaxed. "The stuff grows wild in the empty beach lots along here."

No one took him up on the offer, so he indulged by himself. Carol studied the stranger and noticed immediately that he was about thirty years older than Steve and Bobby. His long gray ponytail combined with a slightly wrinkled face indicated he was in his mid- to late- fifties. He had all the characteristics of a man who'd been beaten down and dropped out. Whatever heights his previous life had obtained, presently his status was that of a wandering generality. Despite this and some of his kooky ideas, the superior intelligence he possessed shone through when speaking.

Spaceman took a long drag on his home-grown cannabis. "So, you want to know about UFOs?" he asked while coughing some smoke out. "My two surfing buds over there have heard a number of my revelations. The main problem is trying to remember. You see, they erased quite a bit of my memory by employing advanced brainwashing techniques. I knew way too much."

"Who erased your memory?" asked Carol.

"The CIA, Naval Intelligence, and the NSA," answered Spaceman.

"What's the NSA?" asked Kim skeptically.

The NSA stands for 'No Such Agency,'" said Spaceman.

"That's the National Security Agency," Steve explained. "The kids help our guys with the advanced techniques and drugs for the mind control. They're always present when someone must be made to forget."

"Kids? What kids?" asked a confused Carol.

"They're not from around here," answered Spaceman. "I guess I'm lucky I'm not dead. They settled for reducing me to a half-wit by using chemical injections and their advanced mind control programs. There are others who weren't as lucky. I knew two Navy Seals that tried to blow the whistle on underground activities at Area 51 in Nevada. Those boys were never seen again."

"C'mon. Our government would never let that happen," protested Kim.

Spaceman, loose now from his smoke, continued spilling out the unpopular truth from his sporadically functioning memory. Kim's reaction was totally normal. It's comparable to children finding out their parents weren't telling them the truth about the existence of Santa Claus. Some kids catch on faster than others, but it still leaves a rotten feeling in their stomachs when they realize that all things are not what they seem. The populous will soon reach that age, and be told by their over-protective leaders the realities.

Spaceman continued, "Unfortunately the military powers that be do not take it too lightly when a soldier breaks a couple of National Security oaths, especially at the highest level. Man, I personally believe this whole thing goes way beyond National Security. People have got to know now that outsiders are here."

"I don't believe any of that," snapped Kim.

Spaceman just looked down into the flames of the fire and began laughing again. "Do you have any idea of the level of security involved with the programs I worked on, baby? I had information the president didn't possess a need to know. Yeah man, we had a good ole time. The secret space program also employed me. If you think Cape Canaveral is America's only portal to space, think again.

"In the old days, our military space capsules in orbit would shoot missiles at alien craft. Being a highly rated Navy pilot with extremely good connections, I entered this program and was accepted," Spaceman coughed as a recycled cloud of smoke came out his nose and mouth.

Carol glanced at Steve showing him a look of disbelief. She questioned Spaceman, "Are you saying NASA knew nothing about these events?"

"Strictly need to know. Since its inception under Dr. Von Braun, very few, if any, were even aware of its existence. Man, those civilians do what they're told. They are so far out of the loop they really don't have a clue. That agency was set up as a cover to keep people occupied and justify siphoning off budgeted funds to the Black Projects and other critical space defense projects. Money is desperately needed to get alien technologies incorporated in our civilization, which equates to our very survival against outside threats. 'How come no one ever told me?' Is that what you're going to ask, man? Well baby, you have absolutely no need to know at this point. What good would it do to reveal the truth and be an alarmist causing chaos and counter-productivity. At least that's how they look at it."

"So Space, what you're saying is we're not getting all the info?" asked Bobby.

"It's not totally a case of people being left out of crucial events. No, that would be like simple, man. Remember I talked about Santa Claus and kids?

Well, more and more people are realizing there is no Santa Claus. These dudes in charge are highly organized and very aggressively spread disinformation through various channels so you don't know if you're coming or going on the subject. Even our own pilots are debunked. Recently, an Air Force colonel, who was attached to the Office of Special Investigation, admitted his directives coming down mandated discrediting their own pilots if UFO sightings were pursued. He revealed pilots must be ridiculed or debunked immediately by any means necessary. Our leaders in MJ12 by now are dealing with many different alien groups."

"What's MJ12?" Carol asked with a growing curiosity urging her on.

"What's MJ12? I see I have to start at square one. A group of scientists, generals, and defense related people were all secretly brought together by then President Truman to deal with a rash of crashes and the unknown beings operating them. At Truman's request in late 1947, Dr. Vannaber Bush, Secretary of Defense Forrestal, and CIA Director George Marshal assembled the proper people to form the MJ group. And believe me when I tell you, there is nothing more secret or classified for the last fifty years in this country. Their unenviable job is in dealing with these groups, who possess different agendas and purposes. MJ has ultimate power along with no accountability to reach these impossible tasks. They are the secret governing body of this country and protect the human race as a whole. Being that they control the military and intelligence groups, they are in total control. I just pray no outside forces are manipulating that control." Spaceman took a long hit off his joint.

"Anyway man, getting back to my pathetic story…My early days as a pilot and astronaut were followed up with a stint in Naval Intelligence and the CIA. You see, I was too deep 'in the know.' I was one of the elite, and therefore became a valuable asset. The next project I participated in was Project Snowbird in 1973. Our research boys were starting to understand how the forty or so recovered saucers we've got operated. The idea behind Snowbird was to have our top pilots, together with top technical people, learn how to fly them and what makes them tick."

"Fly what? Flying saucers?" frowned Kim. "Come on!" she groaned and looked away. "What an imagination."

"That's one mind that just totally shut down," Space said.

"Go on. I'm captivated by your information," insisted Carol.

Kim rolled her eyes and turned to face the ocean.

Space went on. "The Pentagon and MJ 12 have kept these secrets not only to prevent a panic among the people, but they also want to back engineer these alien technologies. Because a child could understand that the first one to figure out how these technologies work, wins."

"Wins what?" asked an enthralled Carol.

"Wins everything, baby. Everything."

A silence settled over the small group. Spaceman's controversial statements were being analyzed by the other three listeners straining to understand. Was he the greatest liar of all time or was there a chance that all his facts and information could add up to truth. He possessed a flashlight in the manmade fog of disinformation.

Trying to get to the matter at hand, Steve asked, "So Space, in your opinion, what did that thing that went down over the water appear to be?"

"Stevie, I'm telling you, it was not one of ours, dude. Trust me, I know. Those flight characteristics are impossible to achieve unless your craft is out of phase with our gravity."

Carol couldn't quench her thirst for answers to these mysteries. Totally intrigued by the revelations she was hearing, she asked, "Spaceman, why did you leave the programs and how is it you haven't been silenced?"

"Give me a minute, doll. I need another hit on this joint." When he was ready, Space continued. "You see, in spite of my damaged memory, I get real good recall when I smoke weed for some reason. As to why I left, it was primarily because I did not like what was evolving from our alliances with certain outside groups. My trust in the leadership became shaken. Things happened that destroyed my confidence in our motives on certain undertakings.

"Being far too outspoken, I became a problem for them. The boys at the top do not appreciate anyone swimming against the current in their river. It boiled down to one final unanswered question: How strongly is our military influenced by outside forces?"

"Outside what? You mean Earth? Extraterrestrials?" Carol deduced.

"Correctomundo. At first my mind didn't admit it could be real until hard evidence crossed my path. Now, the reason I haven't been terminated is because no one would believe my story anyway. People have been conditioned and debunked so effectively over the last 40 years that there is no need for them to stop me. They figure I'd be laughed at and ridiculed automatically, man."

Kim rolled her eyes again.

"The main reason I have not been killed has to do with my step-dad. It's also how I got so far 'in the know.' My dad was head of Air Material Command in 1947 at Wright Patterson Field in Ohio where the Roswell stuff was sent. In that same year, he was one of three generals selected to become original member of MJ12. So you see, my connections went to the very top. I was trusted to enter the inner circle. Eventually, while stationed at the Pentagon, I received 'Eyes Only' clearance."

No one noticed the stunned expression on Carol's face. She looked as if a ghost had jumped in front of her. The words Spaceman had uttered triggered a horrific internal reaction aside from shock; the words supplied a piece to a personal puzzle which enlightened a long-standing mystery for her. The unsettling solution answered one big question, only to create a plethora of others to be pondered. She had suddenly figured out Santa Claus didn't exist. Carol kept a straight face hiding her emotions well and regaining her composure.

Spaceman's stamina weakened. "Like maybe I'm just lucky to be alive, but some of my father's friends are still around. On occasion there will be agents who covertly check up on me. Where I am, who I'm with."

"Yeah, we saw a couple of suspicious guys one time shadowing Space after surfing," Bobby recalled.

"All I know is everything really isn't as it seems with this alien thing," said Steve. "I started listening to Space awhile ago and statements he'd made checked out with some insiders I know who served in Naval Intelligence. Some of these friends adamantly refused to discuss certain topics even though they were retired from the military. This information is extremely difficult to come by."

"C'mon Steve. Do you actually subscribe to this malarkey?" Kim blurted out.

"I know we're being lied to with regards to the alien presence here. And I don't watch the TV news like most people getting large doses of misleading facts and disinformation on this particular subject."

"You may be right," Carol added. "I've never discussed it with you, Kim, but I've read something I took to be pure nonsense. These papers I accidentally saw were discussing aliens. Naturally, the whole thing appeared to be a practical joke. That was until those words 'Eyes Only' were spoken a minute ago. The papers assessing threats from various alien cultures had those very words stamped across the top in big black letters."

"Where did you see this?" asked Steve.

"It's impossible for me to disclose any details now."

"If this isn't pure fantasy…C'mon," Kim said.

"Man, there are only one or two places you could have come across that," Space said. He felt good having someone back him.

Kim looked over at Carol with a shocked stare as if not recognizing her friend after the blunt metamorphosis from the so-called rational world into the alleged fringed boundaries.

Spaceman started to his feet. His eyes welled up with tears and his voice quivered exhibiting a build up of emotion. "Man, that's all it will take. A few brave hearts willing to come forward and speak the truth. If we all stick together, stand up, and speak out, people's right to know will be achieved."

"Hey Space, don't get upset. Everything's gonna turn out fine." Steve tried to calm him down.

Carol also recognized his distress and grabbed his arm in a comforting gesture.

"You can crash in my garage tonight if you like," Steve offered.

"Thanks, baby. That would be cool of you Stevie," he answered.

19

"Well, c'mon. We should be heading back down the beach." Steve occasionally let Spaceman stay in his garage. At least he would have a safe, comfortable place out of the weather.

The group commenced extinguishing the small fire. Nike sneakers plowed the damp sand on top of the glowing hot embers eliminating the limited supply of light. The fighter jets and helicopters which had previously swarmed over the entire area were gone. In their pursuit of the illusive intruder, it appeared as if the ocean's vastness had gobbled them up. A stillness was reclaimed by the moonlit sea.

Everyone trekked back past the tranquil surf in the direction of the party. Steve's small rented beach house lay about a quarter mile further south from John and Cindy's large home on the water. Departing the buried campfire, Spaceman caught up with the group. He commented to Steve, "Stevie man, I like really appreciate the room for the night, bud."

"Don't mention it," answered Steve.

"That damn thing brought back some bad vibes, man."

"Well, it's gone now, so try to take it easy."

Steve and Carol dropped behind the others as they walked. Striding side by side they intentionally slowed in order to achieve the desired privacy.

"How are you doing after all that enlightenment?" Steve asked.

"Fine," Carol replied. "Your friend is a real interesting fellow."

"Yeah, like I said before, most people just think he's nuts and makes up all those fantastic stories. Although, if you seriously focus in on what he is saying and understand the big picture, which means knowing what the military and alien motives are, his stories no longer sound like the babbling of a deranged loner."

"I believe him, Steve. He knows too many names, places, and details to be dreaming this up."

"The time line of events he describes makes total sense the more you investigate and realize how things operate," Steve explained.

"You've done research on the subject?" asked Carol.

"Uh huh in my spare time. Don't get mad, but I'm compelled to ask you again about the experience you related. That statement back there about the 'Eyes Only' document stirred up my curiosity, big time."

"Yes, after the incident I figured no one would take my story seriously. I mean, I didn't realize the validity of the papers myself until tonight. The exception is your friend. He made the light bulb go on over my head, and it all made sense. It appears he was highly involved."

Steve nodded. "I know from my small research efforts that it's almost impossible to get information on alien crashes, UFOs, and military involvement. So inquiring minds want to know, how did you have access to this super secret info?"

Carol stopped walking and looked directly at Steve. "I can't say other than I've come in contact with the document and to reveal the source would severely jeopardize the well-being of a loved one."

"O.K. I'll buy that." They walked on very close, giving Steve the chance to notice Carol's beautiful features reflected in the moonlight. "When you say loved one, you don't mean boyfriend, do you?"

Steve and Carol were now separated from the others by at least one hundred yards of dimly lit beach. Carol stopped and faced Steve, who moved closer in anticipation of her answer. They stood inches from each others' faces as Carol whispered softly, "No." Their eyes were transfixed on one another in mutual attraction.

As though hypnotized, Steve answered, "Oh, good," and boldly kissed her. Carol returned the sentiment with equal passion. The strong magnetic attraction of opposites transcended any difference for both participants and closed off the outside world. A cone of silence was lowered over them as they embraced, pressing together as one. They fell to their knees in the sand. Carol's hands surveyed Steve's broad muscular back. He could feel her warm body pressing up against him. Her long ebony hair flowed over his embracing hands. The relaxed spontaneity of their passionate connection was not questioned by either of them.

Their privacy was abruptly shattered by screaming from the direction of the three advanced scouts up the beach. Though barely visible, their howling voices were easily deciphered, "Out there, look." Carol and Steve drew their attentions from one another to the water directly beneath the moon's glow. There, not more than a mile out and creating no noise, was a round saucer-like craft, pulling a spiral of sea water up underneath its base. Its outer edges displayed colored lights as it strained to escape the black water's grip. A blue strobe light flashed intermittently atop its dome in weird gyrations. Who or whatever it was, it obviously had serious mechanical trouble.

Steve grabbed Carol's hand and yelled, "C'mon," and raced down the wet sand toward the others. If a brick wall had been laid across the beach, they'd have run right into it as all their attentions were locked on the strange sight in the sky.

The UFOs altitude never increased over seventy-five feet. The ship was wobbling out of control. Just as Steve and Carol reached the others, a loud pop erupted from the craft, vibrating across the water's acoustics very clearly. Simultaneously, all the colored lights on the ship's outer edges went totally black and the single blue strobe flashed from atop the circular dome. The saucer still remained highly visible as it was silhouetted brightly against the narrow stretch of lunar-lit sea. The craft's distance from the group on shore could not have exceeded a mile.

While everyone stood there motionless, not believing what their eyes had just recorded, the ship proceeded to slowly lose altitude. Everyone was a bit spooked following Spaceman's dissertation by the fire.

Bobby shouted, "It's gonna fall back into the ocean. It's going down!"

Spaceman observed, "Man, there is something negatively wrong with that bogie."

"What in the hell is that?" Kim asked excitedly.

The answer she requested came from the shaggy Bedouin standing next to her. "That's them, dudes. They're here, baby," warned Spaceman.

A second later the seemly powerless wobbling ship smacked the ocean's surface hard. The resounding echo from the vehicle crashing into the water could be heard up and down the beach front. The object didn't linger on the surface for long. It submerged quickly below the horizon, its strange blue strobe light still flickering for help. The water swallowed it up but the blue flashes could still be seen in the murky depths sinking slowly.

A minute passed before anyone could speak. Steve commented, "That was one hell-of-a-show out there. Do you guys see that blue light anymore?"

Bobby answered, "I'm not sure. I think it's down for the count."

Spaceman jumped in, "Some of these groups use blue strobes for distress signals. Like I'm not totally sure, but that craft appeared to have its annihilation reactor malfunction causing a power loss."

Kim glanced over at Space, rolling her eyes again.

Spaceman said, "Stevie, those are the dudes the military was trying to apprehend earlier."

"It had to be the same one," said Steve. "Apparently it shook off the Air Force boys who are still searching too far east."

"We need to get to a phone to report this to the air base," said Kim.

"Relax honey, I don't think that thing will be going too far," Bobby reasoned.

The group jogged to a nearby public access deck. Attempting to gain a better view, they clambered up the steps. After a few quick scans of the area, no sign of the enigma presented itself. It was all over in the blink of an eye.

Carol let out a sigh. "That was really weird. I can't even believe I saw a live UFO." She thought to herself, peering out over the now sedate beach, how strange this whole night was turning out. First, meeting and listening to Spaceman's odd tales of his clandestine experiences with the country's most super secret alien related projects were exciting enough. But then his revelations actually shone light on her own private mysteries and bringing competent explanations to the reality of an extraterrestrial presence here on Earth. She'd had a brief but exciting encounter with Steve. And finally, a close up look at God knows what, crashing right in front of them and probably stranding some far off visitor on the ocean floor. What a night. And she thought her vacation would be dull.

No one was leaving the observation deck atop the stairs. The chance of gaining another glimpse of this anomaly was a powerful attraction. Spaceman was abuzz. "They've lost power, man. They're stranded out there and I'm telling you, escape is not an option."

"You O.K.?" Steve whispered to Carol. Steve clutched her hand, and she smiled at him.

Bobby judged the crash distance from shore and he thought it could not be more than seventy feet in depth if it was marooned on the bottom. "Steve, we could probably dive the area easily."

"Good idea and I know just the guy with the right equipment to take us out," said Steve. "Captain Al is really into this stuff, being he spots unusual things on the water while shrimping all the time. He'd kill for the chance to try and recover something."

Kim listened intently to the salvage plans. "I don't think it's safe to go near that spot. We ought to call the Air Force."

"Negative, man," countered Spaceman. "Don't call the authorities. I'll help you guys on the dive. If there is an outsider on the bottom, you'll need my help once it's located."

"Sounds good. I'll call Capt. Al once we get back," answered Steve.

"You guys are nuts!" Kim exploded. "What'll you do if the improbable really happens and you come across a flying saucer in the depths?"

Steve said, "We'll assess that picture if and when it develops."

"That would be so cool to recover something from another world. What a rush!" pondered Bobby aloud.

"I know a plane crash victim wouldn't last long in seventy feet of water," said Carol. "Could something still be alive in that craft? I mean underwater with no air?"

A small smile appeared across Spaceman's gray-bearded face. He said softly, "Oh yeah, baby."

Steve announced, "Either way we need to get out there tomorrow and check it out."

"I don't believe this whole conversation," complained Kim.

The group grew silent as each member reviewed the event that had taken place. While pondering the situation, one eye was employed still surveying the beach and ocean, watchful for any sudden movements. Carol was the first to scream, followed instantly by Kim's wail, as she retreated to the rear of Bobby.

Kim yelled in a panic, "Oh my God! What is it?"

Bobby and Steve instinctively jumped back in disbelief. Spaceman stood his ground, not moving a muscle while showing no fear on his face. Approximately twenty feet to the side of the deck rail, jutting out of the high dune grass, appeared an unearthly face. It's unmistakable hairless head and large dark almond eyes were alertly fixed on the occupants standing on the deck. Bobby blurted out, "What the hell?"

Everyone's pulses raced with fear at the startling proximity of this extraterrestrial visitor staring up at the group. Then as quickly as it had arrived, the head snapped from sight. Rustling could be heard in the high marine vegetation below. Fumbling around, Steve found the small flashlight in his pocket and finally brought its brightness to bear on the intruder crouched among the tall reeds.

"A damn turtle," he shouted over the rail.

"Shit, it's turtle season," cried Bobby in relief. "There are the tracks coming in from the surf."

"Turtles?" asked Carol who was comforted to hear a connection with known realities.

"Yeah, the big sea turtles come ashore at night to lay their eggs this time of year," said Steve. "They get pretty big."

"That turtle with its neck stretched up and rotating around those big, dark eyes looked like the real deal," said Bobby. "Jeez, I need to catch my breath."

The annual turtle season had begun along the Space Coast. They come in at night and lay their eggs if they feel it is safe. These monstrous mother turtles are spooked quite easily and will extend their necks up high in the air to survey the beach to make sure it is unoccupied and safe.

Spaceman had an authoritative tone to his voice as he told everyone, "It does resemble one group that I've seen which has the almond eyes set in its head in a similar manner." No one heard Spaceman talking; they all were trying to regain their composure from the sudden shock.

"The joke is on us," said Steve.

"You see? There's always a logical explanation for everything," said Kim.

"Like, a single sea turtle is one thing, man," rebutted Space. "The alien presence on this planet is a whole other bag, baby!"

Steve said, "I'll tell you one thing. That craft that went into the water out there was no joke and warrants investigation at the very least. I don't see any movement; things seemed to have settled down. Let's all head back to my house for a drink, and I'll give Captain Al a call. Maybe we can run a search from his boat tomorrow."

"I'm there," shouted Bobby.

"Count me in, boys," insisted Spaceman.

Carol directed her question at Steve. "What do you think the odds are of finding that thing in all that ocean out there? Assuming, of course, it's dead in the water."

"It could have moved, but Space doesn't seem to think so. If we work a grid in the crash area towing a magnometer behind the boat, our odds are good. I worked with Captain Al on a couple of treasure hunts in these waters. We were looking for wrecks from the 1715 Spanish fleet wiped out by a hurricane along this coast. Anyway, the magnometer should locate something that big pretty quickly. Once a good signal is received, we don our wet suits and dive on the target."

"It sounds to me like you guys are out of your league and asking for trouble," said Kim.

"Nah, it's simple," replied Steve. "The only problem might be how to raise the thing if we do find it. Although I'm sure Al's trawler has a few big winches aboard."

"Like it'll be simple assuming they let you raise them up," warned Spaceman.

"If he's right, by some long shot, and there is something alive down there, then this is too dangerous for me," said Kim.

"Relax, Kim. Spaceman's only trying to scare you girls," exclaimed Bobby.

"Well, it's working," answered Kim.

"I'm not scared," said Carol staring at Steve. "I think the chance to discover whether or not that object out there originated from another planet is too fantastic to comprehend."

Steve moved in closer to comfort Carol but they began kissing. Bobby gave Kim a tap on the shoulder, signaling her over to him. Each showed surprise at the other couple's spontaneous connection. Bobby and Kim moved into one another's arms and nervously hugged and laughed lightly.

Spaceman was not distracted. Reclined on the wooden bench, he hashed over the possibility of becoming involved again with an old nemesis. He was constantly attempting to decipher his blurred memories and sort out details of a dark world very few had access to. A world that in the past supplied no solutions to complicated questions. Tomorrow's search might give him another opportunity to gain answers. He leaped out grasping at the rare chance to confront this so-called intangible and did not show the slightest hesitation in his purpose. Despite disillusionment and withdrawal from past experiences, he still had a burning fire deep down inside to expose the truth in this grand deception concealing all of mankind's basic questions dealing with our past, present, and future. The importance for humans to realize the truth overrides any bogus priorities our leaders have misconstrued.

Steve pressed closer to Carol. "So we're all going tomorrow?"

"Count us in," said Bobby.

"I don't know about this..." replied Kim tentatively.

"Oh, c'mon Kim," coaxed Carol, trying to persuade her friend. "We're not going to find anything, but we are gonna have a great boat ride."

"Well, I guess," she finally conceded.

"Good. Now let's hope Captain Al is available to make the trip tomorrow," announced Steve.

All five travelers passed the noisy, illuminated home of Cindy and John. Heavy conversations and laughter rolled off their deck and onto the sand dunes. After the evening's bizarre happenings, no one desired to return to the party. The revelers went about their merrymaking totally oblivious to any unfolding drama outside the enclosed walls of the celebration. A half mile further to the south the five spotted a small modest home set above the dunes. Large palm trees guarded its perimeter. The structure was one of the original dwellings built on the beach after World War II. As they approached, a six-foot swath in the dunes led to a half dozen weather-beaten wooded steps. Creaking wood squealed as the party climbed onto the deck attached to Steve's house. Everyone received one of the five faded deck chairs available.

"Who wants a drink?" offered Steve.

"No, thanks. I'm half in the bag," said Bobby.

"Yeah. We started early at my house," Kim explained.

Steve went inside and retrieved his portable phone. After dialing Captain Al, he hung up. "No one's answering. He might be out on the water .

"It's getting late, Bobby. We've got to be going," advised Kim. "I've had quite enough excitement for one night."

"I probably should leave, too," said Carol. "I mixed my drinks earlier, and I'm a bit under the weather."

"Are you sure you're all right?" asked Steve as he led her to a darker corner of the deck.

"Yes, I'll be O.K. I just need some sleep."

"I'll see you tomorrow then?"

Carol shook her head.

"Great. Tomorrow should prove interesting at the very least."

Once again they embraced and kissed not wanting to separate.

Bobby interrupted, "Steve, call me as soon as you reach Captain Al and know the details."

"Are you going to be at Mom and Dad's?" he asked.

"Yeah, I have a few things to take care of at the orange grove in the morning. They are both out of town for a week on business."

Steve reluctantly released Carol after one last kiss. "Good night everyone."

Bobby and the two women exited down the loose boards on the steps. Spaceman simultaneously broke out of his daze and managed a "Adios, amigees." Steve led the homeless beach comber into his garage where he flipped open a folding cot for him. After scrounging up a sandwich and a soda for his guest in the VIP suite, Steve asked, "You O.K.?"

"Great man. Thanks, Stevie."

"You know where everything is."

"Yep."

Steve closed the door from the garage to the house behind him. He felt good about performing this bit of charity occasionally. Besides, Spaceman wasn't your run-of-the-mill troubled person. Steve knew somehow he could trust Spaceman implicitly. There were moments when hidden qualities he possessed shown through. It was quite unusual for a man of his lowly M.O. Steve saw that beneath that rough exterior was a fine person.

Crossing the living room, Steve glanced out the front bay window and noticed something out of place. An object was blocking the end of the long, narrow driveway in front of the house. A dark sedan sat halfway on Highway A1A, and the other half on his driveway entrance next to his mailbox. Two figures sat motionless watching the house. Trying to act completely normal, Steve kept walking to the light switch. He turned the lights out and quietly slipped out the back door. Peeking over the fence from the backyard, he observed they hadn't budged an inch. The occupants silently sat there watching the premises. One of the men had a pair of binoculars raised to his face.

Steve decided to confront these trespassers to find out what was going on. In an attempt to get closer, he tiptoed down a narrow, sandy path between heavy growths of palmettos out to the highway. A minute later he emerged fifty feet from the dark-colored car's trunk. Steve searched his pockets for a pen and began writing down the license plate number on his hand. Then with a deep breath, he marched up to the driver's side window and gave it three sharp knocks.

Both men slowly set down their equipment. The closest one to Steve lowered his binoculars. His partner dropped a megaphone-type instrument, the small ear plugs still attached. This thing was a hyperbolic listening device used to amplify sound at a distance. The two men inside didn't appear to be all that surprised by Steve's flanking movements. The window glided down, revealing a Terminator-type character. Both guys wore sunglasses in spite of it being 12:30 at night. The driver's side window had just opened all the way when Steve said, "Hey, I really like your sunglasses. You know, ya need good ones to protect your eyes from the damaging UV rays this time of night."

There was no reaction from the occupants, just a steel, cold stare.

"So, are you fellas lost?"

Another menacing gaze was directed at Steve leaving little question as to the seriousness of this meeting. "Shut up and listen," the driver said menacingly. "Don't go near Commander Whitson."

"Who?"

"The man who entered your home this evening."

"Spaceman?" asked Steve.

"It could be extremely dangerous for you."

"How do you mean?" Steve shouted at the rising window. The car burned rubber as it kicked up sand and pebbles into Steve's ankles. "Hey, who are you clowns?" He picked up a small rock and tossed it in the direction of the departing vehicle.

After rubbing his stinging ankles, Steve walked toward the house reviewing in his mind what had just transpired. There was a good possibility these two thugs had shadowed Spaceman previously from time to time. Steve thought to himself that bizarre inadequately describes the threats he'd received. If Space was telling fairy tales, then why are these guys hell bent on keeping anyone from getting too close to him. Sometimes people's actions do speak louder than words ever could. If Space is telling the truth, then the implications for mankind are mind boggling. Steve knew previously that there was more to Spaceman than his reputation locally as a homeless kook. The information he related exhibited a high degree of accuracy. Steve also realized how well placed disinformation, emanating from the powers that be, could influence and confuse people's own logical thought processes. Steve started concluding it wasn't Spaceman living in a fantasy world but the complete opposite. And the truth was the simple key to it all.

When he reached the garage door, he banged on it yelling for Space to get up. "Hit the button on the wall." Steve entered under the rising door. He saw Spaceman perched on the cot finishing up the last of his sandwich. "Hey, guess who I just met outside?"

Spaceman was too busy eating his sandwich to pay much attention to Steve's question. He shrugged.

Steve continued, "Two of your old acquaintances who are keeping tabs on you, Commander."

Spaceman nearly choked on his remaining food.

"Commander Whitson, I believe?" mocked Steve as he pretended to straighten out boxes in the garage.

"Man, that's a name from another life, Stevie. I want nothing to do with those guys."

"Apparently they don't want me to have anything to do with you."

"Sorry, dude. I really wanted to avoid dragging anyone else into my troubled vortex. I've learned to accept their constant presence and live with it."

"Are those the creeps that shadow you?"

"Yeah. They're NSA or CIA agents most probably. Either way, they're simply following orders originating in the Defense Department or MJ12. They've kept tabs on me to make certain no one takes my information seriously. I've been looking over my shoulder for fifteen years since I voluntarily left the program."

"Ah, don't worry about it Space, they're gone now. Those schmucks don't scare me. Get some sleep, buddy, and I'll see you in the morning."

"All right, man. Thanks."

Steve walked through the main hallway unable to clear his mind. Why in the world would these agents be trailing Spaceman if he'd simply fabricated all these strange stories? The answer repeatedly kept coming up the same. They wouldn't. This conclusion created a chill that suddenly ran down Steve's spine. It raised a topic whose main question asked, "Is the human race prepared to deal with such revelations?" Its effects would permeate across all lines of our civilization: religion, economic, social, and the very fiber of our existence. Acknowledging the actual fact that we are not alone is a complex problem and might take time. It's like pouring cement; if it is not given the proper amount of curing time, it weakens and cracks. Humans are more complex and more vulnerable; therefore, they need more time to avoid damage.

This problem explains the government's determination to implement desensitizing programs through the different communications mediums years ago. A slow feeding of information has taken place while the information age accelerated technology. The impact on our civilization will be greatly dampened by gradual subconscious learning of alien existence by the general population. This will create minimal damage to our fragile psyches. Despite mankind's huge egos stating the contrary, discovering human beings are not the king of the hill anymore is survivable. The Brookings Institute and other government think tanks probably made a correct assessment in the 1950s when deciding on a slow desensitizing implementation on the public. Steve acknowledged this because when the sudden realization that Spaceman's tales had registered genuine, it shook him to his very soul, despite the bravado he had exhibited in the garage tonight. Even with his above average knowledge of this phenomena, it still did a number on his head.

Steve halted by the small bar in the living room and poured himself a large glass of Johnny Walker. The sleeping aid was dispatched within short order. Double checking the locks on all the doors, Steve laughed at their false security and retired.

CHAPTER THREE

As the Florida sun was rising, Steve phoned Captain Al. Al had his fishing trawler tied up at the bulkhead in the canal behind his home. On the Indian River side, the town of Cocoa Beach is a crosshatch of canals that eventually leads out to Port Canaveral and the Atlantic. Captain Al ran the shrimp boat Steve worked on a few years prior to becoming an insurance agent. Al had migrated down from New York to Florida seven years earlier. He formerly ran a trawler out of Shinnecock Bay at the east end of Long Island.

In a word, Al was a hustler. "Anything for a buck" was his motto. He retained his callous New York exterior and established himself as a stern task master aboard his boat. Al's coarse, money-hungry attitude somehow never got in the way of the friendship he had with Steve. Steve, a native Floridian who'd been raised on his father's citrus farm, understood what it takes to be a successful sole proprietor in a small business. This might be the common bond between them. God knows Steve earned every dime he made while working on "Captain Blythe's" ship, as it is known among the crewmen. In spite of this, they still fished and surfed together on occasion.

Al was next to his cellular phone down inside the engine room aboard his boat, The Sea Disk. He was trying to locate a leak on the large diesel engine when the call came in.

"Al?"

"Yeah. Hey, how ya' doin', Steverino?"

"Great. Are you going out tonight?"

"No. I've got the next two days off. Why, what's up?"

"Well, it's got to do with a UFO off the beach."

"Did I hear you right?"

"Yeah, you did."

"Badda bing! I'm all ears. And since you mention it, I captured some outrageous video shots of a craft coming out of the water a couple of weeks ago. I've got my video camera close by all the time when I'm out now. You know my interest in this stuff."

"This involves substanially more than videos, Al. Bobby and I saw something go down right off the beach. Its lights went out as if it lost power. We're pretty certain of the area it's located in. If it's there, we could probably detect it with that old treasure hunter's magnometer I gave you."

"Say no more. Forget about it. I'm there, Steverino."

"I figure if we did recover something, your winches on board might be able to bring it up."

"I'm there, Bro. I can't get going for a few hours. Can you be ready to roll this afternoon around 4:00?"

"Yep. Is it O.K. if I bring a couple of friends along?"

"Sure."

"You remember I told you about that guy, Spaceman? Well, you'll get a chance to meet him..."

"Sure, sure."

"Great. I'm going to bring my tanks and wet suit."

"No problem. I have plenty of gear we can use aboard ship. Oh, uh, Steverino? What's my cut on this salvage operation?"

"Whatever, Al."

"I trust you, Steve, you know that but I'm thinking this thing could be a gold mine. Worth millions."

"We can discuss it when I get up there."

"O.K. Steverino. See ya."

Steve moved around the house, cell phone propped against his head. He opened the garage door to find Spaceman snoring away peacefully on the portable cot.

The next call Steve made was to the Brevard County Sheriff's Office where a cousin worked. Steve's cousin owed him a couple of favors, and he intended to use one now. He asked him to run a check on a certain license tag number, the one attached to last night's visitors' black sedan. The plate was from Florida, and its owner's identification could prove most interesting. The response from his relative was affirmative. His cousin would call when he had something.

Steve put the phone down and headed toward the kitchen when the doorbell rang. "C'mon in, Bobby."

"Morning. What's up with you?"

"I just got off the phone with Al. He's a go on this thing."

"Cool. The girls are going. I don't know about Kim but Carol's really looking forward to this trek. Or maybe it's simply your irresistible charm, Big Brother."

"Oh, that must be it," said Steve.

"So, what's the deal there?" questioned Bobby with a sly smile.

"I don't know. It developed out of nowhere. She's a gorgeous woman."

"Well, don't get too serious. You're asking for nothing but trouble," warned Bobby.

"What's that mean? She's cool," defended Steve.

"You know what I'm talking about. The black/white thing and how people can be. You're probably better off keeping your distance."

"That'll never bother me. If different groups can't get along, what the hell kind of world would it be?"

"I guess you're right," Bobby said, sorry he'd opened a can of worms. Trying to back out of the dead end he'd turned into, Bobby asked, "Anyway, so we're really going looking for that flying saucer. What'll we do assuming against all odds we find something on the bottom?"

"Bring it up with the trawler's winches," said Steve.

"Do you think towing that old magnometer will pick it up?"

"If it's made of metal, I don't see why not," replied Steve.

"This is kind of a wild goose chase then."

"Yeah, well maybe. So we take the girls, pack some dinner, and at least have a good time if nothing else. I have a feeling, though. The way that thing dropped back into the water, it sure appeared terminal. If it's still resting on the bottom, then there's a good chance we'll get more than dinner this evening."

"You're giving me the willies," said Bobby.

"Speaking of willies, you missed Spaceman's Welcome Wagon last night. Two thugs warned me, in no uncertain terms, to keep my distance from Space a.k.a. Commander Whitson."

"Are you joking?"

"No their car blocked the bottom of my driveway last night. It's just another excellent reason I think our sighting last night was genuine."

"Commander Whitson is Spaceman's real name? Did they show you some I.D. badges?

"They told me they 'didn't need no stinkin' badges,'" Steve said in his best Mexican accent. "Seriously, the only thing I got was a warning to stay away from my house guest, and some intense threatening stares."

"Could you tell if they were military?" Bobby asked.

"Well if I tell you, I'd have to kill you."

"This shit's not funny, Steve. Maybe we shouldn't be getting involved with Spaceman. If he's telling the truth, this is some serious shit. Serious enough to be getting threats from government agents."

"Ah, relax. It'll take more than a couple of threats to keep me from talking to Space."

As Steve savored teasing his now overly concerned brother, a shaggy, gray-haired, bearded hippie poked his head out from the door leading to the garage fully attired in the latest Woodstock collection. "Hey man, I would like to take this time to express my gratitude for letting me crash here, Stevie."

"What's up, Space?" greeted Bobby.

"Hey, Bob."

"We're a go for later this afternoon with Captain Al's boat," Steve informed him. "You still going?"

"Yeah, Stevie. I have to."

"You'll like talking to Al. He's a member of the local MUFON chapter in Cocoa, the mutual UFO network."

"That's cool. I'm telling you man, it is like everyday I'm remembering more and more."

"Does this mean I have to salute you now, Space?" asked Bobby. "I heard your rank is Commander."

"Like that is absolutely not humorous, Bob."

"Lighten up, Space," Bobby said. "Listen, I've got an extra long board in my truck you can borrow. Meet us out front on the beach in half an hour. The sets are small, but we're going to try and shred a few waves anyway."

"Are the girls coming soon?" asked Steve.

"Yeah, in a little while. They're sleeping in a bit. Are you going to teach Carol the first rule of beach surfing: if it swells, she should ride it?" Spaceman actually gave off a small snicker.

"You're a riot, you are," Steve said. "Let's go."

The temperature on the beach was about 85 degrees with a slight breeze coming out of the west, which aided in holding up the waves rushing to shore from the ocean to the east. Brevard County was showing off its best weather. Visibility in the water couldn't have been better. The incoming high tide began amputating the beach's overall size by squeezing it up against the grass dunes. For a Saturday, the beach was unusually quiet. Steve and Bobby squatted on their knees applying surf wax to the surface of the three long boards lying on either side of the blanket. Spaceman had already departed, paddling out in his usual slow, cautious fashion. With beard and long hair now soaked, he sat atop Steve's extra board accepting his reign as elderly statesman over all of surfdom.

Carol and Kim emerged through the dunes behind Steve's house. Bobby looked up from his waxing and whispered to Steve, "Jeez, will you check out Carol's suit." Steve caught both girls out of the corner of his eye just as they arrived at the blanket.

Carol knelt down asking, "So is this my stick?" and she planted a big kiss on Steve.

"Hi," he said returning the kiss and dropping the wax from his grasp. "Stick? Are you sure you've never surfed before?"

"No. Kim's been tutoring me on the lingo."

"Oh. So you're ready to show me your stuff?"

Giving Steve a big smile, Carol answered, "Yeah, right after we go surfing!"

"Hi, Honey," exclaimed Bobby as he welcomed Kim with a kiss.

"Beautiful day out here," commented Kim.

"You said it. Let's get to enjoying it because we have to meet Captain Al up in Cocoa Beach at 4:30." The smile slid from Kim's face.

"I'm really anticipating an interesting evening," Carol told Steve.

"Bobby, c'mon. Take a walk with me," suggested Kim, adding a wink and head nod to her request.

Steve and Carol took immediate advantage of the empty beach. They embraced and grappled across the blanket in a whirl of passion.

Fifteen minutes later, both lay on their stomachs side by side facing the ocean.

"You know, Steve, I often wonder why people from different backgrounds and cultures are unable to act civilized to each other. Why can't small differences such as appearances and customs be accepted? We're all the same on the inside. Everyone needs air, food, love, and hope. The diversity people encounter in foreign groups should be experienced and might even be found to be enjoyable and rewarding if they'd let it. Do we always have to be warring with one another or at the very least, segregated? If people would just make a small effort."

"You're right, Carol. Attitude is everything. Attitude keeps different groups separate from one another. You can't understand other cultures if you have no respect and refuse to seek out the good qualities which exist in them."

"Steve, I was just thinking about that thing underwater. What if something or someone is alive inside? How would we treat an alien originating from a totally remote point in our universe? Could humans who maintain a fairly high level of intelligence be able to overcome our prejudices and accept such a radically different being? I've always believed variety is a beautiful thing and makes the world a nicer place to live. After all, you and I seem to be getting along really well." Carol held her arm up against Steve's leg for color comparison.

Steve observed, "That's almost a perfect match with my surfer's tan."

She laughed and said, "See, that's what I mean. We're really not that different."

"Well," said Steve, "I respect you and I'm making quite an effort today to get to know you even better." They both laughingly kissed while embracing together on the blanket.

After a moment, Carol's attention was directed north. She asked, "Is that Kennedy Space Center up there?"

"Yes. You can barely make out the outline of the Vehicle Assembly Building. The building is so large condensation clouds form inside it right below the ceiling."

"Now that's big. How long has the Cape been there?"

"I'm not sure, but they use to shoot captured German V-2 rockets up in 1946-47. I think they stopped the test firings due to complaints from the Cubans that the rockets were landing down range in their country. The U. S. recovered quite a few V-2s captured at war's end. Half of the items went to the Cape, the others ended up at Whitesands near Roswell, New Mexico."

"Isn't Roswell where the flying saucer crashed in 1947?"

"Yes and I'll tell you a related story from a year ago which peaked my interest in the subject." Steve got comfortable as he relayed the story.

"A friend of mine was having a Christmas party. He knew of my interest in UFOs and told me not to miss speaking with his 73-year-old aunt from Roswell, New Mexico. As I started talking with this very intelligent women, I found out that not only was she born in Roswell, but she worked at Los Alamos National Labs. She was high up in the Non-destructive Materials Division. Well, you know how the Air Force denies everything pertaining to the crash and retrieval? This woman, who was extremely sharp for her age, told me in no uncertain terms, and I quote, 'I know they're lying because I saw the official Air Force memorandum stating how they shipped the disc and bodies to Ft. Worth and then on to Wright Patterson Field in Ohio, which was the home of the Air Material Command.' The memorandum was lying on her boss's desk. He was the director of the department. Being from Roswell she said seeing that name on the memo had originally attracted her attention to it."

"Did she question her boss?"

"Yeah, and he asked, 'Doris, do you have a need to know?' This all occurred in the 50s. Doris also knew everyone in Roswell where she grew up. She related a story involving one of the nurses at the air base in '47. This nurse assisted with the autopsies done on the alien bodies brought in from the three crash sites. Supposedly, she was killed in a car crash in England where she was transferred. The family knew the real story. She is being kept in a convent in Wisconsin by the government for safe keeping. To this day, she can't handle the whole thing. The powers that be did not want an unstable security leak talking when they went to so much trouble to bury this whole event."

"They couldn't do that. Could they?"

"Absolutely. Under the shield of National Security, all niceties go out the window. My own research efforts align pretty damn close to many of Spaceman's so-called crazy stories. There have been quite a few crashes and retrievals over the years. Our Defense Department has been highly involved doing one hell of a job keeping it from the public. You have to understand one single fact; it is not only our government hiding the facts, but the aliens themselves who came here to study us. They do not want their presence brought to light in any way. If you can't understand those basics, then you'll never see how silence is maintained so well. Our boys are highly organized and have unlimited funds and resources available. Every security agency in the nation, all branches of the military stand ready to enforce the secrecy using a strict 'need to know' basis. Soldiers don't question; they follow orders."

Carol looked a bit surprised. "Boy, this stuff can really get intense."

"You saw how it overwhelmed Spaceman. I personally can't see how anyone is not interested in the subject. It literally encompasses our whole history, maybe why we're here. I think people are afraid of what may be revealed if enlightened to the truth. I'm not afraid of the truth now or ever. If man is part alien and they've been here for a million years, so be it. Oh, sorry Carol, I'm rambling."

"No, I'm fascinated by all of this."

Spaceman caught a wave some fifty yards off the beach. His 55-year-old legs were hanging on for dear life. It was Space who opened Steve's eyes to the grand deception being perpetrated on the public. His past consisted of much more than that of an ordinary beach bum. He possessed an abundance of integrity and intelligence beneath the innocuous facade he created running from the military. God only knows how much knowledge he actually absorbed in an area of above top secret clearances and classified "Eyes Only" material.

Carol's mind was silently connecting the dots on this huge puzzle, her face reflecting the determination of not resting until the truth is unearthed and exposed. "So where did our saucer go down?"

"Almost straight out," Steve pointed. "Right over Spaceman's head about a mile further out."

Carol wondered aloud, "Do we have a shot at really finding that thing?"

"If it hasn't moved too far," Steve replied. "Whatever it was, it sure seemed to be disabled when it plunged into the water."

"Are there many reports by locals in the area of seeing things come out of the water?" asked Carol.

"Some. I've sure observed my quota."

"What would aliens be doing down there?" Carol wanted to know.

"You'd have to ask them. I think they're keeping an eye on the Cape and the payloads our military puts into space aboard Delta, Atlas, and Titan rockets."

"That would make sense."

"I met a reverend in town that told me he used to work on the launch pads in the 1950's. At a night launch of a Thor rocket which predated Gemini and Redstone, he and two other workers were the only ones close enough to witness a large star-shaped UFO descend to approximately a hundred feet over the rocket. Standing from their vantage point by a fence they noticed a short flash of blue light and the UFO was gone. Seconds later the Thor rocket exploded on the pad. His superiors put a scare into all three men telling them never to speak of what they'd seen, or they might jeopardize national security. Not until forty years later did he feel safe enough to tell me what had happened."

Carol suggested, "Why don't these people go on TV and tell their story to someone?"

"I know the network CEO's receive strict guidelines not to broadcast certain info on this subject from the Department of Defense. National security is a very broad shield. Not only does it provide justifiable protection for legitimate security but also hides a lot of rats and their greedy, dirty dealings. This is done with unaccountable funds. But that's another discussion."

Carol lay on the blanket still reviewing in her head what Steve had said. Her train of thought was derailed when Steve jumped up from the blanket and lifted the two surfboards.

Glancing at his watch Steve said, "If I'm going to show you how to surf before 4:00, we should get out there. Ready?" Space was the only one visible on the abandoned horizon.

"Yep."

Carol had managed to plane the board off and ride sitting on her knees to the inevitable wipe out. The waves were not big and extended a courteous gentle roll allowing for her first successful ride. Steve stood close by in the waist deep shallows and applauded her efforts while coaching her techniques.

"Good job," Steve called out. A second later the board and Carol flipped upside down under the small breakers. She surfaced and tried to laugh but concentrated more on gulping air. Steve grabbed the loose board.

Carol asked, "Did I do it correctly?"

"For the most part, that was pretty good." Steve enjoyed teaching his fearless, vivacious student. He admired her spirit and curiosity. Carol also loved receiving all of Steve's attention as she frolicked in the white water with him.

The perfect day was soon to be interrupted by Spaceman's muffled bellows from behind them. He shouted to them over the splashing surf in an attempt to attract their attention. Space pointed his arms toward the relatively calm deeper water further out. Steve's first reaction was to scan the area for signs of shark movements. Given his nasty experience only a few short months ago, he always remained vigilant to that danger. But the typical fin activity and shadows never materialized. Steve thought to himself that he was overreacting. Meanwhile, Space continued shouting.

Carol uttered, "Did you see that?"

"No, what?"

"Over there. Where Spaceman was pointing a minute ago!"

Steve wondered what he'd missed. This time it didn't escape his line of vision. The tight beam of blue laser-like light flashed up extending from the deep through the atmosphere into infinity. "That's coming from our sight out there," Steve said.

"Oh my gosh. What are they signaling?"

"I don't know. It sure looks like some kind of distress signal."

"But Steve, who could they be signaling?"

Spaceman was paddling toward them for all he was worth as Carol and Steve hustled the surfboards onto the beach in an attempt to procure a better vantage point from higher ground.

Steve threw the board on the sand. They shaded their eyes by cupping both hands to block the sun's glare. Space catapulted from the water in an excitable state.

"Man, they're out there, Stevie. Like I'm telling you, they're here for real."

"We saw it, too," Steve verified. "The flashing seems to have stopped."

"Yeah. I don't see it anymore," added Carol. "Space, what could they be doing down there?"

"I don't know. It might be a signaling laser."

"So these guys are putting through an SOS to the nearest galactic auto club?" asked Steve, trying to loosen up some of the tension.

The blank expression on Spaceman's face clearly showed that the joke did not register with him.

"It has definitely halted sending the signals," noted Carol.

Bobby and Kim jogged toward the blanket with an air of urgency. They pulled up short of everyone hands on their hips, huffing and puffing. "Did you see it?" Bobby coughed as he gasped for air.

"Steve, tell me the truth. Is this going to be safe?" Kim demanded.

"Honestly, I'm not sure. But someone or something is out there, and I for one am prepared to take some risks to investigate it."

In response to Steve's declaration, Bobby reminded everyone that 4:00 was approaching, and they all needed to go. He wanted to get the trip underway before any objections sabotaged the whole thing.

"I'll pick you and Space up in half and hour," said Bobby. "Kim and Carol will be with me."

"Sounds great," Steve answered. He gave Carol a quick kiss goodbye.

They all made their way over the grassy dunes to Steve's house. The group members remained a bit uneasy after witnessing those peculiar underwater lights that penetrated the atmosphere.

At 4:01, Steve and Spaceman found themselves standing at the end of the driveway waiting for Bobby. Space leaned against the mailbox while Steve surveyed the limits of his front yard that bordered A1A. "I've got to do some yard work and trim back the growth," said Steve. "There are wild weeds all over the place."

Spaceman snapped to attention, "Where, man, where?"

"Not wild weed. I mean real weeds!"

"Oh, my mistake, Stevie."

"You know, from what you tell me, Space, I wouldn't mess with that shit especially if you don't believe there's a surplus of brain cells to kill."

"Stevie, like that is true but it is the least of my problems currently."

"I hear ya."

The van came off A1A kicking up dust and dragging dirt and small stones as it slid to a halt. Steve and Carol sat behind Bobby and Kim in the front seats of the luxury van. Spaceman snaked his way to the rear padded bench seat. He promptly laid down and propped his sandle-clad feet in the air against the velour covered walls.

The group sped north on A1A toward Cocoa Beach. Bobby turned to the group, "I've got to hit a gas station. We can load up the big cooler in the back at the same time. Where's a good place to stop?"

Space sat up, "There's a gas-mart past the next light." He was referring to a convenience store whose proprietor was Hindi.

"Carol and I will get the beer while you gas up," Steve said. They turned off into the parking lot of the gas mart. There was a large dump trunk parked sideways across five parking spaces. Immediately behind the truck sat two chopped Harley Davidson motorcycles. While walking toward the store, Steve realized he had left his wallet in the car and made an about face. He yelled above the dump truck's idling motor, "Go ahead in. I'll be right there."

Space and Carol walked into the store. Space greeted the owner, "Hey, Hodgi, what's up, dude?"

In a heavy Hindi accent Hodgi responded, "So where have you been lately, Mr. Mayor?"

"I have administrative duties on the beach, baby," smiled Space. He headed straight for the gourmet food rack and pulled down a couple of Slim Jim's. Carol continued past two large construction workers who immediately had trouble pouring their coffee due to Carol's shapely legs.

She continued to her destination and retrieved two bags of ice from the freezer.

Steve had grabbed his money and entered the store. After greeting the owner, he made a bee line to the beer and soda at the rear of the store. Wobbling and banging into the shelves of food were two unsavory characters who owned the motorcycles outside. Both drunk bikers eyeballed Carol as she went about collecting what she needed for the boat trip. The first trouble-maker snickered some undecernable curse words ending very clearly in the word "nigger."

Steve opened the cooler doors and removed a case of beer. The uglier of the two looked in Steve's direction, "Hey, do you believe they let niggers in here?"

Not acknowledging him, Steve walked to the checkout counter and joined Carol. "Did you find the ice O.K.?"

She answered, "Yes." Her face reflected fear as the two drunk bikers closed in on them.

The ugly one taunted, "So you're with this nigger bitch?"

Listening by the front doors, Space slipped the two Slim Jims into his shirt and exited silently.

At two hundred and forty pounds of muscle, Steve was not about to back away from a couple of loud-mouthed losers. He answered the challenge, "Yeah, she's with me. You got a problem with that, dirt bag?"

Hodgi's complexion turned pale in anticipation of the inevitable conflict. He made an attempt to lean over the counter with not much success due to his small stature, and pleaded humbly to the combatants, "Please, boys. Take this outside. Don't fight in my establishment."

"Oh a tough guy nigger-lover."

The two construction workers had finished getting their coffee and now looked on. The tension had proliferated throughout the entire store.

Steve spoke to them in a calm, matter-of-fact tone. "Normally, I wouldn't waste my time kicking the crap out of the likes of you, but I will make an exception for you two losers." They both looked at one another and began laughing.

Meanwhile, right outside the store, Spaceman walked up to the idling sand truck left by the two coffee-swilling construction workers. He coolly sized up the proximity of the bikers' shiny motorcycles to the tailgate on the huge truck. Giving a quick spin around of his fuzzy-haired head, Spaceman reached in and activated the hydraulic dump mechanism. His mission completed, he slid as inconspicuously as possible from the truck's cab and slithered around the back of the building lower than a snake's belly in a wagon track. Emerging on the far side of Bobby's van, Space hopped in the side door.

Inside the store, the ugly biker growled, "All right, tough guy. You know you'll have to fight both of us."

"Time's a wastin'. Let's do it," Steve snapped. His opponent was taken aback by Steve's eagerness to butt heads.

Carol searched for a way to avoid a fight. "Don't fight them, Steve. Let's just go," she begged.

The store owner pleaded again in his heavy Indian accent, "Oh, my goodness, please gentlemen. Don't do this. 'Dis is very, very bad!'"

Steve led the way to the parking lot and put the case of beer on the curb. Carol continued to implore him to leave.

Following in Steve's wake, the drunken bikers trailed him and smashed the front door open. The first creep tossed his jacket on the sidewalk. While turning to face his enemy, the biker observed a surprising sight. His beady little red eyes popped opened in disbelief as mountains of cascading sand engulfed their precious motorcycles.

"Shit!" they both yelled as they sprinted over to the almost submerged Harleys. In their futile attempt to pull them out, they both came close to being buried alive by the vast piles of sand continuing to pour out of the truck.

While paying for their coffee, the pair of burly construction workers realized their truckload of sand was being emptied. The truck's driver yelled to his partner, "What the hell?" They both bolted out the door.

In the parking lot, each biker was buried up to his waist in sand and started cursing profusely at the construction workers.

The ugly biker screamed, "You're gonna pay for this, asshole!"

Listening to the idle threats, the rather large road workers remained silent momentarily. They were extremely agitated at the loss of their load and didn't require much coaxing to set them off. The driver finally erupted.

Directing his words at the sand-encrusted loud mouth, he said, "You're the only one that's gonna pay, brother. Starting right now!" He let a monstrous right fly. The crack it made landing on the biker's jaw could be heard a block away. The biker's legs were still implanted up to his knees in sand. This caused a hinge-like motion as he folded up like a cheap suit case from the shot perpetrated upon his face.

The second worker leaped on the other sand-clad punk. They wrestled and shouted in an effort to become king of the sand hill. There was sand everywhere.

The owner of the store, who stood a menacing 5'2" in height, arrived at the scene to try and break things up. He shouted, "I cannot have this sand here. 'Dis parking lot is for my patrons only. Please gentlemen, this is most improper."

Steve and Carol looked at each other in disbelief as Bobby pulled his van right next to them. They picked up the beer and the ice and hopped into the side door of the vehicle, escaping the ensuing riot.

The escapees drove north on Hwy A1A toward their destination. Spinning around in his seat, Steve eyed Spaceman lying over the length of the plush bench seat with his feet up chewing on a Slim Jim. "Where were you?"

"What do you mean?" Space asked innocently.

"You, ah, didn't happen to go near that dump truck back there, did you?"

"Nope. I was right here the whole time after leaving the store. I do not like those anti-social types. Have a Slim Jim?"

Steve gave him a smirk and said, "I'll pass, thanks."

Kim leaned over the high back seat, "What was all that ruckus about back there?"

"Nothing. Just a couple of drunken dirt bags causing a little trouble." Steve answered.

"I'm really sorry about all this, Steve," Carol apologized.

"You're sorry? They're the ones that should be sorry, and probably are right about now."

Carol tried to figure out the bikers' actions. "I don't understand people sometimes. We just discussed this on the beach. One group thinks they're better than another. They show no respect, take advantage and play on the visible differences to incite trouble."

Steve said, "Punks like those dirt bags back there need to be taught they don't have to see eye to eye with people of other races or cultures, but peaceful cohabitation is the very least one should strive for. The big lesson to be learned would be that showing a minimal effort to get along pays nice dividends when the other group returns the effort. We all have prejudices inside us. I think it's part of our primitive natural animal instincts. The one distinct difference humans possess is intelligence and a soul. If we can't use these capabilities to overcome the hostile animal instincts, well we're all in trouble." Carol put her head on Steve's shoulder.

"Hey, you guys are getting pretty heavy back there," commented Bobby.

"Just some ideas to live by," replied Steve.

"Right on, baby," reverberated Spaceman from the bench seat in the rear.

It continued to stay gorgeous outside. The weather was balmy and beautiful. The van approached the narrow palm-lined stretch of the highway separating Patrick Air Force Base from the ocean directly across the street. Laying on the beach at this place one could see right up inside the landing gear of the fighter jets arriving only a hundred feet over the dunes and road. Runways come right up to the edge of the highway corralled by the ten-foot high chain link fence surrounding the entire base from the Banana River on the west side to the Atlantic Ocean on the east.

"Carol, see that building there?" Steve asked as he pointed inside the base. "They used to show that before every 'I Dream of Jeanne' episode on television back in the sixties.

"Isn't that Dr. Bellows over there in the parking lot?" asked Bobby with a serious stare.

"Very funny," said Kim.

Bobby said, "I heard that they stored two alien crash victims in cold storage at this base."

"Really?" asked Carol.

"Get outta here," Kim responded.

"I heard that, too," Steve said. "God knows there's been enough crashes over the last fifty years. What about that, Space?"

"Yeah, they used to store some here and at Langley, Virginia. I believe they moved the ones from Wright Patterson in Ohio. They've played musical chairs with them over the years. Secure military installations are their favorite depositories. When rumors grow after a few years, they'll move them."

"You guys are all nuts!" Kim complained.

Space sat up and leaned forward. "Man, then explain to me why every United States Air Force base has a UFO Officer, baby. There are no Leprechaun Officers or Santa Claus Officers."

"I never heard of that," Kim said.

"Need to know," said Space. "Strictly need to know. Believe me, they're like not going to consult with you first."

Kim turned around in her seat as she chose not to listen to any more substantiating facts about the subject.

Most people don't just turn around, they bury their heads in the sand like an ostrich hoping the problem will go away. But it won't. Not only don't the aliens want us to know they're here studying humans, but there are a large number of ostrich-like people out there who will actually tell you, when the subject comes up, that they don't want to know. It's bad enough that the military is in cahoots with the aliens and hides the truth. These ostriches may someday find out that they've become sheep and are on the way to slaughter. The point is by then, it might be too late.

Fortunately, the number of intelligent people who can see through the smoke and mirrors and examine the hard facts is growing everyday, inspite of mind control, continuous disinformation on TV, and other controlled media outlets. The truth may have a cost, although in most estimations this cost is a whole lot cheaper than living a large lie. Truth is an intangible that eventually makes itself known to those people willing to hear it.

The runways were extremely close to the road. A loud noise began filling everyone's ears. Bobby was checking his dash board for signs of malfunctions coming from the van. It soon became quite apparent the high-pitched whine came from outside. In a search for the source of this anomaly the fence line along the base was scanned, trying to relieve the uneasy feeling accompanying this unknown quantity.

"What is that noise?" asked Kim.

Bobby said, "Hey, look up ahead by the fence."

At the end of a runway, hovering in the air approximately thirty feet above the ground, were three Harrier jump jets. A group of officers stood signaling them in what appeared to be a training session.

Steve pointed out the window, "Carol, see them?"

"Yes, I see them. They're pretty cool, aren't they?"

"They just hang there as if the laws of gravity don't apply," said Steve. "Space, you see those jets hovering out there?"

Carol asked, "That couldn't be what we saw last night, could it?"

"Yes. That's probably what we saw last night hovering over the water," said Kim, confident she had a solid explanation for the mysterious sighting.

"Not hardly, baby," corrected Spaceman. "Those vector jets and that main turbo jet engine can be heard a mile away. And as far as underwater maneuverability, it's a big fat zero. No way, Jose."

"Oh, how would you know anyway?" snapped Kim.

"I was checked out on those babies in '67," he replied.

"What are you saying? You mean you flew Harriers in 1967?" asked a surprised Steve.

"Among other things," Space replied seriously. "One elite unit I was with required all the pilots to be able to fly every winged aircraft in the known world."

Kim rolled her eyes once again at his creative mind.

"I told you earlier about Papoose Lake, Nevada. Well, under Project Snowbird in 1973, we made successful attempts at flying recovered wingless craft not of this world. You talk about unusual flight characteristics. What a trip, man."

Spaceman took a short glance through the rear window at the noisy hovering jets and returned his attentions to the more pressing issue of eating his beef jerky.

Steve and Carol looked at one another as if to silently utter, "Do you believe this guy?" Steve did and listened quite closely to the details emanating from Space's memory. The two visitors in his driveway last night only solidified Steve's trust in Spaceman.

CHAPTER FOUR

The van turned down a driveway on Captain Al's property. It led straight past his home to a large bulkhead located in his backyard. Al's boat, The Sea Disc, sat secured to the dock awaiting its passengers. Captain Al stood high up in the wheel house giving a brief wave of acknowledgment at his guests' arrival. The homes in this part of town were all on canals. The 65' trawler dwarfed the surrounding pleasure craft belonging to Al's neighbors. His twin-diesel engines idled in a low roar and indicated plenty of power to drive the boat.

Steve led the way to a primitive boarding plank. He marched up the entryway, a cooler on his shoulder and a procession of bearers close behind. The girls brought the food, Bobby brought the scuba gear, and Spaceman exhibited the most trouble carrying his load, himself.

Up on deck, Captain Al came down to greet everyone. His New York accent led the way. He said, "Aye, Steverino, how have you been, pal? I haven't seen ya in a couple of months."

Steve shook his hand, "Captain Al, what've you been up to?"

"Mostly no good," he stated, not allowing anyone to distinguish if he meant it or not.

"Captain Al, you know my brother, Bobby," said Steve. "And this is Carol, Kim, and Spaceman."

Al shook hands with everyone until he got to Space. Al eyed him up and down while shaking his hand. Suddenly he said, "Spaceman, huh? I heard you used to work in the dark world."

"Yeah, I got around," answered Space nonchalantly.

"I need to talk with you later, pal," insisted Al.

Space gave a nod in agreement.

Not wasting any time on small talk, the Captain barked out orders. While not the most imposing physical specimen at 5'7" in height and two hundred pounds, this slightly overweight fisherman had a commanding presence about him. He meant business while on The Sea Disc and his normal profit driven hustle was about to pursue one of his favorite passions: UFOs.

"All right, Steverino and Bobby, grab those lines, and we can get underway on this salvage operation," exclaimed Captain Al. He slid back into the comfortable mode of task master.

Steve and Bobby both made their way toward the stern cleats to release its heavy lines. On their way down, Bobby spoke quietly out the corner of his mouth, "Arrh, it be the great white whale that Captain Ahab is after, is it?"

Steve laughed, "Yeah, same kind of thing. We're searching for something that doesn't exist."

"I hope we avoid ending up with a similar fate dolled out to the crew of the Pequod," said Bobby.

"Amen, brother," Steve retorted. They wrestled the heavy lines from the dock cleats freeing up the boat.

Bobby continued, "You know our quarry out there has the potential to be far more dangerous than any white whale."

Steve stopped for a moment. "Well, you never make any progress without taking chances. I won't take any foolish risks with the girls here, but I've just got to have answers to what we saw last night. I guess risk-taking is the price you pay for discovery."

Coiling up the rope, Bobby asked, "Where is Captain Ahab?"

"I think he's in the wheel house."

All lines were cleared while the big diesels were revved up then dropped into gear. The boat drifted slowly from the large bulkhead wall. Both brothers joined up with their dates and maneuvered about the boat's cluttered rear deck attempting to stay clear of the nets and equipment. Spaceman had already secured a perch on the railing circling the wheel house deck. He sat there in a relaxed posture smoking one of those funny cigarettes. Aside from rendering him high, the weed also jump-started his impaired memory which he'd probably concluded would be called upon shortly.

Steve and Carol climbed the steps to the wheel house door. Once inside they spied Bobby and Kim down on the port bow sightseeing. Captain Al kept a close watch for channel markers. He turned the boat with a learned precision through the narrow canals which emptied into the Port Canaveral Inlet and on to the sea. Port Canaveral can handle the big ships. Everything from cruise boats to the Navy's Trident submarines tie up there.

Another resident is the highly secret Cape Canaveral Air Force Station located adjacent to NASA's launch pads. On occasion, it requires ships to transport oversized and hazardous materials through this slender inlet. Highly classified materials for our supposedly non-existent Space defense systems and satellites which are not permitted to travel by land near urban centers also arrive here regularly. Cover story on top of cover story ensures sound security and leaves the public totally in the dark on the cargoes. No one ever gets the straight story on the contents of these payloads launched constantly from the Cape's Air Station. Whether it's small reactors to power Star Wars beam weaponry or other more conventional nuke weapons and warheads, the Port area is a very interesting place indeed. Unbeknownst to anyone outside of a very tight security loop, supplies are also sent up to our super secret base on the moon. It's manned by the military and is used as a buffer point against unfriendly outsiders approaching Earth. The Black world thrives at the Cape. The benign shuttle program is a convenient and effective cover.

46

Outside forces most definitely have an extremely high level of concern and interest in any developments taking place at our main portal to space. On occasion, these visitors' presence is noticed and observed not only by the military but also in the visible light spectrum by the local people. The number of occasional sightings of these intruders are very limited even around the Cape. This is due to an intricate and intense effort put forth by the visitors to prevent a human realization that monitoring of man's progress is an ongoing operation. Superior technological capabilities permit their shadowy existence here as elsewhere.

Locals such as Al's fishing crews are at the forefront of sightings over the water. In the late evening hours, his boat most often becomes the lone sentinel plying the darkness off shore. Many times they have halted work to watch and observe unknown visitors who are here to watch and observe us. The waters surrounding the Cape offer quick cover for these high-tech gravity-exempt craft. A number of the more observant residents along the beach have witnessed on more than one occasion the game of hide-and-seek our military planes play with the technologically-superior interlopers from space. Last night's show over the beach front did not follow the usual sequence of events. The group on the beach realized that an opportunity had presented itself for validation of the elusive enigmas' appearances.

As the boat edged its way across the channel, two F-18 fighters whizzed overhead from out of nowhere. The sudden boom forced Captain Al to glance up from his maneuvering the trawler's wheel. The boat moved swiftly with the outgoing river current in the inlet. It ran head-on into a stiff incoming ocean tide and waves from the east. This opposite collision creates a hazardous time to travel this passage. Many inexperienced small boat operators have capsized or become swamped in these small walls of turbulent churning water.

Captain Al's boat, being a good sized craft, pushed effortlessly right over the small wall of surging water in the center of the inlet's mouth. Bobby and Kim sat near the bow spotting dolphins swimming an arms length out ahead of the trawler's sea-splitting front edge. These playful submariners enjoyed interacting with the slower moving vessel. They sliced through the clear blue channel at a torpedo's pace. Almost breaching the surface, they peered up at the strangers from another world showing no malice or aggression toward the alien craft. A more intelligent creature on earth does not exist, with the exception of man. Dolphins have learned to co-exist with the human race which is more than can be said of our tuna boats slaughtering their kind indiscriminately. Respect and understanding for different life forms is not a given simply because a species is lucky enough to possess high levels of intelligence. Negative attitudes and indifferences can twist any intellect toward a distorted view of the universe.

Inside the bridge, Carol surveyed the inlet and caught sight of Bobby and Kim's enthusiastic entertainers swimming back and forth under the bow. Her curiosity immediately peaked upon seeing this phenomenon.

She asked, "Is it all right to go down and join Bobby and Kim?"

"Sure, honey," replied Captain Al. "Use the hand rails, though."

Steve opened the cabin door for her. "I've got to speak to Al."

"O.K.," Carol said and shot down the steps to the front of the boat.

When she was gone, Al asked, "She your girl?"

"I just met her last night. She's Kim's roommate up at school. Carol's a really nice girl," responded Steve.

Al turned and said, "And damn good looking, you dawg. She does seem like a sweetheart. Good luck, pal. Now, let's get down to saucer business. I don't know if you realize the monetary value of recovering something down there. I understand we're just taking a wild shot here, but anything found would be worth a king's ransom. There are people in high tech corporations who would kill to examine advanced alien hardware."

"Al, let's not forget what will happen to us if it ever leaks out we had possession of these materials."

"Oh yeah, we'll cross that quick sand when we come to it. But think of the money, Steverino. Millions! Billions!"

"I've got to be honest, Al. I'm not in this for the money and I know you're not either. I just want the damn truth. We need some answers."

"Sure, I want answers, too. I owe that to the memory of my dad," Al said.

"I mean this thing involves man's origins, who we are, and more importantly, where we're going in the future. Things so tremendously important that our leaders feel they must shield us from the truth."

Al said nothing.

"Listen," Steve continued, "we're getting ahead of ourselves, Al. That ship might not even be out here anymore."

"True, pal, but I believe in always having a plan of attack ready in case a battle erupts."

The monitor for receiving soundings from the magnometer to be towed behind the boat was plugged in and ready to be activated. It was perched atop the control panels near the front windows.

"So the equipment is ready to roll?" asked Steve.

"Badda bing. Forget about it. I've got extra dive equipment stowed below if you need it, Steverino."

"Good. I'm not sure if we brought enough air," replied Steve.

"We won't have a lot of daylight remaining so it's a good idea to get this operation underway. Steverino, you've got to see the tapes I made recently. Some pretty weird stuff has been coming out of the water and I've recorded it all." Al flipped open a drawer by the big wheel which revealed a camcorder and

48

a half dozen tapes. "I bet my shots in these tapes are worth some big bucks if put in the right hands!"

"Al, that's the problem: getting them in the right hands. Speaking of weird, this baby we saw go down let out a loud POP before plunging into the sea. It might be disabled. I've got a strong feeling about this."

"And if we do find it, what is your plan to raise it?" asked Captain Al.

"I've heard the metals on these things are super light-weight."

"That's true," Al agreed. "My winches could probably yank up a load that's not too heavy, Steverino. Let me just say this: we find a saucer down there, trust me, that son-of-a-bitch is coming to the surface, no matter what it takes."

Steve exited the wheel house door pondering their upcoming hunt for the mysterious submerged craft. The excitement of the hunt was slowly building. An excellent chance for proving the existence of a long time debunked reality was at hand. Physical proof probably rested on the bottom only a short distance away.

Bobby yelled to Steve, "C'mon and help me lower the magnometer."

They both reached the stern of the trawler to find the equipment ready to be lowered away. Together they heaved the missile-shaped magnometer up, keeping the thin cable tangle-free. They lowered it off the stern gently watching its descent. At that instant, a supervising Al dropped the engine's RPMs which initiated a slower towing speed. Steve let out cable gingerly until the proper distance was achieved and the line became taut.

"Looks good," said Bobby as he waved the 'Go' signal to Captain Al.

"Yeah," replied Steve. "If it's here, something that size shouldn't take long to locate."

They both made their way to the bridge to wait for any results. The trawler cruised approximately a mile off shore in seventy feet of water when it started its slow, meticulous grid pattern over the target area. All the salvers sat around the monitor in anticipation of an early strike. Spaceman remained perched outside, finishing his memory-altering business.

"Have a seat boys and girls. This might take a while," urged Captain Al. Kim inquired if anyone wanted a sandwich; she wasn't paying much attention to what she considered a wild goose chase. The food and drinks seemed to be secondary on the minds of the focused group.

Carol watched the monitor curiously. "Captain Al, how do we know when we've found something?"

"Well honey, you see these lines on the display screen? That's where your visual will appear. We'll also be notified by a loud beeper in the signal box. Traveling over an object the size of your UFO will cause this thing to scream louder than a long-tailed cat in a room full of rocking chairs."

"This is getting kind of creepy," noted Kim. She leaned over to Bobby, "We'll be back before dark, won't we?"

49

Captain Al released a small frown and turned to face in the direction his boat was heading.

Before Bobby could answer, the cabin door swung open allowing Spaceman to enter. He was pursued by the odor of exotic cannabis fumes in his draft. The smell stood out against the surrounding brine-soaked boat.

"I love that fresh sea air," exclaimed Space.

Captain Al took in a snoot full of the trailing scent and maintained his forward gaze while steering the boat. He said sarcastically, "Yeah, but are you getting any of it?" It was obvious that Al didn't approve of Spaceman's sloppy appearance and smoking habits. Unconventional types rubbed him the wrong way.

"Hey amigo, do me a favor and keep track of those matches you're throwing around," snapped Captain Al. "There's too much fuel on this boat."

"No problemo, baby," came the response.

Captain Al glanced over at Steve as if to ask, "So this is your expert?" Tension began to fill the air as these two opposites began to clash.

Steve tried to divert the sparks from a combustible conversation. He asked Space, "Where do you approximate that disc went down?"

Space said, "We're in the area, man. I thought it dropped in just north of that party at your friends' place. We're looking good right here, Stevie."

Steve pointed toward a small group of white dots on the shore. "There is John and Cindy's place on the beach."

Carol chimed in, "This is definitely the area, Steve."

Captain Al leaned back in his chair, "Like the rabbi said, it won't be long now."

Bobby scanned the horizon. "There haven't been any military planes or ships around at all."

"Beauty," said Al.

Steve said, "Real good break. They must have lost its trail out at sea and didn't notice its last unsuccessful attempt to take off in here closer to shore. It probably didn't have any real altitude and never tracked on radar. Those boys in military intelligence and blue teams don't give up easily on this kind of recovery."

Spaceman nodded in agreement as he munched on a sandwich.

"What's a blue team?" questioned Kim. Her voice contained less doubt and an increased curiosity now that she was part of a serious salvage search.

Steve answered Kim's question, "Space told me Blue Teams are 'Ready to Deploy' units stationed across the country. Their job includes diversions and concealment if a craft was to come down in or near a populated area. Transport and removal by any means necessary is also their responsibility, along with creating diversions. It occurs rarely, but the military has recovered over forty craft since 1947, mostly in remote areas. All involved different circumstances and no stones were left unturned in erasing all traces of it ever happening.

"I still don't believe any of this saucer retrieval nonsense," scoffed Kim, happy to remain in the safe known parameters of her limited reality.

"Al, isn't that how your dad got involved in all of this?" asked Steve.

"That's right, Steverino," Al admitted. He leaned further back in his big captain's chair. "You see, my dad was stationed in the southwest with the army in 1947. He was assigned to the IPU which stood for the Interplanetary Phenomena Unit. My dad only told me these facts on his death bed five years ago. Like a good soldier, he maintained his sworn National Security oaths to the very end.

"In the late forties and fifties, there were quite a few crashes out there. My pop was at the Kingman, Arizona, crash, the one that went down right over the border in Mexico in '49, and the huge ship that appeared on military radar all the way to its demise at Aztec Flats."

Spaceman listened intently. He suddenly spoke, "That one really buried these visits by EBEs in total secrecy at the highest levels. The classification went to 'Above Top Secret.'"

"That's right," snapped Al. "It seems they found things aboard which scared the shit out of the recovery team."

Space became agitated, "Like, man, it wasn't things they discovered. It was quantities of human body parts."

"How do you know that? Were you involved?" demanded Al.

"No baby, that was a little before my time. But some time during my dark career, I read the report on that crash retrieval."

"Who is this guy, Steve?" Al asked visibly alarmed.

"Space is O.K." Steve assured him.

Captain Al continued, "Do you know how many people alive today who would be privy to that information? You could count them on your hands and feet!"

Steve intervened, "Space's step-father was one of the three original generals who sat on MJ12 back in '47 That is how Space was brought into the ultra-high security loop."

"O.K., that explains his knowledge," said Al as he continued to eye Space. "He just doesn't fit the type."

"A lot of water's gone under the bridge since then," reasoned Steve.

Bobby and Carol half chewed their sandwiches nervously while trying to figure the odds of these two guys meeting each other.

A comparable chance encounter equates to a spotted owl meeting a Peregrine falcon in the woods. They are both rare birds indeed, and the probability of them crossing one another's path is extremely remote. The fact is though other rare birds exist and are more common than the general population of the forest is aware. Light does penetrate the deep, dark woods on occasion and in recent times more and more birds are seeing the light and willing to take risks and emerge from their hiding places to start singing. Federal legislation protecting them is needed, however, to assure they don't become hunted and silenced.

The boat made its first turn to remain in the grid pattern, this time moving in a northerly direction. Once on course, Bobby urged Al to relate his father's experiences.

He began, "In late 1948, my father was part of a six-man unit moving a small disc to an extremely remote dry lake bed in Nevada. It was what's knows as Area 51 today. Back then my dad told me it was only three or four hangars. This was before the army dug out all the extensive underground facilities and tunnel systems.[n]

Spaceman's voice interrupted, "Hey dude, the Navy Sea Bees dug out that subterranean complex in 1951."

"Well, thanks for that clarification, pal," Al said annoyed at Spaceman's poorly timed interruptions.

"No problemo, bud," retorted a relaxed Spaceman.

"Anyway, my dad drove up to see a half-dozen of these saucer discs stacked up in this hangar. When he got out of the flat bed truck, he was shocked to see a little man walk past him about three and a half feet tall with a gray complexion. My pop thought he was seeing things. Once inside the hangars, an intelligence officer gathered up the new people from his unit and gave them a simple briefing on the aliens. Everyone was told not to speak to anyone while going about their tasks. He said they all took National Security oaths and it was explained in no uncertain terms the severe consequences of not maintaining silence about what they'd witnessed there."

Spaceman became visibly antsy. He blurted out, "Tell me about it."

"Wow! 1948, that's totally weird," said Bobby. "Who was in control out there? The military or the aliens?"

"My pop didn't really know what was going down," said Al, "and he certainly didn't ask."

The cabin grew eerily quiet.

"That's the sixty-four thousand dollar question," stated Spaceman. With increased intensity, he asked, "Who really is in control and were our guys originally duped by subtle deception? Or are our leaders in cahoots with the outsiders and their agendas because of good old fashioned greed?"

A short loud beep echoed off the magnometer's monitor. The boat's occupants of the wheel house half came out of their seats in response to the beeping sound. The previous conversation was reminiscent of a spooky fireside story told to youngsters on a camping trip. Everyone froze in midstream at the possibility of a hit.

Carol spoke out first. "Is that it?"

Captain Al reached over to the monitor, turned a knob, and said, "Nope. This target's way too small." He examined the graph's feedback. "We'll mark it on the GPS anyway."

"There should be no mistaking our baby," said Steve.

"Have a beer, Al?" asked Carol as she attempted to reduce the tension.

"Sure, send it over."

"Kim, would you like another sandwich?" Carol offered.

"No thanks. My appetite is shot," replied Kim. "I can't finish my first. Food is the last thing on my mind after that story concerning the human body parts found on the crashed UFO."

"Sorry ladies," said Captain Al in mock apology, "but facts are facts."

"So Al, you never had any idea your dad worked with these recovery units?" asked Bobby.

"No, he never spoke about those early years until the end. On his death bed over a two week period, he told me everything. Of course I didn't believe what I was hearing at first, so I taped him. Then it all fit: his past, the secrecy, his always avoiding questions about his military activities. The whole thing started my research efforts which continue to this day. In the end, Pop realized he could no longer be threatened for speaking out. At that point, he clearly possessed immunity from all forms of military reprisals. It's called death. The importance of telling someone the plain truth became his last mission. 'People must know,' he said before succumbing to the Grim Reaper."

"What could they do to him for telling the truth?" asked Kim.

"Well I'll cite an example that was relayed to me. In 1949, the Secretary of Defense, James Forrestal, allegedly committed suicide by jumping from a window. Pop told me in actuality he was killed by the CIA because of his dogged determination to reveal the visitors' presence to the populous. It had been decided by MJ12 that the masses had to be kept in the dark at all costs. I guess they determined at that point in time such a revelation would devastate our society at every level."

Space glanced around the cabin at the astonished faces. He said abruptly, "Correctomundo. Forrestal was silenced. I knew one of the agents who staged the incident by tossing him from his hospital room window to the street below."

"Is there anything you don't know, Skippy?" growled Captain Al.

"Uh huh. Number one is I don't know why you're so freakin' hostile. And number two is why you're calling me Skippy. Skippy is a peanut butter," Spaceman replied as he managed to retain his calm disposition.

"Yeah, really nutty!" retorted Captain Al.

Anticipating the growing friction, Steve stepped between the two again. "So Al, your dad had a pretty interesting military career."

"That's an understatement. He was as loyal a military man as any, but this thing became different from the other secrets. It's too important. To this day they still haven't come clean with John Q. Public."

Bobby said, "A lot of people are beginning to wake up and smell the coffee, though."

"This stuff is too scary. I really don't care to know," said Kim.

"They are frightening, but the implications are so far-reaching. I can't see how people can pretend it's not there," reasoned Carol.

"Keep going, Al," Bobby pleaded.

Al smiled at Carol and tried to regain his train of thought broken by Spaceman's abrupt interruptions. He drew a long drink from his beer and continued.

"All right. One night Pop told me of a very strange incident. He said Washington really tried to bury this one." He threw a backwards glance at Spaceman. "I bet Skippy hasn't even heard this one. Apparently in 1952 an Air Force C-47 Transport plane had departed from an air base somewhere in the Northwestern U.S. Twelve Air Force special technicians equipped with advanced electronic gear were on board for transfer to another base. The tower radioed the plane warning the pilot that a large radar target was approaching head on. Not far from the base over a rough timber lined wilderness area the plane went off the tower's radar as well as the large UFO.

"Anticipating a crash, a second plane was dispatched to search for survivors. What the spotter plane found was beyond anything they expected: the plane was down, all right, but not in small pieces of burning wreckage. Sitting in a clearing among the tall pines was an intact C-47. It was as if some one had plucked it from the sky and gently set it down in the field. There was absolutely no room for a landing. My old man, stationed with the IPU, was flown to the scene. They were the first to arrive at the remote site.

"After hiking through the snow-covered area, the rescuers became completely baffled by what they saw. There were no tracks leading into or out of the small clearing among the pines. But the big surprise came when they approached the craft to search for survivors. Pop described the eerie scene when they discovered that none of the airmen were aboard. It was as if all 12 vanished from the face of the earth. Again, tracks outside in the previous night's pristine snowfall were nowhere to be found. My dad still got the willies four decades later relating that story to me."

Bobby said, "What we're talking about here is a permanent abduction of those men?"

"They never turned up anywhere to my father's knowledge," answered Al. "He found out later that the relatives were told the men were killed in a training accident."

Kim was listening to Al's story intently. She turned to Bobby and repeated, "Honey, we are going to leave before dark, aren't we?"

"Oh yeah, pretty soon if we don't find anything," assured Bobby.

The sun dropped low on the western horizon. It extinguished the previously well lit cabin interior where Carol presently slid against Steve on the long bench seat behind Captain Al. She burrowed underneath Steve's strong arm seeking a comfortable haven. Carol's psyche seemed not only disturbed by Al's stories but they agitated memories from her own past. The uneasiness finally forced a question from her.

"Why would someone take twelve soldiers from that plane, and more importantly, for what possible purpose?"

"A great question that my father had no answer for," Captain Al said.

Kim said, "Who cares why? I don't want to know."

"What's your take on this, Space?" Steve asked.

"Like, man, I don't want to be an alarmist, so I'll just say, any way you slice it, the whole thing is ugly. Let me put it this way, If those 12 guys got frequent flyer miles for where they were headed, each one would own the airline that issued them. It can't be measured in miles."

Carol angrily asked, "What gives them the right to kidnap people?"

"Simply, because they can," said Steve.

"It's similar to the way you can remove one of your goldfish from its tank," said Al. "The goldfish know someone's outside, but they go about their business in their immediate little world—"

Al was interrupted by the scream of the monitor. The high volume of the beep indicated a solid target. Everyone rose to a stiff attention. The bench seats against the cabin walls emptied in a blink as the agitated group circled the instruments.

Captain Al surveyed the graph for a moment and let out a surprised yell. "Badda bing! That's the big dog!" He pointed to the large, round anomaly on the paper.

Steve proclaimed excitely, "There's something down there"

Captain Al replied, "This area of water has no wrecks I'm aware of. Steverino, this could be it. We're at sixty feet on the depth. Is Bobby going down with you to check it out?"

Before Steve could respond, Bobby answered, "Damn straight I am!"

"Oh, be careful you guys," Kim pleaded.

"Don't take any unnecessary chances down there," Carol told Steve.

"We won't," Steve smiled and gave her a quick kiss. He turned to his brother, "Let's drop anchor and get suited up."

Captain Al told the brothers to take his underwater lights in response to the rapidly decreasing visibility. After reeling in the magnometer, the Sea Disk's anchor plummeted into the darkening sea. Bobby slid on his wet suit by the stern

55

ladder as Space and the girls watched anxiously. Steve followed Captain Al below to the lockers where they would procure the two portable underwater lights.

Steve found himself caught up in the hysteria. He hadn't paused to contemplate what it was he might be confronting down there. Not that it would stop him. The operation was set in motion. The very idea of voyaging into the unknown to satisfy his curiosity and prove this elusive ghost really existed had a lock on Steve's physical and spiritual being. Fear and logic were set aside. The rewards greatly outweighed the risks. Or so it seemed.

Captain Al grabbed one light and Steve the other. Al caught Steve as he tried to head back up the steps. "I got a feeling this is it, Steverino. Did you see that circular imprint on the graph? In all my days treasure hunting and salvaging wrecks, I never saw a shape like that."

"It certainly shows up as real unusual," agreed Steve. Perspiration began running down his face in the warm hold below decks.

"We're going to be rich men, Steverino. This thing will be worth a freakin' fortune."

"Let's not get ahead of ourselves until we see what's down there," he reminded Al. When they got on deck, the sun was disappearing behind the coastline. Darkness was upon them.

For the first time, Carol's face registered concern. Her concern for Steve and Bobby overlapped the tremendous curiosity which propelled her into this trip. The dangers now became very real, floating sixty feet above the mysterious shape which appeared on the monitor. Carol ran over to Steve and pleaded, "Steve, don't take any chances down there. If it looks dangerous, come right up. O.K.?"

"Don't worry, Carol, we'll be back in a few minutes once this target is identified."

"Will you be able to see with these?" asked Kim while inspecting the lights.

"Yeah, they're half-a-million candle power each," answered Steve.

Spaceman loitered against some netting by a boom in the background. "Like Stevie, what's the plan, baby?"

Steve replied, "Bobby and I will go down just to identify the object and come right back up."

"If that thing's there, watch your proximity to it," warned Space. "Active fields could be in the immediate vicinity surrounding the craft. Move slowly, baby!"

"We will," said Steve.

Bobby sat on the stern ladder's edge, blowing into his regulator hose. Steve joined him, fully clad in tanks and wet suit. Each held one of Captain Al's lights in hand.

"O.K., keep your fingers crossed. We'll be right back," Steve said descending to a point where he could jump.

"Please be careful," shouted Kim and Carol.

Once submerged, Steve and Bobby switched on the lights. They achieved fifteen feet of visibility in the darker than normal water. From the boat, the scene resembled an illuminated built-in pool walled off and safe from the unknown. But no walls existed here. Their descent down along the anchor line was fairly uneventful. As if they were performing a space walk, their suspended bodies drifted down into the alien world. Despite man's brief technological developments, the ocean's primeval world has remained unchanged. Distant planets in the cosmos most assuredly contain similar environments. The dark side of the moon is a fine example of a close yet relatively unknown environment. Different gravitational forces, rotational rates, and pressure zones are probably as varied as the trillions of solar systems. You don't have to travel far to be exposed to one of these alien atmospheres. They exist in our oceans' depths.

At sixty feet the trip down and back would be a direct one, assuming you didn't linger long on the bottom. Steve saw the mixed sandy rock bottom first. Kicking his feet, he planed out a few feet from the bottom. Bobby was directly above him checking the depth gauge on his wrist to verify their descent. The brothers floated back to back as they surveyed the terrain of the sea floor using the lights. No objects were visible in the lights' limited range.

As if the two weren't edgy enough from the eerily dark moonscape bottom, a six-foot black-tipped reef shark shot past them from the darkness. They avoided a collision with the large fish by only a few feet. At night, the reef sharks get a bit frenzied while feeding and exhibit more ferocity.

The near miss emphasized the dangers associated with entering an unnatural environment. Both divers knew the vulnerability of night diving. That shark grabbed the attention of Steve in particular. His recent attack while surfing precipitated a rapid heart beat and a wide-eyed expression. He knew the quicker they left the water, the better.

Bobby looked at Steve and pointed to his wrist compass. He then pointed in the direction of the target to the north. Swimming in a tight formation they held the lights out in front of their intended route. The lights exposed many small fish scampering to get clear of the approaching invaders. Their pace was slow. It resembled car headlights inching along a thick fog-blanketed road, unsure as to what might be coming around the next bend.

The silent tranquillity of the blackness was quickly broken by the loud vibration of an underwater scream from Bobby. Steve strained to see what it was his brother was wildly pointing to up ahead. It was lights. Someone else was down there.

The lights off in the distance were pointed straight at the paddling pair. Steve watched the two prowling beacons move in unison with their own! This was strange, so he shut off his beam. Only one light now came at them. It was Bobby's light; something with a reflective surface returned their beams back to them through the shadowy blackness.

They kicked onward until a discernible silvery gray horizontal line materialized on the murky seabed. Both brothers' hearts started pounding as they approached the metallic light-reflecting disc. The closer their proximity to this unnatural object became, the clearer its detailed shape appeared. The swimming stopped momentarily. Exchanging shocked glances at one another, the two began surveying the 22-foot round enigma resting quietly in the sand. People were always told this couldn't happen. The same kind of closed minds said, "If man was meant to fly, God would have given him wings." As late as the early 1950s, a noted French astronomer proclaimed a man traveling to and landing on the moon to be pure fantasy. Less than 20 years later, that closed mind was forcibly opened by Neil Armstrong's walk. This saucer was undeniably real, and for a change, the military wasn't the first at the scene.

Light from the underwater lamps revealed a symmetrical disc which supported a smaller dome above. A border containing strange geometric-type writing covered the parameter of the dome's base. Atop the dome were three equidistant lights surrounding a short shaft ending in a small ball. The ball-capped shaft sat directly in the center of the ship. Steve understood the protruding rod to be a wave guide. He'd read these controlled the craft's stability while inside a planet's atmosphere or until the ship powered up and went out of phase with its gravitational field. Tremendous speeds are achieved being out of phase. It was akin to traveling in space but inside Earth's atmosphere. No G-forces affect its occupants because there is no gravity around the ship.

After all his deductive reasoning, Steve happened to glance down at his wrist watch and compass to observe the odd gyrations being performed by the compass needle. He suddenly remembered Spaceman's warning to proceed slowly. Bobby's progress was halted with a grab of his arm by his brother. Neither one of them advanced any further than the ten-foot distance they'd all ready attained.

Signaling his brother to circle the object cautiously, Steve brought his light to bear on the underside to approximate how deep in the sand the craft had gone. On inspection he'd found the disc had dropped gently to the bottom settling on the sea floor.

Bobby completed his circular inspection meeting up with Steve again. Steve removed a small anchor from his belt. His brother handed him the rope and fluorescent orange air bag to mark the location on the surface. They both pumped air from their regulator hoses inside the balloon-like bag causing it to expand upward. The lift bag ascended slowly to its destination above. It would provide a temporary marker for Captain Al. On their knees in the sand the divers buried the anchor in a secure spot next to the craft.

Even with the self-evident danger, the brothers decided to experience a close encounter of the fourth kind—contact. Observing the benign craft in a seemingly incapacitated state, both men approached gingerly floating toward the protruding edges of the disc. Underwater reverberations became audible. However, they did not come from the craft but originated from each other's racing heart beats pounding against their wet suits.

Steve's hand touched first, then Bobby's. The metal on the disc felt silky smooth and warm. There was a temperature variance from the surrounding colder water. Not seeing any immediate threats, Bobby removed his knife, butt end first, and began knocking against the surface in anticipation of a response. If something was alive in there it surely would be intelligent enough to recognize his simple signal. None came.

Crouching underneath the lip of the disc's outer edge, Steve motioned for Bobby to join him. He'd heard these ships were extremely light weight and he wanted to test the theory. Any attempts to haul this thing up would depend entirely on its weight. Space had explained to Steve that these craft did not pick up mass and stability until the different fields given off were actually engaged for travel.

On Steve's signal the two would brace their shoulders under the saucer and try pushing it off the sandy bottom. After a nod to start, they prepared to budge the expected resistance. To their amazement the whole 22-foot saucer moved off the bottom with relative ease. If there was an occupant inside the oversized clam shell, they were definitely aware of the salvage efforts now. The jostling did nothing to precipitate any signs of life as the disc settled silently back into its sandy cradle. Satisfied with the results, Steve gave a thumbs up to his brother, and they departed toward the anchor line.

Their brief stay on the bottom enabled a rapid ascent to the surface without decompressing. About half way up the line, a school of panicked fish shot in between the two divers. Small "pings" could be heard as a result of the miniature Kamikazes ricocheting off the divers' air tanks. Steve and Bobby covered their masks to protect against the onslaught. This barrage of small fish didn't overly concern them; it was what caused the underwater stampede that created alarm in both of them.

Steve saw his brother lunge forward as if being pushed from behind. He swung his light around to see a large gray shadow blow by him. Out of nowhere the living torpedo, mouth hanging open, swung his head back and forth in a controlled frenzy of nighttime feeding. The catalyst behind the panicked fish's exodus had been found. Sharks. Sharks' eyes allowed for excellent vision at night due to light reflectors adjoining their retinas. A fact not making night diving any safer.

As quickly as it had arrived, the intrusion was gone. Steve and Bobby, back to back again, moved upward in an attempt to leave no blind spots in their hasty departure. The short malay instigated strenuous kicking toward the protection of the boat.

On board the trawler, Captain Al had switched on a large halogen light normally used while netting fish. It lit up the surrounding water like daylight. Carol and Kim hung over the rails, searching for a sign of the divers' return. Captain Al walked the deck encircling the wheel house. He yelled down to the women who were leaning over the side.

"Hey, be careful you don't fall in the drink. There might be sharks feeding this time of night."

Kim and Carol immediately responded to Al's warning and slid down off the rails.

"What about the guys?" asked Kim whose voice showed increasing fear. "Will they be O.K.?"

"I'm sure they will," said Carol. "I mean, they know there are sharks around, right?"

Spaceman sat on a large wooden container. "Hey baby, they'll be fine. Ignore Captain Blithe up there. All that bastard cares about is hustling a buck."

Al exited the wheel house just in time to miss hearing Spaceman's comment. "No sign of them yet, huh?"

Everyone scanned the water nervously. Carol spotted the lights first and yelled up to Al, "They're coming up over here."

Al abandoned his station in eager anticipation of the divers' report.

Space followed the girls to the stern ladder. "See, I told you they'd be fine. If that magnometer is correct, sharks will be the least of their worries down there." Spaceman thought to himself the only real question remaining was which group of outsiders had come to grief below.

As Space's mind wrestled with many cosmic questions, the others gathered under the deck lights in quiet anticipation. They waited for answers to a question posed many times in the past by people outside the Defense Department loop in Washington. Is there physical proof UFOs and aliens do exist? The answer to that question rapidly approached the ship's stern ladder.

Bobby's head broke through the surface first. He handed his extinguished light up to Captain Al. Steve's head popped up next. Bobby raced up the ladder, sat down, and began removing his air tank. All he kept saying was, "Holy shit! Holy shit!"

"What?" screamed Carol and Kim in unison.

"What's down there?" demanded Captain Al. "Do we have one?"

Steve climbed on deck and answered Al's question, "It's there all right. We got one!"

"You're kidding," bubbled Carol who was glad to see them back safely.

"We're rich! It's worth millions," danced Captain Al as Steve struggled unsuccessfully to shake his air tanks off.

Carol hugged Steve. "You know, I was really worried about you."

"You were?" he responded, momentarily losing interest in his find. He stared deeply into her brown eyes. They kissed and hugged oblivious to the others standing around them.

"Break it up. We'll have time for that later," Al rumbled. "This thing's got to be raised under cover of darkness."

"You're sure you are all right?" Carol questioned again.

"Yeah. We had a close brush with some sharks but it was worth the effort."

Spaceman edged in closer. "What did it look like, Stevie?"

"Its diameter is about 22 feet across with a dome on top. There's some small blue lights and a metal rod at the center of the dome."

"Any windows or insignia?"

Kim joking nervously said, "Oh right, it said 'Handle With Care.'"

Bobby told her, "No, but it did have writing on it."

Steve agreed, "Yeah, some kind of geometric style lettering around the dome, but it didn't have windows."

"That's real good, baby," Spaceman said. "I think I know its point of origin."

"Hey, Skippy? We can study it later. Let's not putz around. We need to figure out a way for my nets to get that sucker up," Al said.

Bobby had all his gear off. "I don't think we should go back down there right away."

"He's right," reasoned Steve. "In a half hour or so the bait fish will hopefully have left the area taking the sharks with them."

Al was agitated by the delay but agreed halfheartedly. "Can my nets lift that thing?"

"I'm sure they can," replied Steve. "While down there, we both lifted one of its edges and tilted the whole craft. It's pretty light."

"That's correct, man. The fields generated from its fusion reactor provides the ship with stability and mass when operational, baby. When not engaged, its mass is extremely low and hence quite light weight." Spaceman's memory had kicked into gear, and he sounded as if he'd read the information from a technical manual.

Carol's interest was a bit different. The welfare of the ship's occupants caused her to ask Steve if there were any signs of life on the saucer.

"We saw no movements or signals at all. Bobby knocked on its metal skin with his knife handle and got no response. So whatever is inside either can't respond or didn't choose to."

Spaceman stood off to the side smoking one of his cigarettes; he started to chuckle under his breath.

At that moment, Steve and Bobby's wristwatch compasses began spinning like airplane propellers. "Jeez! Look at that…," Bobby screamed.

The group grew silent as they observed this strange anomaly. Captain Al suggested a possible magnetic field was being given off.

"All that means is they still have some power on board," proclaimed Space. "So I'd be real careful bringing those dudes to the surface."

Al in a contradictory protest said, "Ah baloney. Let's jerk that sucker outta the water. Steverino, I'm going to need your help positioning the ship to snag the saucer with my nets. When you boys are ready to dive again, we'll rock and roll. Forget about it."

Steve and Bobby watched the maneuvering and assisted Al in positioning the vessel for its approach. Al felt a loop net would be able to scoop the disc off the bottom. The brothers would have to be on the sea floor assisting the hook up for success. Al would move slowly with the net and stop, once it was snagged. It was essential to have divers in the water. It also was extremely dangerous at night. Al returned to the controls and started the anchor retrieval motors. Barely visible off the stern lay the orange fluorescent float marking their quarry.

The trawler would be brought to a gentle idle once contact was initiated with the net and saucer. Before commencing to scoop it up, Steve and Bobby were needed underwater to facilitate a clean lift. Al told them they'd have ten minutes from the initial snagging to rearrange the net and get themselves clear of the lift.

The Sea Disc was lined up to drop her net and move over the orange marker. Steve had experience with the powerful net retrieval motors and stood by the large roller at the trawler's stern waiting for Captain Al's signal. A wide loop was arranged in the net's weighted end similar to a lasso. Getting the O.K. from the wheel house, Steve engaged the motor allowing the weighted loop to drop over the stern boards.

Bobby stood near Spaceman and commented to him, "This should probably be attempted in daylight."

"No man, Bob. Your captain is right about using the cover of darkness before the military gets wind of our operation. Even though it's a pretty half-ass way to raise it, the time is now if you guys want to retain possession."

Steve slowed the release motor as the net hit bottom. He allowed another 30 feet of line out before shutting the equipment off and locking it down. The boat sat in a low idle awaiting its attempt at a submerged docking. The girls and Space trailed the brothers to the stern ladder. Captain Al scampered down the ladder to see them clear.

Kim and Carol grew very nervous as they watched the boys slip on their black flippers and prepare to dive again. As the work proceeded all participants attained a surreal recognition of the fact that the entire operation might actually succeed.

Kim overheard the plans of attack earlier and asked Captain Al, "Are you sure you can't hook onto it without someone being down there?"

"Not really. My net has to be around it securely."

"We'll only be down for a few more minutes," said Steve.

"What about the sharks?" she continued.

"Hopefully they've moved on with the fish," reasoned Bobby, trying to quiet her fears while convincing himself that it was safe. The thought of descending back into the darkness one more time had Bobby questioning the decision himself. His back still hurt from the earlier collision with the reef shark. Bobby's confidence in night diving was beginning to wane.

Steve slapped his brother's arm. "Don't think about it or we won't go. Let's just do it, Bro."

Not wanting to appear afraid, Bobby answered halfheartedly, "Right."

CHAPTER FIVE

Captain Al stood next to the departing divers reviewing last minute details. "Don't forget, guys, I'll move very slowly until my net catches. You've got ten minutes to set the net around the disc. Get clear after that because I'm going to yank that bastard up." Both divers nodded an affirmative response.

"Please be careful," added Kim as she hugged Bobby.

"Yes, don't take any unnecessary chances," implored Carol. She moved quickly to Steve and kissed him. He looked back at her and responded in kind.

"I'll definitely be back for more of that," he promised as he slid into the dark murk; his brother followed closely behind. They swam toward the illuminated buoy which would guide them down. A beam of light from the bridge focused in on the orange marker floating approximately a hundred feet ahead. Captain Al had the boat in a direct line to cross over the disc below.

Existing conditions seem to favor the nocturnal retrieval. The surface of the water was becoming more tranquil by the minute. This would aid diving efforts in their unconventional salvage attempt. Steve and Bobby ignored the possible dangers from roaming sharks and concentrated on reaching the orange marker. After snorkeling on the surface, they came under the trawler's spotlight surrounding the buoy. Switching on their portable lights, the brothers dove pursuing the thin line to its terminus below. The powerful lights cut through the liquid fog. The light revealed no sign of the schools of fish that were previously swarming the area. With any luck, the big boys following the migration had also departed.

At forty feet a glint of reflected light disclosed the vague outline of the saucer. This surreal enigma had remained stationary at its mooring. Sitting silently in the sand, this mother of all clams showed no signs of life.

Steve landed right on top of the upper dome. He bent over and couldn't help touching the smooth metallic surface to reinforce the reality before him. This ghost was not in anyone's imagination as our military would have us believe. Steve always trusted his senses over any propaganda by so-called government experts recruited to shape people's opinions. He felt people need to believe what their eyes witness in the skies. That's reality. Period.

Bobby had landed on the illuminated dome and secured himself by grabbing the rod-like antenna jutting out in the center. He stared at the lettering encircling the dome and noticed they weren't printed or painted, but had been molded or fabricated in the metal itself. Despite studying the writing closely under his light, he determined it to be not of any earthly culture he'd ever seen. The actual blending of geometric shapes with letters was most interesting.

Glancing at his watch Steve signaled to his brother to get ready for the net's appearance. The brothers swam fifty feet to either side of the saucer and pointed their lights in the direction of the approaching drag net. As Steve stood on the bottom waiting, his mind could not help but wander off, speculating as to what these creatures if alive might be feeling. They'd become stranded and trapped inside this capsule from another world. It must be awful being so far from home facing so many unknowns. Is this how early explorers like Megellan had found themselves stranded in a hostile alien land? He knew the technological advantage wasn't in our favor. Just as Megellan was ahead of his native counterparts, so too were the inhabitants of this advanced craft. Steve was quite sure the marooned intruders possessed high levels of intelligence, but how it would be applied toward humans would only be conjecture. After all, if humans were deemed inferior, might we be treated likewise? It's an old story: one group thinks it's superior to another.

Do these aliens behave similarly to human beings? If they are similar, they may well be as unpredictable as we are ourselves. And knowing man's past track record through history, that could be very scary. It was all just speculation.

The rapid materialization of a large, dark object emerging into the light yanked Steve from his contemplation. It engulfed the sea floor, closing like a solid mesh wall. Their round prize was about to be scooped by the eerily drifting webbing. The dragging loop was perfectly aligned.

Quite patiently the net inched under the lip of the craft, pulling slightly and lifting it almost on end. Al had stationed the girls and Space on the stern to inspect the lines for the slightest tightening. They all screamed and waved to alert Al to cut the engines and idle back. Cutting the engines in the nick-of-time prevented the disc from flipping over. It became evident the upper section of net needed a bit of urging to enclose the whole 22' craft.

The guys took a brief time check and set about using the allotted ten minutes to their best advantage. Al's noose was almost set. Beneath the curved belly of the ship, no securing was necessary. The net was well entrenched when the saucer slid back down on it. Only the top portion required some prodding and straightening. The brothers pulled for all they were worth in an attempt to cover the top half of the disc and created a gunny sack of sorts. Bobby worked on clearing a few last tangles. Steve checked his watch to see a good five minutes remained before the lift. They had to be out of the way by then. One last section of tangled netting was being attended to when it happened.

All hell broke loose. Without any warning, the small blue lights on the dome began flashing. Its strange pulsating light lit up the bottom. Intense vibrations shook the water near the craft. A humming vibration penetrated everything, leaving the two divers very unsteady. The blue strobe flashes continued to grow in brightness, showing no sign of letting up.

Meanwhile, on the bridge of the Sea Disc, Captain Al sat patiently in front of his controls. Shortly he would engage his large diesel engines and pop his prize from the sandy reef. Carol and Kim stood closely observing Al's operations.

Carol asked, "How long until you try and lift it?"

"We've got about five minutes. Then the guys will be clear of the nets." Al's face grew perplexed. He stared at his control panel in shock. Suddenly without warning, he jumped to his feet and exclaimed in a bewildered voice, "Hey, what the hell is going on here? This can't be!"

"What's wrong?" asked Kim.

"Take a look at my goddamn gauges. They're all acting crazy." There wasn't any reason for it, but the speed control lever moved into full power mode by itself. Al hadn't touched anything. The big trawler was moving underway at flank speed.

Immediately, Al tried to pull back on the speed controls while maintaining his footing after the surprise acceleration. The knob would not budge. Carol and Kim assisted Al in trying to pull the control arm back down. It refused to move. Struggling to free the frozen lever all six hands continued tugging in vain.

At the stern, Spaceman found himself jerked off his feet as the boat lurched forward. There was a small tidal wave of foaming water kicked up by the Sea Disc's rapid acceleration. The situation deteriorated faster and faster by the moment.

Underwater, Steve had come over to assist Bobby when the net whipped taut around the disc. Bobby's arm became entangled between the saucer and the lines pressing tightly against the now moving mass. Steve acted quickly to the unfolding events. He grabbed hold of the net with one hand and his brother with the other. Their lights plummeted from their hands out of reach. Conditions had changed dramatically in the blink of an eye. The dark on-rushing water pushed both of them against the net-shrouded metallic monster.

Steve formed a strange picture in his mind. He saw the image of Captain Ahab of Moby Dick fame. At the end of the story, as the whale breached the surface, Ahab was hopelessly entangled on the whale's back. Was theirs to be a similar fate? It appeared the opportunists were quickly becoming the victims.

The disturbing image momentarily paralyzed Steve as they were towed mercilessly through the deep. He wondered if they hadn't repeated Captain Ahab's mistake of biting off more than they could chew. Not willing to leave his brother, Steve knew something must be done to free Bobby's trapped arm from the ropes if history was not to be repeated. Fortunately for them the blue strobe lights activated on the saucer gave off just enough light to see what needed to be done.

Reaching for his knife, Steve barely could make out the piece of line pressing into Bobby's arm. The force of being towed underwater began to wear them down. It was clear there was no stopping this run-away cosmic train. Half guessing at the binding points, Steve plunged the knife in and ripped outward and freed his brother's arm. He held onto Bobby's dive belt with both hands as the brothers were blown loose of the tangled death trap and tumbled away.

Bobby grasped his wounded arm as the two spun aimlessly in the dark whirling wake. Steve turned on a small pen light built into the wrist compass he wore. Putting it close to his face he observed which way the bubbles escaped and adjusted for a proper heading toward the surface. The saucer was nowhere to be seen. Only a faint hint of the blue strobe could be seen advancing further into the abyss. Steve wondered what had gone wrong aboard the Sea Disc. Al wouldn't have moved until the designated time. He'd never lift the saucer not knowing if it was secure. That's without mentioning the fact that two divers were in harm's way. Who or what had flipped on the blue lights? Al couldn't have pulled that one off. Something very unusual was occurring.

Their heads emerged amid the night air free of the sea's clutches. Off in the distance roughly a mile away was the boat. It appeared as a small light and its engines noisily churned away pushing it almost from their low line of vision.

Bobby spit out his mouth piece. "What the hell is that jerk doing?"

"Beats the hell out of me. How's your arm?"

"It's bruised bad. I don't think it's broken. Thanks for cutting me loose, Bro."

"We were just lucky it wasn't worse. The way I see it, we've got two choices. Go for shore or swim toward the boat, hoping that moron comes back looking for us."

"The boat," Bobby decided.

"Agreed. Let's go." The two brothers swam on a relatively calm sea and kept the glowing lights on the Sea Disc in their sights.

At the helm of the trawler, Captain Al, Kim, and Carol all tugged themselves to exhaustion trying to free the throttle control. A panic-stricken Kim shouted, "We've got to stop this boat! The guys are still down there."

Before anyone could answer, Spaceman burst in the cabin door with bulging eyes, "What the hell are your doing, man?"

Carol panted, "He's not doing it. Something's causing the equipment to go wild!"

"Oh shit! I hope you didn't piss 'em off!" Space yelled.

"Who?" demanded Kim.

Space turned away from her without answering the question. A wild-eyed expression crossed his face. His head remained stationary while he spoke calmly to Captain Al. "Hey dude, like your net motors are bringing in line down there."

"That can't be. I didn't turn those motors on!" shouted Captain Al. He jumped to the rear window and watched the retrieval rollers wincing up line unmanned all by itself.

Kim walked to the rear window as Al returned to his jammed controls. In a horrified voice, she asked, "Oh my God! What's that blue light in the water behind us?"

"We've got company," announced Spaceman.

All four spectators watched in disbelief as a large circular-shaped craft came into view. It was completely covered by the mesh lines. The net had a firm hold on the disc and the whole load became rapidly drawn to the stern of the runaway boat. A loud bang sounded when the two came together.

At that point, the blue strobe light shut down. Simultaneously, the boats power shorted out, which put everything in a black silence. Quietly, the trawler drifted, no longer on an uncontrollable rampage. Terror filled the cabin following the first few seconds of darkness. No one knew exactly what had happened.

One minute later the power came on illuminating the cabin. It revealed four people whose eyes had grown larger than silver dollars. Suddenly, the situation returned to normal. The throttle lever was back in idle position and the instruments all recorded their normal readings.

"The guys," yelled Kim leading the way down the steps. A mad rush to get to the stern ensued. Arriving first, Kim and Carol desperately searched the water and netting for a sign of the divers. The odd-shaped saucer floated in the sling barely breaking the surface.

"Do you see them?" asked Kim.

"No…" Carol answered.

"Where could they be?"

Captain Al grounded to a stop. He stood stunned and motionless while gaulking at the day's catch in his net. Dollar signs danced before his eyes. He already was calculating the huge amounts of money high-tech corporations would be willing to pay for its secrets.

Carol interrupted his thoughts of future financial statements by grabbing his arm. "Hey Captain. The guys are missing!"

"Em…They're not on the net so they probably were clear and swam to the surface at our original position. We'll head back and slowly search the area for them. You two go to the bow and keep an eye out."

Carol and Kim looked at one another. "He's not too concerned about the guys."

"No, he's acting as if he hit the lottery." They wondered if the good captain really wanted his partners found.

Al acted like a Las Vegas gambler who'd just hit a million dollar slot machine. He was giddy. This was the mother lode. The Holy Grail had just fallen into his lap.

In the meantime, Spaceman approached the back rail almost afraid to look over. It was as if old demons were about to traumatize him again. He leaned over peering down at the silver outline submerged in a shrouded covering.

He was talking under his breath. "It's them. I'm positive."

Carol responded, "It's who?"

"That's their type of ship."

"Who?"

"The official intelligence communication term is I.A.C. - Identified Alien Craft."

Carol was stunned by what he had said. Those very initials I.A.C. appeared among her father's papers she remembered accidentally reading years ago. Not alerting Space to her shock, she quietly rehashed over past events in her memory trying to make sense of it all.

Captain Al yelled from the bridge, "Everyone on the bow if you want to find Steverino. We're heading back."

"C'mon, we better help out up front," Spaceman told Carol.

The distraction had pulled Carol away from the crisis at hand. She emerged from her past spurred on by a concern for Steve and Bobby. Especially Steve whose honesty and sense of fair play had won her over. All Carol knew was they had to find the guys.

The three reluctant crew members watched for their friends ahead under the bright search light Al swept in front of the boat. The Sea Disc crawled forward retracing its earlier runaway path. They didn't wish to miss or run down the divers, so Al hardly touched the throttle. The slow pace also enabled the novice lookouts an opportunity to spot them. Oceans are a vast place and attempting to locate two small heads at night presents a real challenge.

Al's catch of the day being dragged right off the stern skimmed through the water quite efficiently. Disk-shaped objects have a tremendous aerodynamic capability. Someday when man evolves to using other more powerful and efficient propulsion systems, he will be able to make this advanced shape serve him. A lifting body or wave rider like the shuttle's design shape can't even compare with the dynamics of a disc-shaped craft. In the atmosphere a saucer shape can reach Mach 20 speed range. Comparatively the shuttle's atmospheric limit is around Mach 8. The subject of disc and saucers is not allowed to be discussed outside of a loop of government sponsored scientists. It's suppressed because people simply haven't a need to know such things.

Kim's tears streamed down her face as she tried to spot some sign of Bobby or Steve. Carol hid her concern while comforting her friend. She insisted they'd be found in a few minutes. Spaceman gave out a shout and pointed wildly off the port bow. There up ahead in the water could be seen a tiny firefly-like beacon flashing on and off. Al shut down the big search light creating a natural darkroom. This backdrop allowed the small speck of flickering light to become predominantly visible. Al gave three quick flashes on the flood light. In response the small beacon signaled back three times.

"That's them, man," shouted Spaceman on the bow guiding Captain Al nearer to their position. Kim and Carol were leaning over the rail's precipice, teetering close to an involuntary high dive.

Below in the dark, calm sea, Steve continued signaling with the small wrist light. Finally realizing rescue was at hand, he assisted Bobby who was treading water with his injured arm. Help couldn't have arrived any sooner. Bobby told Steve something was in the water behind him. He felt a swoosh of water brush by him as it past. The Sea Disc's big light suddenly illuminated the area where the two men were swimming. Glancing around they saw two large fins about thirty feet away. The sharks were good-sized Hammerheads and were eying the swimmers as if it was dinner time.

Al's trawler was right next to them now. The light revealed an attack in progress. Both sets of fins knifed along the surface toward the intended prey. Steve and Bobby didn't think they were going to reach the ladder in time. Bravely Steve placed himself between the sharks and his struggling brother. The large buck knife carried on his belt was drawn and ready for confrontation. It never came.

Out of nowhere, a loud bang sounded. Then another and another. Then one more. The sharks jerked off course. They retreated from view in a hurry. Hanging over the bridge railing, Captain Al ejected spent shells from a high-powered rifle. The gun still issued smoke swirls out its barrel. He'd apparently did some fancy shooting to allow the swimmers time to reach the boat's ladder.

Even with the injury to Bobby, both divers got on board with great haste. Waiting arms assisted their exodus from the shark-filled waters. The girls hugged their boyfriends ecstatically. Steve and Bobby dropped to the deck to catch their breaths and to contemplate how fortunate they both were to have escaped the ordeal relatively unscathed.

The exhausted men laid on deck as Captain Al appeared from the stairway. He yelled, "Congratulations, we got it!" With a second thought he removed the joyous tone from his voice and asked, "You guys all right?"

"Yeah, just barely," Steve snapped as he gave Carol another kiss. He freed his lips and continued, "That was pretty good shooting. Thanks. By the way, Bobby had his arm in the net when you pulled out of there."

Bobby terminated his hug with the distraught Kim. "What the hell went on up here? You could've killed both of us."

"Forget about it. I didn't pull outta there. The boat's controls moved by themselves. I'd never leave you guys down there," Al said.

"What do you mean 'moved by themselves'?" asked Steve.

"Everything went completely haywire. I couldn't budge the control levers. The damn thing winced itself from the bottom. My boat only stopped when the blue lights went out on the saucer."

The brothers looked at each other a bit amazed but at least a few questions had been answered. "So it's safe to say they have some power left on their ship," said Steve.

The group stood silent for a moment eyeballing the strange object secured tightly to the stern of the boat. The blue lights and antenna on the crest of the dome were all that rested above the water line. More concerned about Bobby's arm than any UFO, Kim asked him if his arm was all right.

"I think it's just badly bruised," Bobby replied.

Carol studied the alien disc's shape carefully. She commented, "God, that's the biggest clam I've ever seen."

"And worth billions of smaller green clams, honey," added Al.

The fine details of the craft weren't visible even in the trawler's bright lights. It almost refused to materialize and give up its secrets, preferring to remain hidden just beneath the water and perpetrate its false fairy tale reputation as a fleeting cosmic ghost. A mystery brought into our so-called reality.

In true reality, these highly evolved visitors have existed much longer than human history. But then our egos, combined with hidden government and alien agendas, have maintained the grand illusion. As in the tale of "The Emperor's New Clothes," the emperor's many subjects were told over and over by respectable individuals how beautiful the royal wardrobe was. But in reality, it took common logic and plain observation skills of a child to plainly see the emperor had been tricked and actually wore no clothes at all. No one wanted to go against popular opinion and speak out on what they really saw.

This principle works quite effectively for our government. Their agents need to make little efforts in debunking programs because the job is done for them by popular opinion. Anyone brave enough to speak out on UFO encounters and the truth are publicly ridiculed. Someday, when the facts are all tallied, pompous "know-it-alls" will come to learn our so-called reality is in actuality a fantasy existence heavily monitored by outside forces. A fantasy initially created to hide the simple truth and not impact the apple cart on Earth known as humanity. At least not until man evolves enough to defend himself against these outside forces.

Steve suggested that Captain Al douse all the stern lights as soon as possible. The bright lights, which are visible for miles, might attract unwanted attention. There were plenty of military planes criss-crossing the sky, hunting for this thing, and it might be unpleasant being caught transporting it.

The whole group filed into the wheel house cabin to find Captain All opening a bottle of champagne. Once the cork popped, the celebrating captain guzzled down the bubbly. He toasted to success and said, "We've gotten lucky and achieved what no single individual has ever been able to do—capture an intact alien craft."

Steve took the bottle next and chugged a long drink, more to calm his nerves than to celebrate the recovery. Carol took a sip and handed it to Kim who was putting antiseptic on Bobby's bruised arm. The champagne disappeared very quickly as Spaceman finished the last with an abrupt belch.

Steve still worked on removing his wet suit. Many questions still remained to be answered pertaining to the saucer. The questions would be easy, the answers hard to obtain. He yanked free the last piece of his dive outfit and asked Spaceman, "Well, what's your take on this thing?"

Captain Al chimed in sarcastically, "Yes, what is your official assessment of the situation, Professor?"

"Stevie, that is like definitely a Grey's ship back there, buddy. And whoever's inside is alive because the equipment was affected by the fields given off as a result of their attempted escape." He turned to Captain Al, "That's my assessment, Admiral."

"Gee thanks, Skippy."

Steve intervened, "So its a Grey's ship? Is that good?"

"Not really Stevie, but we can get some answers if the little bastards are alive in there."

Kim finished wrapping up Bobby's arm. She warned, "You guys better turn this thing over to the military. You're all getting in way over your heads. I mean it. This is out of control."

"They want it, they can have it. As long as we're compensated for our trouble at the appropriate current market value," reasoned Al.

"Is the money all you care about?" snapped Kim.

"Certainly not. I did this for my father too. But fair is fair and salvage is salvage, no matter how fantastic. Whether its a sunken cargo of bricks or a ship from the Orion constellation, we deserve to be compensated. Aye, what's wrong with hustling a few bucks while we solve some age-old mysteries?"

"We need a place to hide and examine the disc," said Steve. "Bobby, how about Dad's storage barn at the orange grove? That's probably more than enough room."

"Yeah, I'm running the farm for the next week until Mom and Dad return from vacation," stated Bobby who winced as Kim adjusted the bandage on his injured arm.

"Can we get the big truck and flatbed trailer, Bob?"

"No problem, Bro!"

"O.K. We'll move it later tonight around three o'clock. Sound all right, Al?"

"Badda bing. Sounds good so far."

"Will that hoist on your dock be able to make the transfer to the flatbed?"

"Steverino, if that saucer's as light as you say, it'll work just fine. Badda bing. No sweat."

"Good. The sooner we move, the sooner we can try to get inside."

"Steve, do we really need to know what's in there, and can we communicate with them even if we do gain entry?" inquired Carol.

"Carol, that's the reason we came out here. We all have a need to know."

72

Overcoming her fear she nodded in agreement. The thought of what might reside inside the metallic pod brought silence to the wheelhouse cabin again. They were in it now, and realized discoveries never were achieved without experiencing the unknown. Before solving any mysteries though, their booty had to be kept from the marauding military trackers. Capturing the saucer was the easy part. Keeping it would be quite another story.

CHAPTER SIX

Al's boat crawled slowly onward, aiming for the Port Canaveral Inlet to the North. The captain calculated the snail's pace to reduce the chances of losing the submerged prisoner. There was no need to conceal the valuable prize as the majority of its structure rested below the water. Dark skies and the surrounding mesh net also provided a stealthy camouflage. Another passing boat would find it impossible to make out its shape. The Sea Disc cautiously maintained a slow speed exposing only one oddity noticeable on the surface. An uncharacteristically large wake was frothing up wildly behind the trawler. The real danger of detection did not arise from ships. It came from the occasional electronic surveillance aircraft leaving Patrick Air Force Base just South of the inlet. Even though the military's search area centered further out to sea where the disc originally splashed down, they continually passed overhead hunting for the intruder in wider vectors.

The trawler slid past the gauntlet right under their noses. Captain Al guided the Sea Disc and her precious cargo to the inlet's entrance. Both couples sat quietly together enjoying an opportunity to rest and think clearly. Spaceman glanced over his shoulder at the saucer being towed at the rear. Steve reclined on the padded bench. He had Carol resting on his chest as he watched Space's head shaking in disbelief.

Steve asked, "Something wrong?"

"I'll tell you, man. I've been involved in many alien-related operations over the years, but I never took the little bastards out water skiing before."

Steve smiled at his wacky friend and settled back against the seat with Carol for some silent contemplation. Spaceman sat perched on the corner end of the long bench seat nearest the exit. He blew a stream of smoke from his exotic cigarette out a crack in the door he'd left open. Wisely, the smoke was directed through the crack. The outgoing air removed the smell, preventing its drifting into Captain Al's direction.

For the most part, Al was still gloating over his unbelievable luck. The wheeler-dealer in him had already predisposed of this high-tech gold mine to some major corporation for a king's ransom. A fantastic pay-off of this magnitude would soon have him on easy street. His ship had come in, or at least he had believed so.

He asked, "Steverino, what are you going to do with your share of the salvage money?"

"I haven't had a chance to think about it."

"Jeez, how many ways do we split it?" asked Bobby.

"Wait a minute, guys. First let me remind you we'll have to dodge the military. Then if we aren't killed by whatever is inside that thing, and assuming some corporate interest deals with us, our shares can be determined then."

"I'm just looking down the road, Steverino. We need a plan. that's all," reasoned Al.

"First plan will be to find out if someone of something needs help in there."

"Steve's right," said Carol. "They could still be alive in there and probably wouldn't go along with your selling their craft. Did you ever think the military might not be the only ones searching for them? What if there are other ships and they got their distress signals and are coming after them?"

Space, who was listening, quietly answered, "That's a viable scenario, man."

"Precisely why we need to bury this hot potato," said Al.

"Badda bing, pronto!"

"Once we get it to my father's storage shed on the farm, we can make further plans," advised Steve.

Everyone agreed with a slight nod of the head except Kim. She didn't falter in her stubbornness. She believed unquestioningly that it should be turned over to the proper authorities.

(Washington, D.C.)

The Naval Observatory in Washington, D.C., provided the usual meeting place for a group of specialized and powerful policy makers called MJ12. Admiral Dirk's communication from Langley, Virginia, had sent a briefing on the current incident to the National Security Council earlier in the evening and presently began updating the search's progress to the other MJ12 members via phone link ups.

"That's right. The bogey hasn't been located at the present time. It has simply vanished from our tracking ships. I've got every available asset in the area out there about ten miles off the coast of Cape Canaveral."

J1 and the other members sat contemplating the admiral's words arriving over the speaker phone. As with most of the members at the meeting, J1's normal position was Director of Central Intelligence. This group, who created policy relating to extraterrestrials, encompassed some of the most powerful and knowledgeable men in the country. Managing this ongoing problem demanded very high security and the integration of every defense agency into a unified response team.

"Admiral, it is imperative that this craft be found to determine if our advisors are providing us with accurate information on these hostile incursions we've been intercepting."

"Understood, J1. It'll turn up. I'm committing a much larger force to the search. If the target's down there, we'll get them."

"Good hunting, Admiral."

75

Admiral Dirk hung up to read a dispatch from the *Florida*, a nuclear trident submarine, which had been on maneuvers near the crash area. The message read: "After initial success with sonar contacts, the object departed the area at unattainable underwater speed. It was picked up once more on an erratic course before totally disappearing. Presently there is no sign of the target. Will maintain position with battle group until located."

The admiral looked at the two officers standing by him and simply said, "Shit. Those S.O.B.'s were hit by one of our SDI weapons, survived, and still managed to give us the slip. Are our deep water electronics craft on station?"

"Yes, sir. If they can't locate the bogey, it's not there," answered the Lt. Commander.

"Get me Patrick Air Force Base at the Cape," commanded Admiral Dirk.

"Yes, sir."

(Captain Al's dock)

Captain Al carefully negotiated the back waterways of the Port Canaveral Inlet. The trawler crept into the canal that Al called home. House lights could be seen in all the rear windows of homes lining the route. One side of the narrow waterway contained mangroves and thickets of brush. This was a wildlife refuge which was quite uninhabitable. Contrasting sharply was the other side containing some of Cocoa Beach's finer homes. At this hour of the night, no one was outside. The Sea Disc made her approach slowly, almost drifting into its berth behind Al's house. Only the low churning of the idling diesel engine was audible in the silent night air. Al's large steel hoist stood guard over his extended dock space. The long rusted gray arm stretched out above the water. It appeared like a gallows, waiting to raise its victim.

Al aligned the netted prey directly beneath the lifting mechanism. The brothers had secured the boat's lines to the dock. Steve and Al then gathered a selection of straps and ropes to be used with the hoist. Al explained the best way to raise the saucer. Steve found himself back in the water swimming under the disc. He lay long straps along the saucer's bottom, bringing the ends to the surface where Al snapped the steel ring ends on the cable's hook hanging down from the hoist arm. They would attempt to lift the light craft, net and all from water to flatbed trailer. It was a distance of roughly fifteen feet up. Bobby and Kim were on their way in the van to retrieve his father's truck and trailer at the farm on the main land. Despite Kim's urging to seek medical attention for his injured arm, Bobby refused to stop until the alien craft was safely hidden.

Captain Al loosened the net at the trawler's rear retrieval unit once it became apparent the small crane-like hoist had a taut hold of the saucer. Gently, the hoist motors were engaged. To everyone's relief, the net-entangled grayish colored disc emerged from the murky canal. The dome surfaced first. It revealed the strange foreign writing circumscribed about its base. Then the entire saucer rose

76

up into the still night air. Salt water cascaded from it in every direction. Carol, Steve, and Al stood motionless as if in a trance. Their thoughts raced out of control. Question after question was generated. Where'd it come from? Who's inside? Most importantly, why is this bizarre craft here?

Spaceman didn't share a lot of the other's amazement. He had some insights but searched for more important answers. His quest entailed a much bigger picture.

"I can't believe my eyes!" exclaimed Carol.

"Believe it, baby," Space answered in a casual tone.

"It's not the first recovered alien ship, but I'll wager it's the first privately salvaged one," declared Steve. He walked close to the craft and knocked on its metal skin.

Al reminded everyone that secrecy was paramount. He emphasized the fact that no one can know they have the saucer until they are ready to sell it.

"He's right," said Steve. "We've got to get it in the barn quickly. Speed is essential. Not only to prevent detection, but also in the event someone's alive inside that oversized frisbee."

Carol showed continued concern for any potential occupants. "Yes, let's hurry. They may be in trouble."

Five minutes later the roar of a tractor trailer could be heard in the street out front. Bobby's head hung out of the truck's cab as he tried to align the huge trailer over Al's sandy driveway. The oversized flatbed crept closer to the canal. Steve guided his brother's path through the dark to the bulkhead where the small crane hoist stood. The trailer's back wheels pushed across the last head wall. A loud hiss signaled the truck's air brakes were engaged. Its large engine shut down as Bobby and Kim jumped from the cab.

"How's your arm, Bob?" asked Steve.

"Seems O.K."

"He needs to go to a doctor and..." Kim stopped in mid-sentence. She just gaulked at the suspended alien craft. "That can't be real," she stated in disbelief as she noticed the unearthly design and writing.

"Can we get it up there, Al?" Steve asked as he studied the elevation of the hoist relative to the truck bed.

"It'll be close," was his response. "When I get it up there, you guys pull my net loose. There's plenty of slack now."

The jumble of nets, straps, and chains that encrusted the saucer hung from it helplessly over the water. "Hey, Skippy. How about lending a hand over here on these straps?" yelled Captain Al. He stood prepared to lift and swing the saucer onto the truck.

Spaceman didn't respond to the name. Finally, he acknowledged Steve's wave and joined the group surrounding the truck bed.

"This thing is pretty damn light, so we just need to guide it to the middle of the trailer bed," instructed Steve.

Bobby and Space stood nearby. Carol and Kim watched further back for any indications of any problems.

"Here we go," shouted Captain Al.

The hoist motor strained momentarily and all too easily the straps pulled their prize high enough to barely clear the trailer. The 22' diameter left considerable lengths of overhang protruding off each side of the truck. Once it was centered, Al joined the others attempting to free the net.

"Piece of cake! Badda bing," crowed Al in victory.

The craft's super light weight made it possible to release the net beneath it using only a couple of simple levers. There were two black tarps tied to the front of the trailer which normally covered loads being transported. They would be invaluable for concealing this contraband. All the straps and netting came loose without a hitch. Each member of the newly-formed recovery team tugged on different corners of the two black tarpaulins in an effort to conceal the entire 22 feet of the domed disc.

Unfortunately, even with the two large trailer coverings draped across the irregular-shaped saucer, a small exposed area at the rear displayed the bottom section of the ship. Not concerned with its shortcomings, the cohorts unrolled the strap rollers attached to the side of the trailer. After tossing the securing straps over the tarpaulin-encased disc and fastening them to the opposite rails, Al and Steve placed a few sections of chain around their captive.

"Badda bing," uttered Al pleased with the completed spider web restraining the saucer. "Dad would be proud."

"Like a military Blue Team couldn't have done better, man," said Space.

"It isn't going anywhere," Steve said checking the straps.

"Stevie, if this sucker takes off, the truck's going too."

Kim looked at Space and commented, "That's a comforting thought."

They needed to remove the ship from its vulnerable position before daylight when prying eyes might ask questions. Steve checked his watch and announced, "Al and I will wait until two o'clock before leaving for the barn. Meantime, Bobby, why don't you go get some x-rays of that arm at the emergency room. We're done here for now. Let's all get some sleep and we'll meet at the barn first thing in the morning."

Spaceman said, "Stevie, I'll hang with you, dudes."

"O.K."

"C'mon honey, Carol and I will run you over to the hospital."

Bobby was about to argue against it, but Kim wouldn't hear of it. "O.K.," he relented.

Steve made his way to Carol and pulled her behind the truck. "You probably need some sleep after all this excitement," whispered Steve.

"That's if I can sleep."

"Well try and everyone will meet in the morning at my dad's farm."

Steve and Carol embraced tightly, kissing good night. "Be careful, honey," Carol pleaded, unwillingly breaking away from his forceful attraction to join Kim and Bobby.

Bobby and the girls borrowed Al's car. Upon pulling away from the sandy driveway, they missed noticing the dark sedan secluded behind a large hedge row on the street. The car contained the same two ominous characters Steve encountered the night before. Their training and knowledge would instantaneously allow them to recognize the object tied down on the truck bed, and its tremendous importance to national security. The agents' discovery would prove highly dangerous for everyone involved in this most unusual salvage operation.

The alarm clock rang out awakening Steve, Al, and Spaceman from their brief nap on Al's living room furniture. Two o'clock arrived without warning.

"All right boys, it's time to move," Al said yawning.

"I'll drive," recommended Steve. "We'll try to go unnoticed using a back road I know."

"Good. Let's roll," Al said.

"Where do you want me, man?" asked Space. The effects of the inhaled cannabis were beginning to wane.

"In the cab with us," answered Steve. "In case something goes wrong."

Al glanced at the groggy Spaceman and rolled his eyes. Despite Space's bouts with mental short-circuiting, his presence and knowledge were invaluable to this project. There were too many unknowns associated with every aspect of this venture. Presently, the urgency to safely secure their trophy became the only priority.

Steve climbed into the tractor cab starting up the Cummings diesel engine. Space leaped onto the side door step and watched over the truck's progress. Captain Al stood in the side yard, guiding the super wide load past his house.

The edge of the covered saucer barely skimmed by a couple of large Australian pines. Every bit of roadway would be commandeered to transport this odd-shaped load. The protruding sides were elevated enough to allow a car traveling in the opposite lane passage. Trucks would be another story. Spaceman volunteered to ride shotgun on the trailer wall behind the cab. They wouldn't be moving very fast so Steve agreed. But Space was instructed to yell out at the slightest sign of trouble. He agreed and climbed behind the aluminum trailer's front wall. He tucked in behind its shield-like protection to block the wind. The show was on the road, and they didn't look back. They hadn't realized their armed escort lingering a safe distance behind observing them closely.

The two NSA men left their headlights off to maintain a discreet advantage as they traveled the dark, deserted roads. Both mysterious agents slid on night vision goggles in unison. The extinguished headlights in no way hindered their pursuit plans. With primitive stealth, they stalked their unwary prey. Total advantage went to the two elite intelligence men. For now they patiently followed, content to watch events unfold ~~and the players develop~~.

In the truck cab, Al grew more excited with every passing mile. "Steverino, now I know how my dad felt in the late forties when he belonged to the Interplanetary Phenomena Unit or IPU back in the heyday of recoveries."

"Yeah, any one of the military's blue teams would be proud to have us. They may have more assets available but the bottom line is we've got one, Al," concluded Steve who anticipated success.

Captain Al high-fived Steve and let out a loud, "Yes! We're gonna be filthy rich, pal. Badda bing!"

"Everything's going well so far. Let's concentrate on not getting caught."

The odd-shaped load moved over the causeway bridge to the mainland utilizing both lanes. Spaceman clung to the trailer wall with both hands catching the breeze in his shaggy gray beard. From his perch, he could see the abandoned streets of late night Melbourne. The silence did not deter him from his vigilant sentry posture. Rumbling off the bridge and down Route US1, the truck continued toward its destination. They had yet to encounter one single vehicle.

They turned down the first side road that led to the orange grove. Branches hanging down began smacking against the saucer's edges. Steve took up the whole road in an attempt to avoid any damaging branches. Their journey's end was less than half a mile down the road.

Peering into his rear view mirror, Steve caught sight of two sets of headlights. One materialized out of nowhere and the second set accelerated behind him.

He said to Al, "We've got company."

"Oh shit!"

At the same instant, Spaceman shouted down at the open windows warning of the approaching lights. The impending lights trailing them added a flasher and siren to the chase.

"Steverino, we're dead meat."

"Just stay calm, Al. I'll handle it." While trying to maintain his current speed, Steve noticed the engine's lack of response. It coughed and sputtered as if ready to stall out. An intense vibrating noise could be heard from the trailer.

Spaceman leaped off his perch in the rear. He stood on the cab's running board, his head and shoulders lurching in through Al's open window. "Let me in," he pleaded. "The saucer's trying to start up again!" Al pulled the struggling lookout inside.

With one eye on his rear view mirror, Steve made out their pursuer to be a local police car. Something very strange was going on back there. The police car's headlights were no longer on the back of the truck. The beams were being bent at right angles in mid-air and extended off into the woods at the side of the road.

"Take a look back there. That cop's headlights are being twisted."

"I see 'em," said Al. "His lights are in the woods. What the hell is that all about?"

"Like, the disc is generating a local field effect when it starts up, man," responded Spaceman.

"Who asked you?" snapped Al.

"Hey guys, we have no power," said Steve as he vainly tried to get the truck's motor running. With no alternatives left, he simply guided the powerless big rig over as close to the shoulder of the road as possible.

A few seconds after coming to a stop, the violent vibrations ceased. Steve locked the brakes and said, "I'm going out. Stay here, guys." He climbed down and walked under the saucer's tarp-covered seven-foot overhang to the awaiting patrol car.

The bewildered Melbourne patrolman walked toward him with one hand on his gun holster. "Sir, you know this load's way over width limits?"

"Billy, is that you?"

"Steve Wilcox?"

"Yeah. How are you?"

"Great. I haven't seen you around in a couple of years. You're not working with your dad on the farm, are you?"

"No, no. I'm selling insurance out on the beach."

"So what the heck is this thing you're hauling?"

"Oh, it's a satellite dish for my dad. I'm helping move it to the farm just up the road."

"I see you've got red flags on the edges, but this is really dangerous at night. Since you've only got another quarter mile to go, do me a favor and get this thing off the road ASAP."

"Sure, Billy."

Steve's old neighbor turned to leave. As an afterthought he turned back around and said, "I almost forgot. What the heck happened to my headlights back there? The beams were in the woods."

Spaceman had left the cab and advanced beneath the saucer's slightly exposed underside hanging off the truck's tail lights. "Uh, Officer? That was simply the reflection of your lights being refracted off this highly polished disc surface."

Steve tried to stay cool in the wake of this unexpected intrusion.

Steve's old friend spun around to try and identify the new voice. In a contradictory tone, he said, "But my lights bent before reaching the satellite dish, maybe a hundred feet behind your truck."

"Precisely, Officer. This phenomenon occurs due to the photons breaking down and putting out an illusionary effect."

Befuddled by the answer, the policeman asked, "Who are you?"

"Oh, he's a friend and local expert on satellite dish hookups," stammered Steve. "John, this is my old neighbor, Billy." The officer nodded and Spaceman waved.

"Well, listen Steve. Get this monster off the road and tell your dad I said hello."

"I will," answered Steve. "Thanks, Bill."

The police officer marched back to his patrol car not all together satisfied with the answers given. However, he trusted his old neighbor's words. The Wilcox name was good as gold among the local people. Space stood there reveling in his performance. He fought to prevent a smirk from creeping across his weathered face.

The sweat was rolling down Steve's neck. He glanced in Spaceman's direction and noticed one of those special cigarettes lit and hidden behind his cupped palm. Nervously Steve called out, "C'mon, John. Time to leave."

"O.K. baby."

A short distance away the two government trackers sat safely in their black car observing the whole fiasco. Like most intelligence operatives they lurk in the dark recesses watching others take the heat and probably snickering at their predicament. After all in their business, morals and decency get thrown out the window. It's the nature of the beast. The almost total lack of accountability extends tremendous leeway to many irresponsible actions. The two agents had obviously turned their lights on after spotting the cop, and their presence had gone undetected by the preoccupied officer. Once again with a dark mirage-like stealth, they followed down wind of their prey.

The Melbourne patrol car crept away from the scene with its flashing lights extinguished. Back in the truck cab everyone was breathing a bit easier. Steve started the truck up with no problem at all. As they headed back down the road, he leaned over toward Spaceman who was riding in the back. "Do you know what would have happened if he smelled that joint? What were you thinking?"

"Sorry, Stevie. Force of habit, man."

"Thank God you did some fast talking out there."

"I'll bet," Al frowned.

The big rig rambled down the narrow side road only a few mail boxes from their destination. Steve inquired, "Space, what really bent those headlight beams?"

"You mean the actual physics?"

"Yes."

"Simple. Amplified gravity produced when the ship powered up a few minutes ago for an attempted lift off, dude. You see the three gravity amplifiers on board put out a field effect in the form of electromagnetic gravitic waves that are much stronger than the Earth's own gravitation power measured at 3 X 10 power negative Tesla. It's like when you look up at a star at night. The star's actual position might not be where you think you see it due to its light traveling too close to a planet or another star. These planets or stars also give off large quantities of strong gravitational waves which warp or bend the light traveling by on its way to you. Very strong amplified gravitic waves given off on the truck a moment ago bent the police car's headlights. The electromagnetic factor shorted out your truck engine. Simple. Even the captain here could understand it."

"Makes sense to me," said Steve.

"Hey smartass. How do you know all this crap, anyway?" snipped Al.

"It's a long story, baby."Space finished up his memory enhancing cigarette and tossed the remains out the window.

Mr. and Mrs. Wilcox were away from the orange grove on a two week vacation. Mr. Wilcox had left Bobby in charge of the large operation during his absence in the short off-season. Not much was transpiring this time of year and the big tractor trailer crept unnoticed past the gates. The bizarre cargo filled the yard as Steve maneuvered for space to back the entire load down into the huge storage barn's sunken bays. Only one employee, a migrant worker turned night watchman named Pepe, approached to challenge the truck. He aimed his flashlight at the cab. Immediately upon spotting Steve behind the wheel, he stopped and waved. The truck window rolled down, allowing Steve to yell, "Hey Pepe. How's it goin?"

"Bueno, Mr. Steve," he responded with a big smile.

"I've got to leave this satellite dish in the barn for a while."

"O.K. Mr. Steve. If you need my help, give me a shout."

"Thanks, Pepe."

The storage barn's main door clattered open. A button inside the truck controlled it remotely. The lights came on as the door rose to reveal a spacious warehouse used in the sorting and shipping of oranges. This was a lot bigger than any ordinary barn. You could park a jet in there, or any other flight-worthy vehicles for that matter.

After clearing some farm equipment out of the way, the big rig retreated down the sunken concrete loading ramp. The truck's trailer supporting the saucer was now level with the loading dock platform. Their plan of attack was to pull the saucer straight off the truck bed and directly onto the concrete floor using a huge lift normally reserved for lifting large bins full of oranges onto trailers.

Al looked around and said, "Steverino, your dad's got a nice operation here."

"Yep. He's done well. Listen guys, when you loosen up those straps and chains, leave them on the disc. Just bring the ends where I can get at them. I'm going to drag the thing off with that big forklift."

"Good idea," said Al. "Don't damage this little beauty."

"You couldn't damage that metal, man, with a runaway locomotive," stated Spaceman in a subtle attempt to remind Al who the expert was.

"Oh, is that so, Skippy? And, uh, I suppose you could tell us why?"

"Like, as a matter-of-fact, I certainly could. These metals were manufactured in the zero gravity of space where no warping or settling occurs. The near perfect vacuum causes the molecular structure to be packed much tighter together and crystallize more perfectly when formed, man. Hence, you get a much lighter, stronger material. Dig?"

"This guy's gettin' on my nerves, Steverino," quirked Al.

"All right, c'mon guys. Let's get those strap ends over here."

The two big fork prongs jutted out in front of the forklift. They contained small holes in the ends where Steve placed steel pins to hold the strap rings. These rings slipped on the pins enabling the huge forklift to tow the saucer backwards off the truck.

With a loud roar of the powerful lift engine, the straps snapped tight and initiated an irritating skidding noise caused by the craft's bottom chafing and grinding along the aluminum trailer bed. Aiming for the loading dock, Steve hit the gas and the disc popped up over the small crevice separating concrete from truck. Motor revving, he continued to drag the craft further into the building. The minute their prize became centered on the concrete floor, Steve jumped down to free a tangled strap. Al rushed over to help tug, but it was in vain. Spaceman saw he could assist as the third man and got up into the forklift's seat. He moved the powerful machine forward which created slack that freed the tangle.

"O.K.!" yelled Steve.

Space started turning the vehicle while backing up. He was looking totally to his rear when the turning vehicle pushed the straps up front initiating the saucer to spin. Al and Steve leaped clear of the out of control load.

"Just go straight back," screamed Steve.

"I gotcha, dude," acknowledged Spaceman.

The words had just departed from Spaceman's lips when the huge forklift lurched forward like a runaway tank. Both Steve and Captain Al dove clear once again as Space slammed into the disc driving it through some metal bins. Before he realized the control knob was in the "Forward" position, the entire procession crunched up against one of the building's large steel support beam with an echoing crash. The whole storage structure of the barn shook as if they'd been caught in an earthquake tremor. Dust floated down from the vibrating ceiling.

"Whoa! Whoa! Shut it off!" shouted Steve as he reached up to the controls and pulled out the key.

"Bummer. Sorry, Stevie. I must have hit "Forward" instead of "Reverse.""

Shaking his head in disbelief, Steve said, "Come down from there."

"If that putz damaged this saucer…" grumbled Al as he inspected the disc for the slightest scratch. To his amazement, he couldn't find one imperfection. "That was a pretty good collision, and I can't even find a smudge on this thing's surface."

"I'd better check for damage," Steve said.

"Like, don't sweat it, Stevie. That thing's indestructible, baby," Space explained.

"Not the saucer. My dad's building!"

"Oh, sorry man."

The heavy forklift prongs were lowered down gently on top of the saucer's dome as a symbolic gesture of restraint if nothing else, in case another unannounced start-up was attempted by its occupants. If they had a fully functional craft and desired to leave, not much could be done to keep them. Everyone sat staring in wonderment at the highly evolved and yet simple craft. It still hadn't registered in their heads exactly what lay before them. The tremendous disinformation program put out over the last 40 years by the Defense Department and MJ12 was very effective in planting doubt among the populous. Even the more highly focused people who knew a lot of the true facts were affected. Mind control works extremely well, especially when assisted by advanced outside forces.

Space walked in a large circle closely scrutinizing the outer edge of the disc. He surveyed the surface meticulously.

Al tapped Steve on the shoulder and asked, "What in the hell is he doin' now?"

"I don't know. Let's ask him." They walked over to him. "Space, what's up?"

"This type of disc usually has a retractable doorway located over and under this leading edge here. We might have a tough nut to crack if no one's alive in there to open up, Stevie."

"It sure isn't showing any signs of cooperating," said Al.

"So Space, if there are Greys inside, what's their story?" asked Steve.

"That's a good question, man. They're, like, very deceptive. They've got an uneasy treaty with our military. There's not much trust and a lot of questions unanswered. From my own experience, I think the little bastards are no damn good."

"These creeps are in our saucer?" Al asked. "Don't worry, boys. If they won't play ball, Captain Al knows how to deal with them. Badda Bing." He lifted his shirt revealing an army 45 pistol tucked in his belt.

"I don't think we'll need that," said Steve.

"Just in case. Just in case," answered Al.

Spaceman continued studying the writing along the upper dome of the ship. He halted upon reaching a conclusion and said, "It's one of theirs, all right. Definitely Greys."

Al and Spaceman followed Steve into the farmhouse. They returned with portable cots. The plan was to sleep beside the saucer to keep an eye on it. Everyone was exhausted and needed sleep before figuring out the best way to open up their mysterious captive. Each cot had one blanket. It was agreed that one person would remain awake as the watchman while the other two slept for two hour shifts. After drawing straws, Spaceman was to stand guard first.

Bobby and the girls stayed over at Kim's apartment. They had phoned to say they'd be by early in the morning to help.

"Wake me in two hours, Space," said Steve.

"No problemo, Stevie."

Al had already passed out on his cot. He was followed shortly by Steve. It wasn't more than ten minutes later when the watchman himself plopped over on his cot in a sound sleep.

The scene was one of total silence broken occasionally by Captain Al's intermittent snoring. A better place to hide something of this size could not have been secured on such short notice. The entire operation mimicked many earlier military recoveries. From the 2:00 AM transport down side roads, to the cavernous hangar-like atmosphere inside the barn, this operation was identical. The oddly-shaped craft originating from another corner of our universe, sat eerily still. Its purpose for being here on the blue planet was unknown. What lurked inside of its impenetrable metal skin also remained a mystery. Two unsuccessful escape attempts pointed to something alive within which tended to validate Spaceman's claims. This craft was obviously incapacitated in a very serious way and sooner or later its occupants, if alive, would have to accept their unwelcome fate. Unbeknownst to the three sleeping terrestrial guardians, the time for contact would be sooner rather than later.

CHAPTER SEVEN

Around four o'clock in the morning, the storage barn's interior took on a strange appearance. Something began to stir. The large chamber gave off an unearthly crimson glow. Increasingly, the scarlet tint engulfed everything, including the three heavily snoring sentinels. The intruders' metallic refuge, which previously separated two different civilizations, began to come apart. Like magic, an opening appeared precisely where Spaceman had predicted it would be.

As our ancestors in the past described similar scenes as fire-breathing dragons, so too did this red-flamed light radiate from the beast, although the present day evolution of scientific knowledge has demanded a different explanation be formulated for these anomalies. Same occurrences, different generations. Our ancestors explained these visitors within their known parameters just as we do now with present day limited comprehension of the advanced outsiders. Mankind will slowly take his first steps and gradually understand the enormity of life forms existing beyond the restraining gravitational pull of the Earth. Alien civilizations have risen and fallen eons before our own dinosaurs appeared. All things are relative, but even a child could easily deduce that other more evolved groups exist and traverse this universe. It's like comparing stone age man's spear weaponry to our nuclear tipped missile. At that particular point in time cavemen hadn't evolved long enough to implement such unbelievable technological power. The same comparison stands for our methods of space travel today as opposed to other advanced civilizations who manipulate time and space to achieve impossibilities by our present primitive standards. People's faulty conceptions of reality and the cosmos need to be prepared for the coming radical changes.

Steve, Al, and Spaceman were about to be smacked right in the face with that reality. The intense light radiated from the ship's retractable doorway resembling a furnace whose door was left open. No heat was present at all, just the weird red glow projecting outwards. All three cots lit up courtesy of the artificial campfire.

Then, it stood in the doorway gazing out at its alien surroundings. The four foot tall figure moved forward with a limp. It struggled to reach Al who slept closest to the craft. Childlike in appearance, it winced in pain after finally reaching the cot where Al lay asleep making loud air sucking sounds. Striving to maintain an erect posture, the being simply succumbed to his fatigue and blacked out, falling directly over Captain Al's stomach.

Al felt the impact and started speaking in a subconscious dialogue. "No honey, I'm not seeing anyone else. I swear!" His hand slid down to investigate the excess weight resting on his abdomen. At that moment, he caught sight of the strange red light illuminating the barn. Almost afraid to investigate his lower extremities, he picked up the creature's hand to count six fingers extending out. Shear terror filled his head as the clammy skin pressed against his hand.

"What the f—! Shit, Help!" Fear overtook him and his body performed an electrifying leap in the air. The small boarder flew in the air also. Fortunately he landed back on the cot.

Steve and Spaceman awoke immediately and spied the light pouring from the inner ship.

Steve gave off a loud, "Oh no!"

Spaceman screamed, "Don't panic. Stay still, dudes." The advice came too late.

An ear-deafening bang echoed the length of the barn. Al, terrorized by his surprise wake up call, pointed his all ready smoking .45 at the unconscious alien slumped over his cot. There was a round hole in the bedding surface where Al's bullet had come extremely close to hitting its intended target.

"Don't shoot!" yelled Space. "Don't shoot, man!"

Steve pulled the gun from Al's hands. "Easy Al, calm down. If he was going to hurt us, he could have done it while we slept."

"Yeah, O.K. Steverino. That makes sense, I guess."

"Just put the gun away, baby," Space advised.

Al was visibly shaken by the encounter.

The group edged closer to the cot. Curiosity gripped them all. They cautiously observed the red stranger for any signs of life. Steve felt sympathy for the small being. He wanted to help him, but wasn't quite sure how to go about it.

"Is he dead?" asked Al.

"Good question," answered Space.

"I wish there was something we could do," noted Steve.

"Yeah, well I guess you were right, Skippy, about the Greys being inside."

Space had a bewildered expression on his face. He glanced at Captain Al and said, "Something is wrong here."

"What do you mean 'something is wrong'?" murmured Al.

Space knew the occupant who disembarked and the type of craft did not match. "Stevie, man, something weird's going on here."

"Like what, Space?"

"Do you see the color of his skin?"

"Yeah?"

"And the bones and muscle structure?"

"Yeah, so?"

"He appears more human-like. This guy's definitely not a Grey, man."

"What the hell is he, Einstein?" growled Al impatiently.

"I'm not totally sure."

The discussion quickly adjourned when it became evident the visitor had moved his head. A short cough erupted, putting everyone on guard. His eyes remained shut. He must have been pretty banged-up physically, judging by the way the saucer entered the ocean. Steve approached first, his desire to assist this unfortunate soul overcoming any fears. Al and Space trailed behind. They stopped and observed Steve putting both his hands to his own temples.

"What's the matter. Got a headache, Steverino?"

"No. Did you guys hear what he's saying?"

"I didn't hear anything," answered Al.

"I've got to get something out of the ship for him."

"Don't do it, pal," Al warned.

"Let him go, man. It's telepathy. That's how 95 percent of the aliens communicate," Space said.

"He's guiding me to the ship. I can hear him speaking in my head. He's physically unconscious and says he needs a small gold wand which came loose from the belt on his space suit in the crash. He'd like me to try and locate it."

Steve walked to the retractable doorway, crouched low, and proceeded inside the red-colored cabin. Everything was so small. The control room resembled a child's video arcade. In front of a large monitoring screen sat a high back throne chair of tremendous beauty. Its entire length was inlaid with gems of various colors and sizes. They appeared to be actual diamonds and precious stones of exceptional beauty.

Steve noticed another being lying face down on the circular floor in a very terminal position. The voice coming to his brain confirmed his speculation that this individual was dead. Following the directions, Steve searched around the floor for the small gold wand. Space and Al weren't far behind. They climbed into the ship and ducked to prevent knocking their heads on the ceiling. Spaceman seemed to know his way around the vehicle. Al just looked on in awe.

"Is he still communicating with you, Stevie?" asked Space.

"Yeah…"

Space pointed to a dark corner. "There. On the floor over there."

"I got it. This is what he needs," replied Steve as he scooped it up and headed for the hatchway.

Steve hastily exited the disc. Al still studied the fantastic chair, oblivious to anything else.

Space caught sight of the dead alien and approached the body cautiously. He reached down and grabbed the being's silver space suit and flipped him over onto his back. He was dead, alright. His belt also contained a gold wand attached to it. Space inconspicuously pulled the device free of its Velcro holder and deposited it in his pants' pocket. He slyly turned to make sure Al hadn't witnessed the pilferage.

Al said, "Will you look at this thing? If these are real gems and colored diamonds, we're stinkin' rich! Badda bing! The big time."

"I heard about these chairs but never had the pleasure, baby."

"Pleasure is a good word, Skippy. If those golf ball-sized stones in that chair are for real, we've got the mother lode."

"I know, like, you're not interested, dude, but his chair also controls functions that operate this ship. The perfect oscillating crystallized pattern in its structure is needed to control frequencies with great accuracy."

"You're right, I don't care. Hey, c'mon Skippy, let's go find some tools to loosen these babies."

"We gotta check on Stevie, dude."

The small alien instructed Steve to place the device in his hand and close his fingers around it. Trying to aid the injured visitor, he cooperated. Upon placing the wand in his palm, a dull glow appeared over his entire body. It worked similarly to a fresh battery jump starting a stalled motor. Their little guest's eyes blinked open, exhibiting a human-like design. He did not possess the dark almond-shaped eyes of the Grey race. Whatever he was, his lineage seemed hauntingly similar to humans. If not for his enlarged head and six fingers on each hand, he could pass for an adolescent homosapien.

Blinking his sapphire-colored eyes, the little fellow awoke. Steve was startled by the sound of car doors slamming outside in the driveway. He glanced at this watch to see it was 6:30 AM. Sunlight was just beginning to cast its brightness over the farm.

"Al, quick, check who's here," Steve whispered.

"Gotcha."

As Al ran to identify the new arrivals, the small visitor sat up on the cot and exchanged glances with Spaceman and Steve. He finally spoke from his mouth. Straight away, he pronounced his gratitude.

"Thank you for assisting in my revival."

"You're welcome," returned Steve. "Are you alright?"

"Yes, for now."

Al came trotting back followed by Bobby, Kim, and Carol. They all stopped dead in their tracks upon viewing the scene before them. The childlike visitor sat upright curiously observing the procession through his big blue glassy eyes. Kim immediately started for the door, but was unable to break free of Bobby's grip on her arm.

Spaceman motioned for them to approach. "C'mon, it's cool."

They moved hesitantly closer as if in a haunted house awaiting a ghost to pop out and send them fleeing to the exits.

As if her skin was crawling, Kim asked, "What is it?"

No sooner had she spoken when the small guest answered," I'm known to your people in the Pentagon as an E.B.E. - Extraterrestrial Biological Entity. I believe your Dr. Bronk coined the phrase in 1947 while serving as an original member of your MJ12 Group."

"You speak English," noted an amazed Al.

"Oh yes. We monitor your communication and media transmission. I am quite familiar with your culture."

"How come we don't pick up your transmissions?" asked Al.

"Our signals are pulse waves and coded. So, even if you could pick them up, they'd have no meaning without an interpreting computer."

"Who are you and what culture do you come from?" asked Steve.

"I live underground on the Red planet you call Mars. Our race once lived on the surface but are unable to now."

"Hey Red. What do you mean you can't live on the surface?" asked Al.

"My name is not Red."

"Don't take offense, pal."

"To simplify understandings, you may call me Red. The answer to your question is that our atmosphere became altered. Our civilization was thriving five hundred thousand Earth years ago. At that juncture in our evolution, we had achieved a prosperous Bronze-Age culture not unlike your Egyptians."

"So there really are Martians?" Carol asked.

"I am part of a small colony still living there, yes."

"This can't be real," Kim blurted. "It's grotesque."

"I think he's kind of cute," proclaimed Carol who was intensely captivated. "Just another of God's diverse creatures."

"Yeah, right," said Kim being far less accepting.

"Hey," said Bobby. "I've seen pictures of the stone face and five sided pyramids taken by the 1976 Viking Explorer. It was on T.V. Two ex-NASA scientists removed some of the shots showing these structures clearly there."

"Yes," Red responded. "Your Defense Department calls it Sedonia. It is the ruins of our old capital city."

"Wouldn't the 1993 Mars Explorer have gotten pictures of this region?" asked Carol who brought up a valid point.

"Your Pentagon terminated that satellite intentionally," said Red.

"That's true," said Steve. "My friend out at the Cape told me the pictures originally coming back to the Jet Propulsion Lab were unbelievable. He said a rogue group pulled the plug on the Mars Explorer."

"Correct," answered Red.

Kim was listening intently. "Why would they sabotage our own probe?"

"Because your leaders are not ready to enlighten your populous," said Red. "And more importantly, the E.B.E.s your Pentagon has signed an agreement with do not want their presence known under any circumstances."

"No shit," said Steve. "I know the Explorers' picture taking quality was fifty times more powerful than the 1976 Viking shots of Mars. So-called National Security interests took over and the plug was pulled on the satellite which maintained the status quo of silence pertaining to extraterrestrial life."

"I read somewhere that NASA said those shapes on Mars were carved by wind erosion," said Carol.

"Negative, baby," replied Spaceman. "The two dudes who leaked the Viking pictures had them independently scrutinized using infrared and computer imaging, man. And surprise, surprise. The head had two eyeballs and its mouth had two rows of teeth. Now that's one hell of a wind."

"Next they'll tell us Mount Rushmore was formed in a blizzard," ridiculed Bobby.

Everyone pressed closer to the small visitor they called Red. The curious crowd saw a chance for honest answers to age-old questions.

"Go on, Red," encouraged Al.

"Tell us. What destroyed the atmosphere on Mars?" asked Steve.

"The proper question should be 'Who'," answered Red. "You see, our planet was changed by a large asteroid colliding into it. Its effects were catastrophic. The atmosphere changed and water disappeared as the planet's axis shifted. We've come to learn this event was not a random act of nature."

"What do you mean?" asked Steve.

"The comet was intentionally diverted at us to achieve the present situation: living underground in small communities or colonies totally dependent on our benefactors. They're known to you as Greys."

"Are you saying the Greys destroyed your civilization by using a comet to alter your planet?" asked Carol.

"Correct."

"Why?" they all wondered.

"Because it served their purpose. They have been visiting our planet as well as yours for a very long time. They consider our planets as part of their frontier territory. Being the more advanced civilization, they utilized us for their genetic experimentation. Their work failed and they tried to erase all mistakes using the comet. It also made the whole debacle appear to be a natural cataclysm which covered their dastardly deeds. This way other groups could not protest such an intervention. A small surviving group of our people was retained by the Greys to continue genetic evolutionary work. These remaining members of my race live underground and are subservient to them."

Carol exchanged astonished glances with Steve. Kim couldn't shake her years of programming which told her this wasn't possible.

Carol listened to the sad tale. "Sounds as if troubled race relations aren't exclusive to Earth. Slavery is a terrible thing. To lose your individual sanctity and freedom because one group feels superior is a crime."

"I must unconditionally agree with your assessment," said Red. "We've been dominated by the Greys for hundreds of thousands of years. You would think beings with that much intellect could respect the sovereignty of less developed civilizations instead of exploiting them."

"Arrogance and greed," said Carol.

"Do you know the Greys?" asked Red.

"No, but intolerance seems to be a universal malady."

"You are a wise human."

Red was half-bent over the cot. A small drop of liquid appeared to drip from his large eyes.

"Don't worry. You're free here," said Bobby.

"Red, why have you come here?" Steve inquired.

"It is said that history repeats itself," Red continued. "To begin, you must understand the Greys have altered your evolution already. As we speak, they are in the process of selecting the exact size asteroid to guide toward Earth."

"Wait a minute. That'd kill thousands and thousands of people!" Bobby moved forward in alarm.

"It would do more than that," interrupted Spaceman. "We'd go the way of the dinosaurs, baby."

"Correct. That is the point. To prevent this occurrence, I was sent here by the Alignment. They consist of many united forces who are guardians against any aggressive interference of evolving civilizations in the cosmos. They assisted my escape in the Grey saucer. I cannot stress the immediate urgency of my mission. The Greys have influence with your military and have them using your SDI weaponry to shoot down friendly ships. In actuality, it is the Greys who are your greatest threat."

"But why? Why would they want us dead?" questioned Carol.

Red went on to explain that humans are no more than a single link in an ongoing chain of experimentation. He told the group that the Greys first introduced Phase I Neanderthals approximately two hundred thousand years ago. Forty thousand years ago, Phase II, Cro Magnom, the present makeup was brought in. Phase III Hybrids are now assembling and preparing for settlement of Earth.

"Wait a minute," said Steve. "Who or what are Phase III Hybrids?"

Red explained that they are crossbred genetically engineered products of Cro Magnon humans and Greys. Humans must be aware of the alien abductions taking place over the years. The harvesting of sperm and ovum is not in people's dreams, as the military's disinformation experts want everyone to believe. Greys are not going to all this time and expense without a strong purpose and agenda. Their program of interfering with natural evolution will no longer be tolerated by the Alignment. "They've sent my partner and me to terminate those plans before they are executed. You see, the Greys cannot introduce their hybrids until the petry dish has been cleaned, to use your terminology.

"The comet or asteroid must be meticulously selected for consistency and size. When it slams into your Earth at 60,000 miles per hour, your life-giving sunlight will be blocked out and everyone will perish. The atmosphere will clear in a year or two, allowing a fresh start for the Phase III Hybrids. Unfortunately, Cro Magnon, meaning you, will be extinct."

Red said he was here to prevent just such an occurrence from taking place like the one that sadly went too far on Mars. "Your leaders need to be alerted to their allies treachery. This is why I was almost killed on arrival. Greys that are advising your Defense Department probably designated my ship as hostile."

"So that's what these little bastards are up to," shouted Spaceman. The information seemed to make a great deal of sense to him now.

"This is becoming way too complicated for me," complained Kim.

"Do you remember the Hale Bop comet which passed closely to Earth recently?" asked Red.

Everyone nodded.

"That comet was deemed too large for impact and ruled out in the final hours."

Steve said, "Funny thing. On the internet there were reports of an object trailing in the comet's wake. Not only that, but they said the comet changed course thirty-four times. Comets do not correct their own course telemetry."

"Quite correct," said Red. "Two ships are used to achieve this control over a comet. One resides in the super vacuum directly behind the hurling mass, and the other uses a steering beam from the target itself. The ship, which will administer course corrections on the incoming projectile to Earth, is presently concealed only a few miles from your dwelling here. Upon final approach of the comet, they will instantaneously depart to a safe distance to avoid the impact residue."

"They're here now?" asked Al excitedly. "How can we stop 'em?"

"Remain calm," said Red. "My task is to place a homing device on or in the vicinity of their mother ship. It must be done within a certain time framework. An Alignment ship will vaporize the Greys using an ion beam from deep space at the allotted moment."

"Sounds like an episode of 'Flash Gordon'," said Bobby.

Spaceman sucked in a freshly lit cigarette. "No, it's real and serious shit, Bob."

"Serious?" said Al. "If that comet hits us, Badda bind, we're on the endangered species list. Our freakin' military needs a wake up call."

Not wanting to agree with the captain but forced to, Spaceman coughed, "He's right, dudes. Our small friend over here is going to need all the help he can get. I knew we could never trust those goddamn Greys."

The whole audience at this bizarre debriefing was fighting cerebral shutdown. That's when the mind refuses to believe a threatening situation exists. It's akin to an ostrich placing his head in the hole where he's safe. Or so he thinks.

Kim fearfully grabbed Bobby. "We need to report this to someone. I'm really getting scared."

"I know. But we can't call the military yet. They might not believe their so-called allies are really our biggest enemies. Let's wait a while. Spaceman will know what to do."

Kim could only give him a doubting frown in response.

"Let's put it to a vote," said Steve. "Who's willing to help our friend here?"

"Do we really have a choice?" asked Captain Al.

"No."

All hands rose in the air but Kim's.

"Good. We'll help you, Red, but let's wait until the cover of darkness to move."

"This is good news," Red responded as he wiped the small tear from his oversized eye. "With a little assistance, I know the Greys can be stopped."

Carol hugged Steve upon seeing Red's reaction. They were still a bit stunned by the unbelievable story Red had just revealed.

"I'm sorry to bring you all this bad news," admitted Red.

"It's not bad news yet," said Steve. "Do you know where this ship is located?"

"Yes. Only a few miles from where we stand. That would have been my destination before your military shot me down."

"Don't worry, man. You can count on us to help," assured Spaceman.

"Hey Red, are you hungry?" asked Bobby.

"No. We do not eat food as humans do. My digestive tract, as you call it, has been genetically engineered for generations. I may not appear very different on the outside, but there are vastly different organs inside for the purpose of a sickness-free long life. Our sustenance is derived from a nutrient-rich water we drink. I have some in my ship."

"What about your comrade?" Carol thoughtfully asked.

"Yes, a tragedy. He will be encapsulated and hopefully sent home."

"Can your ship still fly?' asked Al who hoped his prize was permanently stranded.

"The gravitational amplifiers have sustained irreversible damage, I'm afraid."

"That's too bad," said Al, who slyly hid his joy over the reply quite well.

"Your Star Wars umbrella is quite an effective defense system," Red commented.

Everyone sat quietly absorbing the insights of Earthly events witnessed by an outsider. This was a new perspective, not one forced fed to us by the evening news, but one that is refreshing, non-slanted, and giving off a strong bouquet of truth. Though a negetive message, it was honestly delivered.

"These particle beam weapons which are fired from orbiting satellites destroyed two comrades of mine in an earlier attempt at warning Earthians of the planned treachery. This incident occurred off your Long Island, New York. Our ship had made its way into the ocean after hitting your atmosphere. As it circled a U.S. attack submarine it encountered just below the surface, an SDI satellite opened fire on it. Our ship was destroyed along with one of your commercial airliners. Apparently the jet liner was slightly off course and the photo electromagnetic particles from the weapon destroyed all electronics on board. A fire was induced throughout the electrical system which ignited the fuel tanks causing a catastrophic explosion."

"You don't mean the plane crash that was in the paper a while back?" shouted Carol.

In a mild voice, Red said, "Yes. Correct."

"Holy shit," said Al. "So that's the blue streak of light observers on shore saw before the fireball."

"Correct," said Red.

"I can't believe it," said Kim.

"I can," added Steve.

"Yep," is all Spaceman could conjure.

There was no telling what kind of information Red was privy to. He seemed to be extremely enlightened on classified subject matter. Things he shouldn't know.

"I'm sure the Greys or another group assisted your Dr. Ted Eller in developing these weapons at Los Alamos. As Earthians say, 'One hand washes the other'."

"Hey, I like the way this guy thinks," Al told Steve. "We need to talk, Red."

"If we don't stop the Greys, man, there won't be anywhere for you to spend those millions you plan on getting for that saucer, baby," Space advised Al. He rapidly put things into perspective.

"He's right, Al," Steve said. "For one thing, Red's got to be kept from the military. And secondly, we must help him in any way possible to locate and destroy that hidden ship."

Red watched the expressions on everyone's beleaguered faces. Their thoughts were registering in his head without a word being spoken. He said, "Most of you are willing to help me locate the enemy ship. Locating the targets position is simple; getting to it is not. And that is where your help will be needed. I possess a device that can hone in on particular substances contained in their craft. If necessary, their ship can also be pinpointed by using my device in conjunction with your global positioning satellites."

"You can tap into our GPS satellites?" asked Al.

"Correct."

"And you won't even receive a service charge?" Bobby joked.

"I highly doubt it," answered Red. "You humans are capable of joking at the oddest times. It is a good quality. But this mission cannot fail. Surely you understand the devastating consequences of failure."

"Yes, we do," answered Steve for everyone.

Red explained to his hosts that he needed some time to tend to his dead comrade and prepare for tonight. Steve had retrieved a local map out of his father's tractor trailer on which Red could transpose the Grey's location. Since the saucer before them was irreparable, they would have to seek out the Greys by ground routes.

"Red, we'll meet you back here after lunch to go over the plan of attack," explained Steve.

"Lunch? Oh yes, nutriating."

"Are you sure there is nothing we can get for you?" asked Carol.

"No, but thank you. Everything I need is in my craft."

"If you need us, we'll be 'nutriating' in that house over there." Steve pointed toward his parents' farmhouse.

All the salvers marched quietly across the loading yard to the Wilcox home. It was a large farmhouse which gave testament to a successful business. The family was not only prosperous, but well-liked by everyone. Even the migrant workers admired their boss's fairness and generosity.

Once inside the spacious and beautifully furnished rooms, Bobby and Kim headed for the kitchen to survey the lunch provisions. She was visibly upset while Bobby's immature nature interpreted the whole incident as a big adventure. He tried to coax some calmness into her demeanor but was having little luck.

Space pulled Steve to a side room and shut the door.

"Stevie, we've got to help him find that ship. The military is backing the wrong horse. The race is fixed. And it's fixed for all of us to lose big."

Steve exhibited signs of brain overload. He half-listened to Space while Red's earlier statements were being reviewed in his mind. "This guy sounds logical to you, doesn't he?"

"Absolutely, Stevie. His info is very accurate."

"There's really no choice then," Steve stated. "At dusk, we'll take the van and hope we can find that saucer."

Emerging from the side room, Steve was greeted by Carol's comforting embrace. Their eyes met in a troubled stare. She said, "This can't be happening, can it?" Her jittery voice betrayed her well-concealed fear.

"Space believes the situation to be exactly as Red relayed it. In any case, tonight the truth will be known. I want you and Kim to remain here."

"No way, Steve. I'm going. Kim doesn't have to, but I'm in. This thing concerns all of us, and I've got personal reasons why I must go."

Steve wondered what those personal reasons could be but didn't press her. "I'd prefer you didn't go, but if you're that hell bent on it, so be it. Besides, if we don't locate that ship, no one will be safe."

"Thanks for understanding, Steve," Carol said as she kissed him. They moved to join the others for a quick bite to eat.

Following a two hour discussion regarding the information Red had disclosed, the group left the farmhouse and made their way back to the disc. The subjects covered in their impromptu meeting entailed many aspect of the human-alien connection. Consequences of their little salvage recovery would impact every thread of civilization's fabric. They had no idea how all-encompassing the subject matter could be.

Implications on mankind's origins alone were staggering. Now the impossible job before the secret MJ12 and Defense Department became clear. The vast dimensions of a diversified universe with seemingly limitless variations of intelligent life were awesome. The task of sorting out allies among enemies could also be quite confusing and dangerous. Different agendas and intentions have to be identified within a web of deceptive highly intelligent alien civilizations. This job is extremely daunting and a national security nightmare.

The task at hand was simple and straight forward. Stop the Greys' ominous plans or else. Martian culture had been annihilated many years ago. To prevent repeating that process of long-range genetic engineering on Earth, a concentration of efforts was needed in assisting a small benefactor named Red. He mentioned powerful forces known as the Alignment who sponsored him and would perform the actual shooting that eliminates the threat. In spite of this United Nations of the cosmos, it appears certain groups still persist at interfering with other cultures' evolutionary development to satisfy their own irresponsible desires. Arrogant beings like the Greys show intolerance toward humans and indifference to our suffering.

After the meeting adjourned, all members departed to see Red. They tiptoed through the storage barn door so as not to disturb their foreign guest. The collapsible hatchway on the disc had vanished. Red sealed himself in his comfortable refuge. Spaceman walked up to the spot where the doorway once stood and gave the dull gray metal's surface a slow knock followed by four quick ones. He remained silent for a minute, half expecting a two-knock reply.

"What are you doing, Skippy?" complained Al, getting annoyed by his mannerisms.

"The doorbell is out of order, baby," came the answer.

"You call me 'baby' one more time and the only thing outta order will be you," threatened Al.

"What do you do with all that hostility, baby?" taunted Space.

Al protested to Steve, "This nut's our expert?"

"All right you guys, chill out," refereed Steve.

Tempers cooled rapidly when an unexpected high-pitched squeaking sound pierced the large room. A crack suddenly developed in the saucer's leading edge that lifted the upper section while lowering the bottom section. Everyone grew silent as though watching a master magician perform tricks.

"Oh God," squeaked Kim as a red glow hit her.

"Can we go in?" asked the ever-curious Carol.

"I'm sure we can," said Steve. "Yeah...He's inviting us in to inspect his ship."

"You mean *our* ship," corrected Al.

"You guys can't hear him?" asked Steve as he held onto his head.

All shook their heads in a negative response.

"Of course not. We've all got different frequency brain wave transmissions," reminded Spaceman as if everyone should know better.

Carol led the way up the small narrow ladder. The human visitors found the height differential once inside to be substantial. The low arched ceiling was never built to accommodate our species. Kim lingered outside and argued with Bobby over her entering the strange craft. Seeing the others were all on board, she capitulated.

It became cramped very quickly as six large humans huddled around the control panels in front of the centerpiece throne-like command chair. Red spoke from his mouth as he explained to everyone various functions of objects inside. Of particular interest and catching everyone's attention was a large hologram-type map of the stars. Stars and planets on this flat screen seemed to be in motion. It was bizarre. Distances and positions changed slightly as the actual heavenly bodies rotated or orbited in space.

"Where are we on this map?" asked Carol who was obviously awed by its eerie appearance.

Red pointed, "Here. And this is where the allies'ship from the Alignment will be positioned to fire on the Greys."

"Can we see the Greys' home planet on this?" asked Steve.

"Yes once we switch to their sector." The change was made. "It is Alfa Mensae in the Orion Belt over here next to the two Zeta Reticulae."

"If I ever run out of gas in that neck of the woods, I'll be sure to keep an eye out for them," joked Al.

Red blinked his glassy eyes as he found no humor in the comment. "This ship is not powered by fossil fuels," he said.

"What then?" asked Al.

"Matter and anti-matter combined together in an annihilation reaction which is one hundred percent thermodynamically efficient."

"Sounds hot," said Al.

"The heat particles are controlled inside that small containment sphere behind you." Red pointed at a bowling ball size metal container on a pedestal in the absolute center of the craft. "The tremendous heat is converted to electric power and sent via super conductors to the gravitation amplifiers. No power is wasted."

"I'll bet that little ball can produce some heavy duty juice," Al said.

"Substantially more than one of your nuclear power plants. Correct."

"So this is what the future holds," commented Steve.

"Possibly."

"Do you get a lot of localized warping of time and space once the gravity amplifiers engage?" asked Spaceman. "I mean, do you go out of phase with Earth's gravity on the 0 - 180° longitudinal spectrum for gravitational waves?"

Red gazed at Spaceman in bewilderment, "You know of their technology?"

"Yeah, baby. I was part of Project Snowbird sponsored by our military. I test flew one of these babies years ago. We didn't travel very far back then, but what a rush, man. What a rush!"

"Fascinating," said Red. "If I may use one of your Earthian sayings, 'That's pretty cool, dud."

"That's dude, baby," Spaceman instructed.

"Ah, correct," he replied.

Carol snickered at the mispronunciation. Recognizing the developing relationship between Red and her friends, Carol asked herself why the hostile Grey aliens couldn't coexist peacefully with humans. A small amount of communication and understanding could work wonders. These thoughts urged her to pose a question to Red. "Do you feel it possible to have a meeting of the minds with the Greys to try and prevent hostilities and destruction?"

"Extremely improbable."

"But why?"

"Simply, they have no intentions of recognizing universal laws of sovereignty and showing respect for less evolved life forms. Continually they disregard Alignment mandates in this area. Their proficient deceptiveness allows them domination over other groups. They accept no one as their equal."

"That's too bad," Carol said.

"Correct."

Al, more immediately interested in his salvaged vehicle, surveyed the small walkway around the cabin. He noticed a tube resembling a stovepipe running from the ball-shaped reactor on the floor to the dome-shaped ceiling above. "Hey, Red. What's this pipe?"

With a joint smoldering between his lips, Spaceman answered, "That's a wave guide."

"Correct."

Spaceman continued to empty out his past knowledge in his drug-induced recall. "The adjustable antenna on the roof stabilizes the craft by controlling the magnetic and gravitic waves. It directs the waves at low Earth orbit before all three amplifiers kick in for space time flight. The aliens interact with nature by manipulating the fabric of space. Since its builders work with nature closely, success is found quicker. Our own misguided scientific community likes to swim against the current. Those schmucks out at NASA and the Jet Propulsion Lab in California still think creating a reaction mass to propagate motion for travel is the way."

"You mean rockets," said Steve.

"It's all wrong, man. Primitive shit like rockets. They simply need to pull their heads out of their asses and use space time gravity travel. It would eliminate slow, dangerous, inefficient and expensive rocketry."

Red looked perplexed, "I have not heard of these humans capable of fitting their craniums in their rectums. This appears incorrect."

The group smiled. "No, that's just a joke, Red," Steve explained.

A growing cloud of cannabis smoke swirled into Red's small nostrils inducing a small sneeze. Space apologized, "Sorry, little buddy."

Steve asked Red if he'd completed plotting the coordinates on the town map given to him earlier. He held it up and pointed to the exact spot the ship was hidden. The crowd gathered around to learn of the location.

Bobby studied the map closely and shouted, "Shit! That sits dead center on the old abandoned gator farm off Route 192. That can't be more than five miles from here."

"Are you certain that's the spot?" asked Steve.

"Yes," answered Red. "I've borrowed one of your GPS satellites briefly to cross check my own methods of detection."

"That old gator farm has been abandoned since before we were kids," said Steve.

"Is it possible to gain access?" questioned Red.

"We'll get you there, Red. What's the plan?"

A concealed compartment folded out from which Red withdrew a black metal disc which measured a foot and a half across. The object resembled a large film canister but was highly polished and reflected light like a mirror.

"To be brief, my job is to place this targeting disc on or very near the ship. Once achieved, I'm to depart the area with the greatest of expediency. At precisely 9:00 PM Earth time, this evening the allies will carry out the termination sentence with a beam from deep space."

"You mean, 'Fire all fasers' like on Star Trek?" asked Bobby.

"Correct analogy," said Red. "That was my favorite Earth show to monitor years ago."

"How powerful is this beam?" asked Steve.

"Anything within a one thousand foot radius of the disc will turn to gas vapor. My friends, if you can assist me in reaching the target, the mission's probability of success should be very high."

"What if we won't take you there?" asked Kim.

"I cannot force you, but your own self-preservation should be more than enough motivation to assist me. You see, if I fail, Phase III Hybrids will claim the title of Earthians in a few years."

"Say no more," Bobby said over Kim's protests.

"You'll get there, pal. Don't worry," insured Al.

Darkness was only an hour away. The farm's big 4 X 4 Suburban was selected as the vehicle of choice. Present conditions of the old back roads leading to the abandoned gator farm were unknown. Due to the gravity of the situation, all involved would participate, even Kim. Bobby and Kim decided to follow the Suburban in a back up vehicle to the site. Steve, Carol, Al, and Spaceman loaded inside the larger vehicle and drove around in front of the storage barn doors. Bobby's van brought up the rear. Their small passenger waited patiently on the other side of the barn doors.

Keeping the guest's presence a secret was paramount. It became clear that maintaining secrecy must be a nightmare for the military.

There wasn't much daylight remaining as Pepe, the Wilcox's groundskeeper, trotted over between the 4 X 4 and the barn. He was breathing hard. The urgency in his step indicated he had something important to tell Steve. His timing could not have been worse.

One of the big bay doors opened slightly, allowing Red to make his way past the stunned employee. Pepe's jaw dropped as he watched in disbelief. The four foot silver-suited alien gave a short wave to him while passing by and hopped into the truck's open door.

Red had donned two dark oval lenses which covered both eyes in anticipation of a higher degree of sunlight outside. How the two pieces remained over his eye sockets with no apparent supporting structure was a mystery. To humans he looked strange before, but now the dark lenses gave him a more bizarre, insect-like appearance. Pepe's jaw hadn't budged. With his mouth still wide open, he made a quick sign of the cross and mumbled something in Spanish. Steve jumped from the truck to calm things down and provide a feeble explanation to their shocked employee. Before he could speak, Pepe snapped out of his comatose state and said, "Mr. Steve, there is something going on out in the trees."

"What do you mean?"

"I rush back here to let Bobby and you know."

"What, Pepe? What's wrong?"

"Some men come in the groves. They wear suits and talk on radios."

"How many, Pepe?" asked Bobby.

"Maybe six or eight and three cars on the road in front. They not see Pepe. I run here right away to tell you."

"O.K. thanks, Pepe," said Bobby. "We'll handle this. You better go hide in the old tool shed until we call you."

"AH carrumba!" he shouted and departed quickly.

Bobby looked at Steve, "Spaceman's friends?"

"That's my guess. Let's get out of here the back way by the irrigation ditches."

"I'm with you, Bro."

The minute everyone entered the two vehicles, two dark colored unmarked cars raced in from the main driveway on a collision course for the departing group. Dust and dirt shot into the air from the sliding, spinning wheels. Steve slammed down the accelerator adding more smoke to the dust storm in progress. He simultaneously caught sight of two familiar faces in the vehicle attempting to cut him off. They were Spaceman's surveillance agents. Steve hit the brakes causing their car to overshoot his Suburban. He turned the wheel again and accelerated through the blinding dirt clouds. A loud crash ensued, echoing from the impact of Steve's truck bumper piercing the agent's rear quarter panel. The combined force of this broadside and the already leaning government car, caused the latter to roll completely over on its roof.

Unable to wait around, the escapees found an opening and took off towards the old drainage ditch road. Bobby was right behind in the van. Almost immediately a loud rotary sound could be heard booming outside. Captain Al leaned out the back window and shouted, "Oh shit! There's a chopper on our ass!"

"Hold on!" shouted Steve who pressed down even further on the gas pedal.

The dirt roadway was rough at high speeds and forced the truck's suspension to buck and bounce fiercely. Bobby and Kim were enduring an even tougher ride unable to stay on a smoke laden road to the rear. As the escapees rounded a turn in the orange grove, two gun-toting strangers stood directly in their path. Closing in on the pair quickly, their headlights revealed neither man was budging.

The Suburban swerved at the last minute narrowly avoiding a collision. One agent's machine gun scraped against the doors of the truck in the near miss. Steve peered through the rear view mirror until finally spotting Bobby's van lights knife through the dust and bounce back into formation.

There was the smell of real trouble chasing them. It was no longer a game. The risks of their endeavor were quite real. Obviously, as real as what they had fished from the sea floor. In all these cases involving ETs, the government doesn't mess around or leave any loose ends. When anyone goes up against their unlimited resources, it's a lost cause. And yet based on what Red had revealed, all involved were glad they hadn't called the military. They understood what was at stake. The consequences of not acting on the doomsday information would have a permanent finality for mankind.

Carol put her window down to see the helicopter. "It's right over us. It looks like soldiers are on board."

"I was afraid of that," Steve replied.

"They've got our saucer, goddamn it," cussed Al. "I've lost millions. Millions down the toilet."

Spaceman delighted in Al's misery. "Yeah, man, but think of the tax liabilities you've escaped."

"Shut your damn mouth, you nut job! It's because of you the military is up our butts."

"Guys," Steve shouted above the rotor blade noise, "if we don't lose this chopper, tax liabilities will be the least of our problems."

Steve turned at a small fork onto a more remote trail. A thick canopy shielded out the now starlit sky allowing cover from any aerial pursuer. The Wilcox farm bordered on large tracks of land belonging to a wildlife refuge and the roads could get real ugly fast. In one of Robert Frost's famous poems, he describes a road not taken. It was just taken by the escaping group. It became quite evident why no one traveled this road. The side of the truck barely cleared the dense swamp-like vegetation. This was a tighter fit than O.J. Simpson's black glove.

"We've got a shot at losing them now," said Steve. "No one knows about this old road."

"What road?" asked Captain Al sarcastically.

Obviously Steve was using memory recall to penetrate this backwoods abyss. Both headlights were on bright although their affect was nil. Leaves and branches were all washing over the hood. Powerful aerial search lights intermittently pierced the dark canopy above providing a constant reminder of exactly how close they were to being caught.

"Is Bobby still back there?" Steve asked anxiously.

"No, I can't see his headlights anymore," answered Carol.

"I'm going to stop. He doesn't have four-wheel drive. They better ride with us."

Coming to an abrupt halt, the group noticed the loud helicopter rotors had faded somewhat. Off in the distance from whence they came, could be heard the popping of automatic gunfire.

"Oh my God. They wouldn't shoot at them, would they?" cried Carol.

"Man, this is national security. They'll use any means necessary," Spaceman abruptly reminded her.

"We're going back," Steve decided.

Red pulled himself closer to the front seat. "That would not be wise."

"Well, wise or not..." Before he could finish the sentence, Bobby's headlights came screaming out of the thick brambles almost slamming into the

Suburban. Steve jumped onto the truck's running board and yelled, "Hurry, get in!"

The ever-present rotor noise had returned. Sporadic light flashes could be seen in the sky. Bobby and Kim abandoned the van and ran along the muddy overgrown trail to the awaiting arms of Al and Spaceman who yanked them in the already rolling truck.

"You guys O.K.?" asked Carol.

"Shit, they tried to shoot out my tires from the air!" yelled Bobby.

Kim, in a traumatized state, muttered, "I knew this would lead to trouble."

Unbeknownst to the fugitives, the Blackhawk helicopter in pursuit was equipped with forward looking infrared radar and night vision capabilities. Translated, it simply meant the Suburban was not about to lose this high-tech aircraft and its specialized squad of commandos.

Nevertheless, Steve decided to try his luck on a nearby highway. The turnoff leading to the road was rough. Everyone left their seats, bouncing and hitting their heads on the truck's ceiling. The truck struggled up a slight incline. They were out in the open on a two lane highway across from a dairy farm. Before attaining any speed, their progress was greatly hindered when bullets strafed the ground directly across their path. Machine gun fire rang out all around them.

"They mean business, Steverino," said Al.

"It's called 'Deep Shit' and we're in it alright."

While enduring the raucous chase, Red quietly detached the gold-colored wand off his belt. "Steve?"

"Yeah…"

"Please engage your vehicle in reverse when I tell you."

Steve turned to watch Red hang out the window and aim his small device at the large helicopter preparing to block their exit by landing in the middle of the road. Pointing the pencil-shaped wand at the chopper, a beam of blue light appeared. It struck the engine compartment beneath the rotor blades which caused an instantaneous seizure. The craft dropped the remaining three feet to the concrete. The resulting loud thud vibrated the roadway and could be felt in the truck.

Steve picked up Red's telepathic signal and was already speeding in reverse. All four brakes locked up which initiated a cloud of white smoke that engulfed the spinning vehicle. It came to rest in a perpendicular position with the street lanes. A sideways view of the distant chopper under a street light showed dazed soldiers popping out of its open door.

The soldiers were probably in better condition than their craft at this point. Steve aimed the Suburban in the other direction and sped away.

"Red, how'd you do that?" asked Al.

"It is an extremely simple EMP device."

"What?" questioned Bobby.

"Electromagnetic Pulse weapon," was the answer. "It is quite non-lethal to humans, but highly disruptive to any electronic system."

"Like a helicopter motor?" asked Carol.

"Correct. Your military has had a form of this technology for a few years now at your Eglin Air Force Base in Florida. Their devices are nowhere as compact as this multi-functional instrument. When you hold my device in your hand, it processes your brain waves. That person's wishes are carried out to the potential of its power limits."

Al computed the tremendous demand for an item such as the wand and started to see dollar signs. "Hey Red, you interested in selling me one of those beauties? I'll start the bidding right now."

"I cannot. It would be in violation of Alignment guidelines for evolutionary intervention."

"You don't have to make up your mind now. We'll talk later, pal."

The fugitives moved at a high rate of speed from the coast toward their destination west of Melbourne's city limits. At five miles distance, in a swampy forested area, lay the property which fifty years ago had supported a thriving alligator farm. The Wilcox brothers used to visit its deserted out buildings as boys. Its old wooden structures in the middle of the swamp would always provide an eerie stage for their adolescent adventures and pranks. The props were dangerous as well as real. Many local large reptilian residents patrolled the area in search of a meal. No doubt leftovers from the farm's heydays.

Presently, the place was inaccessible and reclaimed by the surrounding terrain. The only people entering this inhospitable place would be poachers. People just don't go into swamps. Outside of the ocean bottom or polar ice caps, this place was perfect for maintaining a secluded hideaway. Just what the doctor ordered for a cunning intruder to have his presence go unnoticed.

CHAPTER EIGHT

There were not many distinguishing landmarks or features to indicate their proximity to the target. Steve and Bobby knew they might have trouble finding it due to the passage of time and the fast rate of growth occurring in the underbrush. Creeks and streams snaked across the marshes eventually ending up flowing north with the St. John's River to Jacksonville. These waters were responsible for the bayou-like terrain. Civilization hadn't yet tamed the soggy impenetrable swamp. Settlements such as Orlando to the west and Melbourne in the east simply circumvented its uninhabitable boundaries.

"That's it!" shouted Bobby.

"Are you sure?" questioned Steve who couldn't see anything but thick vegetation. "Check with Red."

Red leaned in from the rear seat and held up a small box in his six-fingered hand. "Yes, we must turn and proceed south at this juncture."

Red's presence in the back seat almost passed unnoticed during the ride. He was becoming one of the gang, more or less. When the roof light turned on and his six-fingered hand came into view, the fact he was not human arose briefly. He grew out of a different garden, an alien civilization from a neighboring planet. And yet, in spite of the obvious physical differences, an acceptance was established. There was no hostility or prejudice toward the stranger. Carol noticed this immediately. She thought to herself how promising to see two vastly different races work together for a common good. A mutual respect seemed to be silently acknowledged by both parties. About the only prerequisite to achieving this kind of understanding is desiring a will to make it happen. It's not magic. Quite simply it means making an effort and showing respect for someone different from yourself.

The remnants of the farm's sandy driveway entrance was barely visible on the highway's shoulder. Unless expressly searching for its vague lines extending into the adjoining underbrush, you'd never know it existed. They forced the Suburban's bumper against the vegetation trying to rely on Steve's memory as guidance. After only a few minutes of feeling the wheels straining to get a hold on the soupy ground, the vehicle halted momentarily. They had entered only a matter of thirty feet in distance through the insect-laden brush. Some reconnoitering was required before proceeding into further trouble. Everyone could see two large lightning damaged trees standing guard over some rotted fence posts that barely supported two equally decayed gates. The "No Trespassing" sign fared no better in the elements. It wasn't discernible through the heavy coating of rust trying to conquer it entire surface. The old gate was recessed off the main road by at least a hundred feet camouflaging its existence from all passersby or travelers.

A four foot drop in elevation could be felt after leaving the pavement. Steve was concerned about flooding in the old driveway and wondered if it would be passable. Even with four-wheel drive, they'd have a rough go of it in this muck and mire. His father's truck would surely be lost in the marshy, flooded roadway.

Assembling in front of the gate, the group fanned out briefly to assess their situation. Prospects of riding to the site were downright non-existent following a closer examination of the partially submerged driveway. Only a small path following the highest edge of the original roadway remained dry. Even this thin catwalk didn't show signs of offering a very solid footing. Recalling an earlier excursion here during the daytime, Steve remembered the road ran approximately three quarters of a mile in length. And judging by the first couple hundred feet, its present condition was highly suspect.

Al studied the ground revealed by the headlights. "Can the truck make it in, Steverino?"

"I really doubt it. The wheels are sinking in right here."

"Yeah. Forget about it. It doesn't look too good, pal."

Spaceman walked over while studying the flooded conditions. "Are we going wadding, man?"

"It sure looks that way," said Steve.

"Did you bring your rubbers, Skippy?" taunted Al.

Spaceman ignored his comment as Carol approached Steve.

She asked, "So we're not driving in?"

"No. We'll never make it. I think you and Kim should stay here inside the truck."

"I'm going with you, Steve," Carol said firmly. "This involves us all."

Kim chimed in, "You're not leaving me here," and she clicked on her flashlight.

"It really might be safer for you here, honey," Bobby warned.

"No way. I'm going too."

Steve adjourned the debate and said, "Alright, now that that's settled, everybody stay close together behind Red."

Bobby retrieved two lanterns from the Suburban and lit them. The light given off would enable them to see where they stepped.

"Red, you ready, little buddy?" asked Space.

"Correct. Ready."

He studied the black box he carried and pointed down the dark, overgrown path. The short Martian handed over the thin targeting disc, which would be placed near the hostile saucer, to Spaceman for transport.

"Guard this well until we reach the target, please."

"No problemo, baby," replied Spaceman who gladly accepted the responsibility.

Red informed the group to keep all noise levels to a minimum because his instruments indicated the Greys were very near. He felt the ship would be underground, possibly just below the surface. The Greys never remained on the surface for any length of time. The exposure risked discovery and that went against all visiting alien directives of "out of sight, out of mind." For the more sinister aliens, it means an enemy can't stop you if he can't find you. The benevolent groups remain concealed to prevent interfering with our society and evolutionary progress.

Red's free hand pulled the gold-colored wand from his belt. Its multi-functional capabilities allowed him to scan the darkness for any small perimeter sensors left by the enemy.

"They are definitely present up ahead."

"Do they know we're here?" asked Steve.

"Not yet."

Red became the point man, out in front with his wand device guiding the whole caravan. Steve and Carol fell in behind him with the first lantern. The rest rounded out the formation hailing the second Coleman lantern. They moved gingerly along the narrow strip of soggy road that still protruded above its wet swampy surroundings. Looking like a work crew from a southern chain gang of old, the party's lanterns eerily glided among the hanging subtropical fauna. Strange noises echoed out of the blackness they traversed. The travelers hoped these unidentifiable sounds originated with the local animal population and not a more foreign source.

Kim struggled to keep up with Bobby. "I think I saw a pair of eyes out there."

"It's probably just a raccoon," reasoned Bobby as he slapped a mosquito. No sooner had Bobby uttered those words when a deep, low grunting sound penetrated the swamp. The grunting was loud and closeby.

"Sounds like an f-ing big raccoon," said Al.

"That's no raccoon," exclaimed Kim. "What is that?"

"It's a large gator," said Steve.

Al immediately spun around nervously and placed one hand firmly atop his pistol.

"Ut, oh," said Steve.

"What? What's wrong?" asked Bobby.

Steve shone his extra flashlight ahead on their intended route beyond the lantern's range. It exposed the road's total submergence in a low spot. There was no road. Fifty yards ahead the road climbed up out of the murky black water again.

"Shit," mumbled Steve.

"It's probably not very deep," suggested Carol.

"Correct," said Red as he pointed his device at the water. "Thirty inches in depth. I will cross first."

"You better let me go first, Red," offered Steve.

"I appreciate your concern, my friend, although it is unwarranted. My suit and power stick will greatly enhance my defense capabilities while investigating the hazardous life forms in the water ahead."

"After you," conceded Steve who interpreted hazardous life forms to mean the large gators they heard grunting minutes earlier.

Red held his power stick above his head. A purple glow encircled the alien's entire body. He turned and hand-signaled the others not to follow. Then Red, silver suit and all, marched forward sinking chest deep in the muck. The unearthly glow surrounded him like a second skin. It was visible underwater as well. Presumably the purple glow that completely encased Red was the result of some type of field—a force field molded about his body. Electromagnetic particles, being gyroscopic in nature, had been programmed to conform or spin within certain boundaries. The aliens are able to direct atomic and subatomic particles in a coherent pattern of movement. Possibilities for this technology are limitless.

The water covered Red's waist, a level just slightly over a human's knee cap in depth. He slowly plowed forward creating a small rippling wake. His efforts were illuminated by the nervous bystanders' flashlights on the bank. The little guy moved further out, courageously determined to achieve his goal of locating the hidden saucer.

"Large hostile life forms?" Bobby asked Steve. "Does he mean gators out there?"

"I don't know, but let me have your gun."

"Be careful, Red," Carol shouted at the shrinking form.

A large log floated to one side of their alien ally and suddenly sprang to life. The huge jaws and rows of teeth flashing in the light were unmistakable. Lunging straight for its intended victim, the attacking reptile kicked up a huge plume of white water. Red did not even flinch, standing absolutely motionless before the erupting chaos.

The twelve foot gator attempted to clamp down on its intended prey's lower torso. Meanwhile, Steve had the gun out, ready to fire and was just about to squeeze the trigger when a flash of sparks shot out, exploding near the alligator's mouth. Violet-colored sparks blew out in every direction. Red's attacker bounced backward like a rag doll. The stunned reptile sat still momentarily while trying to figure out what he'd just latched onto. No prey in his domain ever fought like that. Red remained totally stationary while the attacker whipped his long, scaly tail thus propelling himself to a hasty retreat below the surface.

Red glanced over his shoulder at the astounded onlookers. He managed a slight smile from his tiny mouth.

"Wow, that's awesome!" said Bobby.

"I saw it, but I still don't believe it," added Kim.

"You alright?" yelled Steve in a muffled voice.

He waved in acknowledgment and then signaled for the others to proceed.

"It's now or never," Carol exclaimed to Steve.

"Let's do it," he replied. "Stay close and watch you don't lose your shoes in the mud."

"Yuck," complained Carol while sinking into the soft bottom.

"Oh God," Kim mumbled as she watched the murky water climb over her knees.

"Keep moving. Don't stop," advised Bobby.

Red stood on the opposite bank, observing his companions' crossing. Al brought up the rear and swung the last lantern around to detect any movements. He'd freed his pistol from its holster and was waving it at an invisible foe.

The procession neared the dry ground when three deafening shots rang out, sending shivers through the group's jittery nerves. Al clasped the smoking gun, a result of three pot shots he'd taken at what he believed to be a pair of eyes in the distant water.

"What the hell are you doing?" asked Steve.

"I saw a set of gator eyes coming at me."

"That noise will blow our cover, baby," warned Spaceman.

"If I get eaten, I won't need any cover, baby," returned Al.

Steve said, "He's right, Al. We don't need to announce our arrival."

"Quite correct," added Red whose purple glow had disappeared.

"Sorry, Steverino. It's just that those SOBs were getting too close for comfort."

"Forget it. Let's stay together and keep moving. It's not much further. The old farm sits on high ground; at least we'll be dry."

Water-logged below the waist and mosquito bitten above, the struggling band marched on. Large trees suddenly appeared which lined the narrow roadway's approach to the long since abandoned entrance. Like many old southern farms, the trees heralded the nearing of the main house. The groups' destination was within reach now. No signs of life, extraterrestrial or otherwise, were evident as they entered an open area in which large, dark, square objects stood guard silently. Straight ahead, the outline of the old two-level farm house came into view. Its deserted geometric shape stood at odds with the natural jungle-like surroundings. Four or five big wooden sheds bordered the driveway that led to the house. These overgrown dilapidated sheds were once the site of the farm's gator harvesting. Presently, a harvest of weeds alone occupied the premises.

The spooked procession of investigators cautiously tip-toed further inside this miniature ghost town. They were alert for the tiniest of movements. Underbrush blocked their view of the many alley ways and buildings. The vegetation had completely swallowed up a couple of sheds leaving only their tin roofs exposed.

Steve turned and told all to be quiet. This place gave off a dark and sinister atmosphere. It was an excellent backdrop for filming a movie like "Night of the Living Dead." The only thing missing was a cemetery and some creepy ghouls running loose.

All three lanterns were extinguished and only a couple of small flashlights used. Red's silver metallic space suit gave off an unnatural illumination in the moonlight. Everyone followed this highly reflective beacon towards the house. His hand stretched out in front, using the power stick's sensors like a blood hound to reach the exact subterranean position where the Greys rested.

Red moved confidently, his precise mechanical movements leaving little doubt in the others' minds that he would successfully locate their lair. Closer and closer they drew to the old 19th century clapboard farm house. Evidently, this ramshackled structure hid more than spiders and snakes.

Spaceman began receiving bursts of memory recall from his past. Something here triggered memories of past events involving information pertaining to Greys he'd been privy to while working with Naval Intelligence for MJ12. It was an assignment at a remote farm site in the 1960s. The job as a Blue Team member was to recover a crashed saucer, a big one. His team had found two cows aboard the craft. No, the aliens didn't need milk for their coffee. Something far more sinister.

In the laboratory section of the three hundred foot long ship, they discovered human-like fetuses were being placed inside one of the cows five stomachs. An attempt was being made to adopt the cows as surrogate incubators for the growing fetuses. It was determined later that these hybrid fetuses were removed early from human females that were previously inseminated during abductions. These actions violated the secret treaty President Eisenhower signed allowing them to do medical exams on some humans only. Much deception and lying was involved in a very complicated story.

It was those types of incidents which started Spaceman questioning himself years ago as to just what was transpiring on planet Earth.

Space blinked his eyes at remembering the traumatic events. It all fit—Red's recent revelations of the Greys' treachery and hybrid Phase III humanoid introduction to Earth. The timeline puzzle was coming together. Spaceman's disjointed memory made a definite connection concerning the true alien agenda behind the Greys. He realized the magnitude of allowing these beings to go unchecked with their indifference to the human condition. Our military couldn't help, being unable to properly assess the Greys' actual true intentions. Their deceptive facade had our defense systems shooting down potential friendlies and embracing the actual threat, the Greys, as an ally. Everything rested with Red and his small entourage of volunteers.

"Hey, wake up, Skippy," whispered Al. "Have that disc ready when Red needs it."

"Uh…, what? I, like, got it, man," replied a startled Space, escaping from his thoughts.

Red entered the front door forcing a loud squeak out of its rusty hinges. He advised the others to remain outside. The wind blew hard which caused some loose boards to rattle. A storm was approaching from the east. Swaying tree branches whipped back and forth in the wind creating more urgency to their task. The breeze swept through the decaying farm buildings manifesting an unholy atmosphere only a vampire could relish. There was a hidden malignancy here that had to be found.

They stood together on the front porch side-stepping the many loose planks in its floor. Kim whispered to Bobby, "Let's get out of here. I'm really scared."

"We will in a minute. Once Red finishes."

Spaceman's presence went unnoticed. He'd wandered along the side of the house with his lone flashlight. As he approached the building's rear, he noticed a cluster of plants growing against the foundation which caught his attention. Cannabis. Beautiful specimens were thriving all along the backyard. Space bent down, tore off a few choice stems, and tucked them in his jacket.

Steve held Carol tightly to shield her from the wind's gusts. She said, "I sure wouldn't want to meet up with these Greys out here!"

"Me either," he replied. "I should check on Red inside."

The broken front door creaked slightly open, exposing Red's oddly-shaped head. He signaled to come in. Anxious to escape the brisk wind chilling their water-logged pants, they all filed in quietly. Steve's flashlight exposed the cavernous living room they stood in. The weathered interior was furnitureless and creepier than the outside. Everyone surrounded Red who knelt down near the floor boards and pointed to his flashing device.

"They lie directly below us," he said.

"You mean under the house?" asked Bobby.

"And another fifty feet below the surface, yes. Quickly, where is the targeting disc?"

Steve looked around with his flashlight and asked, "Where's Space?"

"That nut's outside," replied Al.

"What's that noise?" asked Carol.

A violent tremor shook the entire foundation of the house. Blue light filled the room from wall to wall. Red rose to his feet. He had a fearful expression showing. The gold power stick he held unexplainably flew free from his grasp. It hit against the old plaster wall on the opposite side of the room. Before Red could retrieve it, a small ghost-like arm came through the wall's surface scooping the wand up and then disappearing again. The startled group jumped back in terror. Directly before them appeared to be a movie projector screen with four figures on it. But it was the wall and the moving figures that stepped out into our dimension. All four stood motionless in the blue light.

They were definitely Greys. Each carried a small black box which enabled the space between their bodies' atomic structure to pass through the wall's atomic structure in a temporary harmless meshing. No emotions were visible; however, it was easy to see they weren't pleased by the trespassers' unannounced arrival. Red was hit immediately by some kind of immobilizing blast.

Outside the house, Spaceman saw the flashes of blue light. Pulling himself carefully up to a window ledge, he witnessed the Greys neutralizing everyone in a brilliant flash of light. He immediately knew the score and dropped down slithering back to the sheltering bushy undergrowth. Lying perfectly still, he waited to be discovered.

No one came, and ten minutes passed. Space emerged from his fear-induced catatonic state ready to venture to the window again. The night had regained its tranquil silence, encouraging him to steal another glimpse. He peeked into a dark room, very dark. Risking detection, Space flicked on the small flashlight he had. No one was left in the empty chamber. His comrades were gone, abducted right before his eyes.

The situation was rapidly worsening. Space knew he had to leave before he was taken captive also, leaving no one to go for help. There was no telling how long his friends would be kept alive by their subterranean captors. The sinister spacecraft was well concealed and rested in its shallow grave beneath the old abandoned house. This bad seed arriving from the coldness of space was buried and needed to take root. Its long term plans to claim Earth's bounty for its own hybrid offspring were peaking. But before this could come to pass, the dominant species on Earth needed to be forced into involuntary extinction. Or perhaps the more accurate word would be extermination. This ship was a crucial mechanism in that evil end.

Realizing what lie in the balance, Space crouched low making his stealthy retreat from this devilish lair all alone. The Greys' dark purpose had finally crystallized for him. There was no going back now. Desperate times call for desperate measures. This meant the military had to be told. The risks for approaching them were totally warranted. Hopefully they'd believe his story. They had to.

Space had remained in the dark so as not to be detected, but as he groped blindly down the muddy driveway he decided to take a chance and shed some light on his situation. He clicked on the flashlight allowing for some orientation through the gator-infested swamp land.

Staying on the narrow spit of road, Space ran until arriving at the dead end. He found wading across the submerged section of roadway mandatory, being his only route to safety. He sucked in a deep breath for the inevitable sprint through the shallows. A brief scan of the muddy waters turned up no sign of any predatory eyeballs—at least not on the surface.

With nothing staring back at him, mankind's sole guardian lunged forward toward the opposite bank. The blackish liquid bogged him down in the sludge. His running became short, slow steps. Swamps are the last place to be at night if you can help it. You're vulnerable to attack from any number of dangerous creatures in ambush. A loud splash rang out, followed by a second. Whatever had entered the water was big. The gators they'd tangled with previously were probably still patrolling for dinner.

Having no shot at stopping an attack from one of these creatures, Space utilized his only option: run like hell. The noise he'd heard put some giddy yup in his step. A small beam of light emanating from his flashlight found the opposite shore. Underwater, the mud had relieved Space of his sandals, but he wasn't about to stop now.

Finally the murky soup gave way allowing the ground to rise up. Barefoot now, he hurriedly tight-roped along the narrow path- way out. It was difficult to stay on the road equipped only with a small flashlight. In spite of the conditions, he pushed on and ran at a good clip. Up ahead was a long, thick branch across the road. The middle-aged beach comber sprinted at a fever pitch and hurdled the debris. During his midair leap, he noticed the large stick moved with him. Halting momentarily upon landing, Spaceman turned to see the huge rattlesnake he'd barely cleared. The serpent proved more startled by their unplanned meeting than his human counterpart.

Another five minutes of jogging on the damp trail finally led to the rotted wooden gates. Just beyond them sat Steve's locked Suburban. The keys were with Steve, and Space wasn't totally sure he had time to break in and try to hot wire it. Had the Greys seen him? Were they coming after him? He knew putting distance between himself and them was a priority. No doubt existed as to their subtle deceptiveness and abilities. Past experiences working with the military had made it perfectly clear these creatures should never be underestimated.

Soaking wet and shoeless, Spaceman headed straight on to the paved two lane highway. He resembled a shipwreck survivor. Scratched and bleeding from the many Spanish swords growing along the tight trail, he created quite a sight. With no other options, Spaceman began walking along the road. As he reached inside his ripped jacket to secure Red's targeting disc, his hand felt something else. He had totally forgotten about the power stick he pilfered off Red's deceased partner in the barn.

Spaceman strained his memory concerning this exotic piece of alien hardware's various functions. These devices had been read about by his assessment team while working for the Office of Naval Research in the old days at S4 in Nevada. At that particular point in time, the wand was only slightly understood. Lawrence Livermore and Los Alamos National Laboratories had been back engineering the device's operating principles. As with all recovered alien technologies that are filtered carefully into our growing high tech civilization, security is intense and on a "need-to-know" basis. Some directors of these programs don't even know where their own projects originated. But the Pentagon and Defense Department do. Aliens.

Spaceman tucked the small wand back inside his ripped pocket totally prepared to experiment with its potential if the need arose. Right now he knew procuring the military's assistance was the only avenue left in saving his friends and everyone else.

(Saucer in the Swamp)

Steve felt a tingling race down his spine as shadowy figures glided silently around him. This foggy dream persisted for a surreal fifteen minutes. During that time, small individuals were sensed congregating in close proximity to his position. Awakening, he found his friends all perched on a large, bench-style seat and taken over by a trance-like state. They gave him no signs of recognition. All sat with their eyes opened and stared into space.

The room holding everyone contained no windows although what appeared to be an oval-shaped doorway was present in their small holding tank. Arching in a curve, the six-foot ceiling dropped in height to four feet away from the doorway. Steve noticed the similarity to certain rooms on a submarine with its curved hull. This indicated to him their cell was aboard the subterranean saucer they came to destroy.

Bobby sat nearest to Steve. He reached over, slapped his brother, and yelled to him to wake up. The efforts met with absolutely no success. Bobby was still breathing like the others but would not be revived to consciousness. Steve tried to remain calm amidst the zombie-like mannequins that sat around him. He thought he saw something move in the stillness. It was Carol. Her head twitched slightly. Then a minute later, her eyes flickered open. Steve bent down in front of Carol, shaking and shouting her name. She awoke and became immediately frightened by the odd surroundings. Carol was calmed by the sight of Steve's face.

"Are you all right?" Steve asked tenderly.

Carol hugged him tightly. "Yes, I think so. How are the others?"

"They seem to be in a drugged state or something."

"Any sign of those little gray creatures?"

"Not since I blacked out. We must be in their saucer underground."

"Steve, are they going to kill us?"

"I don't know. It doesn't look too good. Hey, where's Red?"

"He's not here!" exclaimed Carol.

"I didn't even realize he was gone. The Greys neutralized him first in the house. I'll wager he's not exactly getting a warm welcome."

"You'd win that bet," a strange voice said inside Steve's head.

Surprised by the sudden comment, Steve asked Carol, "Did you hear that?"

"No what?"

"I'm receiving telepathy in my head again, but it's not Red talking."

"You're quite perceptive for a human," the voice announced.

"Who are you and what have you done to our friends," shouted Steve at the empty purple-tinted metallic walls.

"They're only in a temporary sleep state from wave hypnosis."

"Show yourself," Steve demanded. Carol, who didn't hear anything, just watched Steve's rantings.

The movie projector effect commenced once again on the front door. A small figure holding a black box in one hand peeled off the wall like a cartoon character. Two subordinates, also carrying black boxes, stood to each side of the first creature. The guards carried gold wands in their other hands which resembled Red's power stick. All three of these cartoon characters' faces left no one laughing. They didn't possess the human qualities that Red did. You noticed the four-fingered insect hands immediately. Their noses consisted of two flattened slits. Greys were smaller and more fragile in stature than Red. Bug-like eyes gave an inhuman appearance and you never knew if eye contact was being made or not.

The leader's big, black almond eyes stared at Carol and Steve void of emotion. Speaking from his tiny mouth, the alien came directly to the point. "So you came here with your Martian neighbor to destroy us."

Both Steve and Carol were dumbfounded, and they listened quietly in disbelief. After a moment, Steve spoke out, "No, not to destroy you. Only to stop you from destroying our civilization."

There was silence as they seemed unable to refute Steve's point. They also had no intention of discussing it. "You are to be congratulated. You've figured out what your powerful military in Washington could not."

"And that is?" asked Steve exhibiting some resistance.

"Why, that they are being deceived, of course. That humans are not our allies, but our pawns in a much older and larger game of manipulated evolution."

"But why?" questioned Carol.

"Why? To add a stronger genetic diversity to our genetically engineered bodies. This healthier DNA infusion can only be achieved by evolving naturally. Our bodies have been genetically altered for thousands of years to enhance and prolong life. We have no disease, no pain, and these bodies last for seven hundred Earth years."

"So what's your problem? Why do you need us?" pushed Steve.

"Our people have very little pain or sickness, but conversely there is little happiness or joy as less evolved species such as humans experience. We also desire a wide range of emotion which is important to our future survival. A zest for life itself is lacking. Hence, human qualities developed since we brought your species from the bipedal apes wandering your planet a million years ago to the present Cro Magnon will be utilized in our quest. Many corrections have been made to your kind over the years. Eventually, Greys will be cross-engineered human hybrids. Phase III is ready to be introduced to Earth, which means Phase II must be terminated. Just as we replaced your Neanderthals with Phase II Cro Magnon forty thousand years ago."

"And what? We're Phase II?" Steve yelled.

"Unfortunately, yes. You two are the only privileged humans to receive this information."

"You're too kind," Steve answered sarcastically.

"Regrettably you'll not be alive long enough to repeat it."

"You have no right," screamed Carol. "There are billions of people living on Earth. We're not your property."

"We do have the right because of our hand in your creation."

"That crock of bullshit has to be against universal laws," shouted Steve. "There are many other outsiders that will stop your violations to humanity."

"Yes, that is a possibility. Others do not agree with our methods. But it won't be you or your friend from our colony on Mars who deter us."

The leader paused. He seemed to be communicating through telepathy. In response, the oval door behind them swished open and two Greys dumped Red's unconscious body on the floor. They departed while the leader pointed at their friend exhibiting a coldness to his stare. He spoke through his mouth for their benefits.

"Mistakes were made on his planet a half million years ago. Presently the remnants of his race remain subservient to us having to live beneath the surface in small colonies."

Carol said, "More like slaves."

"Objectives must be met. Survival for the Martians totally relies on our support. We have genetically altered them somewhat over the years also. However, our ongoing project here on Earth will be totally successful due to the planet's much more resilient environment."

Carol became visibly upset. The revelations started taking a toll on her psyche. Precisely one reason the government keeps people in the dark. Tearing up, she said, "Don't you have any respect for life? Why can't you coexist instead of destroying? Didn't you ever question this age-old mission as being flawed?"

"Flawed? It is not flawed."

"It's wrong!"

Silence returned to the room.

The alien hesitated slightly and said, "It must be carried out. No one may question the mission. The purpose is clear. A small asteroid has already been diverted toward Earth's orbit. This ship will control the final approach to impact. Your Judgment Day has arrived and our ongoing experiment allows for only one verdict to fall on your species."

"Damn your genetic crap! We'll stop you. Never underestimate the human spirit," Steve proclaimed while inching closer to the nearest guard. Lunging out and throwing the guard up against the wall, Steve knocked the wand from his hand. The guard still held the black box and blended into the walls' surface and disappeared. Steve's head slammed into the metal barrier while his arms grabbed at thin air. He learned the hard way that without a black box to control spacing between subatomic particles of matter, it can really hurt.

Carol shouted, "Steve, look out!" but the warning came too late. The leader side-stepped clear as the second guard let out a short stun blast from his power stick's bulbous tip. Steve was thrown into the air and came down upside down on the floor. His stunned expression transformed into unconsciousness.

"That was foolish," commented the leader. "It never ceases to amaze me— the amount of arrogance and aggression in the human animal."

Carol came rushing over and cradled Steve's head. "You're the animals with your cruelty and indifference."

"I thought you might understand our purpose, but I see that much more evolutionary time must elapse to achieve the desired DNA results. I bid farewell to your extinct species."

Carol looked at him with defiance burning in her soul. She flipped him a final silent gesture with her hand. Her last glance caught a short smile crossing the alien's confident face, and a second later the two Greys teleported into the wall.

Carol began sobbing, her crying going unnoticed by her sleeping comrades. Alone in the cold metallic room, she wondered if what just happened was all a bad dream. As much as she wished it to be a nightmare, the information she received from her father's brief case years ago told her the complete opposite.

CHAPTER NINE

Spaceman trudged down the lonely road, not a single vehicle in sight. His immediate destination was to be Patrick Air Force Base located out on the beach. Even if they didn't believe or trust him initially, the UFO officer designate stationed at the base would definitely dispatch a discreet search team to the area to investigate. After mentioning a few key code words, Spaceman would procure the officer's attention in a hurry. Black helicopters would soon swarm over the site unleashing Blue Team commandos to investigate. Uncovering a Grey's ship was one thing; convincing the military brass that the Greys were not friendlies would be a slightly tougher task. The proof lie under the old farm house in the form of his captured friends, in particular, Red. It was important though that the utmost of expediency was exercised to insure that this living proof remained that way, living.

Two lights appeared on the flat,dark horizon. Space tried in vain to spruce up his motley appearance. He wet the ends of his scraggly hair and tucked in the ripped shirt and jacket. The approaching vehicle's headlights caught sight of him. They slowed down so as not to run over the vagabond hitch hiker. A weathered pickup truck emerged from behind the lights. It pulled a small boat on a trailer in the rear. The passenger window was open and revealed two crude characters dressed in worn fishing gear. They appeared to be intoxicated.

"Where you headin' to, Bud?"

"Out on the beach, man," replied Space. He began to worry they would leave without him. "My truck blew a tire, and I don't have a spare. I just need a ride over the bridge."

"That's where we're headin' if you don't mind ridin' in the back."

"Nope."

"Jump in, partner."

"Thanks, man."

Spaceman leaped over the sides of the truck landing amidst a lot of rusty junk and old fishing gear. Muffled snickering could be heard coming from the cab. Spaceman was simply happy to get moving, even if it was in the company of these "good ole boys." A heavy odor of liquor drifted past his nose verifying the condition of the driver. Spaceman contemplated the ride might get somewhat bumpy.

The truck began traveling noticeably faster than the posted speed limit. These guys were obviously drunk and wanted to give their passenger a little thrill ride. Space laid down as close to the bed floor as possible. He began to bounce up and down while catapulting into the pickup's side walls. Gravity slammed his back down a couple of times, almost rebounding him over the side and onto the roadway. He held on for dear life. The small boat in tow didn't fare much better on sharp turns. Above the engine's winding hum, raucous laughter could be heard. Every so often, they'd glance back through the window at their guest's situation, enabling them to feed their twisted sense-of-humor.

The dirty old pickup truck raced across the bridge spanning the Indian River. They finally reached the stop light on Highway A1A. Although still glad for the ride, Space now possessed a number of bumps and bruises to add to his growing collection. The drunken fishermen turned off the road and came to rest in a grassy lot. Pulling himself from the corrugated truck bed, he heard the driver yell, "End of the line, partner. You can't get a ride like that in a taxi," and the two burst into laughter.

Crawling to the rear, Spaceman threw his battered body over the tailgate. There was just enough visibility from the truck's tail lights to see the retaining pin which held the trailer hitch together. Quickly he pulled at it until it snapped free in his hand. The hitch sat loosely on the ball connected insecurely to the truck.

"Hey get clear, buddy, or I'm gonna run you down."

Spaceman rolled out clear onto the grassy field.

"Not even a thank you. Some people," cracked the passenger as they both rolled in hilarity. Clouds of smoke thrust in the air upon their hasty exit. The vehicle raced away as if it were on a quarter mile drag strip spewing dust and smoke on him.

Spaceman struggled to his feet but was unable to straighten up after the punishment he'd just absorbed. He watched the boat and trailer tilt oddly and then disappear into the darkness at high speed. Tossing the retaining pin into the weeds, a slight smile temporarily interrupted his quiet desperation.

The urgency of his mission along with its tremendous all-encompassing importance jerked Space back into focus. Another half-mile up the road rested all his worldly goods in a makeshift beach camp he called home.

One item from the camp was needed. His bicycle. The rusty old two wheeler, which he had rescued from a local dumpster, would carry him the final three miles to the Air Force base. Spaceman had become quite a colorful character cycling that beauty around Satellite Beach. Steve installed a basket in the front and one on the rear for his convenience in transporting necessities. Yes sir, why would the sentries at the Air Force base question his word, pulling up to the gate in such a suave manner? But that was precisely the reason he remained alive after a premature departure from the intelligence community's black world. They saw no threat. Of course at one time his father's high connections had helped, too.

Spaceman pedaled until his legs felt like they were on fire. He rode along the shoulder of A1A with the Atlantic Ocean on his right. The torrent of white water in the surf was a precursor of the approaching storm. Wind gusts swept briskly across the highway impeding Spaceman's progress. Concentrating on his pedaling, he became unaware of the slow moving dark sedan lingering safely behind him. It had evaded his detection since retrieving the bicycle a short time ago. Two old friends had been awaiting his return to the beach after almost being killed at the Wilcox farm. They now were prepared to come down on him and exact a merciless vengeance. Tailing their target at one hundred yards' distance, the two watched in anticipation of his final destination. The agents never confronted Spaceman but always lurked nearby in the shadows observing. This time would be different.

The air base and flight line came into plain view on the left side of the highway. Sitting together on an auxiliary runway behind the high security fence were the three Harrier jets Spaceman had witnessed practicing maneuvers earlier in the day. Pedaling harder against the stiff northeast wind, he suddenly had a stroke of brilliance. The doubt harbored in being able to convince the military of the truth in a timely manner; helped push ahead his decision to take matters into his own hands. After all, time was running out. A decisive plan had to be implemented in stopping the Greys...

Spaceman crossed the dangerous highway, and rode onto the grassy embankment at the foot of a large wire fence guarding Patrick Air Force Base. His thoughts turned to remembering the operating procedures for the Harrier he'd flown back in the late sixties. Spaceman quickly lit up one of his cigarettes to achieve maximum recall. He didn't need the smoke to figure out a way through the chain link fence. It would be his first priority. Putting the matches back in his coat pocket, he felt Red's power stick. The time to experiment had arrived.

While reading top secret briefings on similar instruments, it was determined these alien devices ran on thought impulses. This multi-functional device worked similarly to our biofeedback machines but with a much higher degree of control. But reading extensively about it and actually controlling its operation were two very different things. Spaceman gripped the short shaft feeling an immediate pulsing connection almost like he had another limb responding to his wishes.

As Spaceman pondered how to test its power, the black sedan stalking from behind swerved recklessly across traffic skidding to an abrupt stop barely two feet from him. Out popped the two counter-intelligence agents, and they didn't appear to be in a good mood. Each man tried to catch their breath while towering over the middle-aged beach comber.

The first guy asked, "Commander, how are you?"

Space didn't answer right away, but held the power stick nonchalantly behind his leg out of view. The joint pinched between his lips smoldered around his beard like a small brush fire.

"Commander, smoking pot is against the law," the second agent said.

"Yes, and you've been a very bad boy," added the first creep.

"Listen, dudes. You can't stop me now. Our national security is in great peril."

"We know. That's why we've got orders to take you in or terminate." Both men produced pistols sporting silencers.

"Man, you'd waste me after our long relationship?"

"Nothing personal, Commander, but either you come with us or orders are orders."

Space gazed at the ground growing madder by the second. "I'm doing your jobs, man. You dumb bastards! I've uncovered an alien threat on a scale involving much more than national security."

At that point, Spaceman squeezed the wand while concentrating on a defensive power field to surround and protect him. Almost immediately, the purple glow Red exhibited in the swamp encased his body. The two assassins tried to grab Spaceman with shocking results. They shook as if being electrocuted by a high voltage charge. Both attackers were vaulted into the air, slowing down after hitting the chain link fence and sliding to the ground.

Spaceman said to himself, "Pretty damn cool, but flying should really be left to the birds." The two limp bodies dropped, landing face down on a bristly mat of well-manicured grass.

The agents were out cold so Spaceman advanced on the ten foot high military barrier. He squeezed the stick and concentrated on walking to the other side. Where his purple glow came in contact with the fence, sparks were given off. Clinking and popping noises briefly erupted. A moment later, Spaceman found himself on the inside looking out through an exact imprint of his body field in the fence.

"Wow," he said aloud. "This is getting better by the minute."

Spaceman had his back to the fence when a couple of dull thuds shook his electromagnetic body armor. Swiveling toward the commotion, Space saw one of the agents standing and unleashing a clip of silenced rounds into his back. The crewcut clad shooter looked on in total amazement at the gun's ineffectiveness. The remedy to this problem rested in Spaceman's hand. Another squeeze on the power stick transferred his wishes to stun the agent unconscious. He directed the short burst into the target. ZAP. The counter-intelligence officer was out like a light. Just another government employee sleeping on the job.

Spaceman reveled over his new toy's simplicity of operation. It was very user-friendly. He'd read years ago these devices contained a miniature annihilation reactor inside supplying quite a potent power source. The device paralled many saucer reactors but in miniture. So there was no shortage of energy to engage the many functions it offered.

Becoming focused again, Space saw no one guarding the three Harrier II Marine Jump Jets temporarily parked together on an auxiliary runway next to the main fence. They sat quietly unattended which seemed highly unusual. Not asking any questions, he broke for the closest aircraft.

His approach was cut short abruptly by two headlights clicking on near the third jet. The sentries jeep arrived just in time to witness Spaceman climbing the ladder to the cockpit. The field's violet halo still covered his person.

"Freeze!" yelled one guard.

"Halt or we'll shoot," the second shouted shouldering his M-16.

Ignoring their commands, Spaceman used the power stick to raise the canopy. By now, he half expected to hear the thud of bullets flying. And not disappointing him, both soldiers, adhering to rigid training procedures, opened up on the strange glowing wild man. The shots weren't silenced and rang out, pinging against the field's impenetrability. Each sentry checked his weapon to assure it was functioning properly.

All hell was breaking loose. Not even bothering to look, Spaceman held the power stick over his shoulder in their general direction and thought, "Stun. Stun." A split burst forked out of the device hitting both men and freezing all movements. As the soldiers lie on the ground motionless, base security was radioing back trying frantically to get a response from the two neutralized sentries. There wouldn't be much time to achieve his escape.

Climbing inside the cockpit using the small footholds, Spaceman hoped he could remember how to work the vectoring nozzles which diverted thrust from the powerful Pegasus main engines. After all, thirty years was a long time. He drew in on his cigarette to stir up memories. Much of the cockpit's layout and avionics on this AV8B had changed from the original Harriers he'd flown though the basic controls remained constant. His flying skills might be a bit rusty but there was no going back now.

With his hair flying in the breeze, Spaceman tossed his cannabis out and pointed the power stick at the control panels. He began thinking, "Start the engines, turn on the engines." Small veins of purple-colored current surged from its tip and spreading across the entire instrument board. The engines, still warm from the earlier training flights, kicked on with a high-pitched whine. Red's wand had bypassed all the security locking codes like a thief would hot wire a car. Space let out a loud, "Yes." Pausing a minute, he studied the clusters of instruments and controls. The canopy was lowered and sealed out the stiff cross winds. Vertical landing craft can be very dangerous when hovering in heavy winds, especially if the pilot's been on a thirty year hiatus.

For Spaceman, the risk of being killed was far less certain than doing nothing and allowing the Greys to enact their well-camouflaged genocide. Death is death for humans. If only the military could be made aware of these creatures' plans. But that wasn't the case.   He knew he must leave immediately or be apprehended. Base security was most assuredly responding as he sat there.

His left hand held the vectoring nozzle control which directed the jets producing vertical lift. Spaceman added thrust and the fighter bomber lifted straight up, slightly tilted to one side. Grabbing the wrong knob caused the plane to drop a good three feet to the concrete. The craft bounced violently on its extra springy landing gear.

"Shit," he mumbled. "O.K. Now I remember, man." A loud increase in thrust shot out and the jump jet rose up to a height of twenty feet. The wind buffeted the hovering craft violently as Space guided the bucking ship over the main fence. The approaching rain storm contained above average wind gusts which began lashing the beach front.

Highway A1A seemed relatively quiet this night. Not many vehicles witnessed the strange events taking place in front of the air base. After clearing the tall fence, Spaceman set the jet down in the south-bound lane of the highway to the surprise of an astonished truck driver coming the other way. The driver's face was white as Space waved a peace sign at his fellow traveler. Even though the Harrier has narrow wings, they came dangerously close to the big truck passing by in the fourth lane. A small car behind him swerved off the road not quite believing what he was about to encounter. Barely touching the roadway, Spaceman roared along its surface like an oversized hot rod. His intentions were to stay low off the base's radar screens for as long as possible. He noticed he was rapidly approaching a signal light spanning the highway and that meant wires. The time for challenging the wind in flight was just ahead.

Nearing the signal light he observed a blue flashing strobe light on the side of the road. It was the beach police at the scene of a car accident. He quickly prepared for a vertical lift off. Spaceman's Harrier rolled up to the light behind a couple of waiting cars. On the right hand side, the accident became visible. A small boat trailer had broken loose and hit a cinder block wall. The vehicle was transformed into a twisted pile of rubble. Two familiar figures stood next to a rusted pick up truck talking to the officers. They spotted Spaceman and pointed wildly at him and screamed.

The canopy was cracked half open, so Spaceman yelled over the slow idling engines at the furious redneck fisherman pointing his way. "Hey baby, you can't get a ride like this in a taxi, either." The befuddled cops didn't know whether to restrain the two pissed off fisherman or try to stop the jet. By that time, the noise from the blaring Pegasus engines was getting everyone's attention. Not hesitating, the jump jet jumped. The plane rose up with a mighty blast streaming out of the vectoring nozzles. This added more air flow velocity to the already unstable gusts of wind circling the pedestrians on the ground.

Spaceman taunted the fishermen one last time with a thumbs up through the bubble canopy. He slowly realized that his newer version of the Harrier had considerably more ease of operation built into its controls than the original models. It was like riding a bicycle; you never forget. Rising up and clearing light poles and phone lines, the veteran pilot caught the wind at his back and roared off toward the river and mainland.

(Swamp)

In the dimly lit recesses of the curved metallic room, Carol shook Steve's head resting on her lap in an effort to revive him.

"Steve, please wake up," she pleaded. Her desperate request finally brought results. Steve's neck twitched revealing a signal of hope. Lifting his head from Carol's grasp, he shook off the cobwebs and leapt to his feet and searched for an invisible foe.

"They've gone," said Carol. "Are you all right?"

"I think…,"

"Steve, we've got to get out of here and warn the military."

"Military?" he replied. "Even if we could escape, there's no time to go through channels trying to convince them of the truth."

"But there is a way."

"What do you mean?"

"Remember when we were on the beach the other night, and I didn't want to speak about my past incident with UFOs?"

"Yeah…"

"I accidentally discovered my father's briefcase contained alien-related documents and pictures of crash sites."

"That's impossible. No one carries that kind of material around unless they're a major player in the Pentagon."

Carol's eyes widened when he mentioned the Pentagon.

Steve's bewildered expression turned to one of intense curiosity. "Just who is your father, Carol?"

"Preston Cole."

"Preston Cole? Preston Cole, the Chairman of the Joint Chiefs in Washington?"

"Yes."

"Holy shit! That's pretty major. Why didn't you tell me this earlier?"

"Well, I wanted to, but for my personal safety, I was asked not to ever speak of it."

"That makes sense."

"If I could make one phone call, we'd have a fighting chance of explaining the Greys' real intentions."

"I can't believe it. Are you able to contact him?"

"If I could get to a phone. There is a private code number which will connect me to him by a direct link up at the Pentagon. He told me only to use it if I found myself in an emergency situation."

126

"This definitely qualifies. I kind of doubt there are any pay phones in the hall outside, though."

"We've just got to find a way to escape."

"There's only one person who knows if that's possible," said Steve pointing at their unconscious Martian ally lying on the floor.

They crawled over to where Red was thrown like a sack of potatoes. Having lived with the Greys for years, Red was everyone's only hope for escape. His unique knowledge of their captors' operations and security procedures could shed some light on a way out. The Greys appeared to have roughed up Red pretty well judging by the abrasions over his head and face. They dealt out extra punishment for any subjugated groups trying to revolt against their dominant authority. Red also was attempting to expose and foil their unsavory plans on Earth by working with the united alignment.

As Red lay there face down, it became apparent how identical his torso and limbs were to humans. If you ignored his head's proportion, it was uncanny the human resemblance. He was quite different when compared with the insect inspired physique sported by the Greys.

These small Grey creatures put new meaning in the saying, "The meek shall inherit the Earth." Although they are meek physically, their mental capabilities are those of titans. A millennium of genetic engineering to maximize brain power rendered them superior. Not being born as humans are, but having bodies grown in labs genetically, their souls are merged with the new bodies in a process which is most unnatural in nature. The ingenious process of transferring the soul energy to a pre-made physical body, offers much longer life but has taken a tremendous toll on feelings, emotion, and the soul's very health itself. A mother and fathers nurturing care has been substituted for a cold fluid filled container or test tube.Not being a natural process, the individuals of their society are simply unhappy.

In searching the cosmos for desired physical qualities to incorporate into their people, they crush and destroy others, carrying on genetic experimentation and playing God. These conquerors of the universe do not march in with traditional weapons of war causing destruction. It is a much subtler undermining of cultures from within. Why make war when controlling a few key figures through more advanced technology (implants) can save vast qualities of limited resources and still achieve the same objectives. Their methods of deception, mind control and superior intelligence work well over less evolved peoples. The victim doesn't even realize he's been victimized, until it's too late. The Greys' victims are like a herd of sheep out in a beautiful pasture grazing without a care in the world. But unbeknownst to the sheep's consciousness, they are there to serve someone else's dark purposes.

Such was the fate of the Martian peoples many years ago. Infiltrated, subjugated, and almost completely terminated. If only it weren't too late for humanity. Powerful allies who recruited Red stand ready to oppose the Greys. Irresponsible interference in evolving planets does not go unnoticed or unopposed. Very powerful forces balance the powers of the universe as they do on Earth. An equivalent example would be the Spanish Conquest of the New World. They enslaved the native populations to serve their interests which were gold and silver mining. The first groups to arrive took the best assets available.

For the Spanish, the assets were precious metals. For the far more sophisticated aliens, it is the genetic assets contained in humans themselves. In both cases, the assets could be taken by the more powerful advanced group. Remote regions, whether it be in the sixteenth century jungles of Central America or the wilderness of space, might becomes right. And when no higher authority is present to monitor the situation, respect, individual rights, and universal laws will fall by the wayside. Some things never change whether on Earth or Zeta Reticuli in the Orion Belt. At least under the treaties and organizational unity, the wide variety of intelligent life in the cosmos can make an effort at living in harmony. Because without effort expended or rights observed, we cannot live together and no one is safe.

Red's eyes blinked open. Steve and Carol helped him sit up and steady himself.

"Are you all right?" asked Carol.

"I believe so."

"What did they do to you?" questioned Steve.

"They tried to retrieve my memory cells pertaining to the Alignment's involvement in this. But those cells were rendered irretrievable before I left for Earth."

"So they got nothing?"

"Correct."

"Will the others wake up?"

"They should very shortly."

"Thank God," said Carol.

"Is there any way out of here, Red?" Steve asked.

"It will take some thinking. They took my power stick. While unconscious a minute ago, I attempted telepathy to the allies waiting in deep space. Ordinarily our minds can travel great distances, except for the fact that our captors here are scrambling my signals. It works similar to your Air Force jets which jam ground radar signals. All wave energy operates on like principles."

"How far can telepathy travel?" asked Carol.

"There is really no limit. Your own people are on the verge of realizing they possess these capabilities, despite the Greys' determination to covertly keep these powers debunked and suppressed."

"I knew there was always something to that," said Carol listening intently.

"Correct. Your CIA has scratched the surface of these capabilities with their remote viewer units. Once the ability to control the various frequencies is mastered, instantaneous communication with the stars will be established for humans."

"Right now we need to figure out an escape route or we'll never reach that juncture in the future," Steve reminded them.

"Correct," agreed Red. "We must also secure the targeting disc from your friend to assure it is on or near this craft at the designated firing time."

"That's right. I forgot about Space and the disc," said Steve.

"He's probably escaped and is bringing help," Carol suggested encouragingly.

"I don't know. Let's hope he seeks out the right people if he did make it." Steve said with a murmur of doubt resonating in his voice.

"He wasn't captured. We know that," Carol insisted.

"Correct," added Red.

Carol went over to check on the others in the group while Steve whispered to Red with a deadly serious stare, "What are our real chances of getting out of here?"

"Mathematically, the same as an ice particle on the surface of Mercury."

"That good, huh?"

"Yes."

"Well, we're not giving up Red, so keep on brainstorming."

Steve was aware of the deadly position the group was now entangled in, as well as the limited time left to act. If they didn't get help soon in stopping this ship, escaping wouldn't really matter. While Spaceman's intentions were good, Steve had resigned himself to the statistically remote chances of the group's salvation appearing from his direction. A grim outlook settled throughout the dimly lit chamber.

Carol still wandered about her snoozing comrades. She continually shook Kim with no response.

"They will not awaken until the subatomic magnetic particle spin effect subsides, and clears their temporary trance state which should be shortly," said Red. "Do not worry, Carol. Remember our plight. We have the entire Alignment with us preparing to take action."

Carol tried to stay calm, "Thanks for your concern, Red. I'm kind of glad Kim's asleep because she'd be very upset at our predicament."

Steve paced back and forth trying to whip up an escape plan. "Where there's a will, there's a way," he mumbled to himself.

Red watched his restlessness. "Steve, please sit down and relax. We will deduct a logical solution to our incarceration."

"That's easy for you to say. If they kill you, you'll just drop your soul energy into another preformed body. When we're dead, we're dead! Who knows where our souls are going to end up?"

Red shut up as Steve slumped to a sitting position in frustration. Carol dropped down next to him and gave him a comforting hug. In the eerie silence, Steve glanced back at Red who stared straight ahead in deep thought.

"Hey Red, I'm sorry I blew up."

"That's O.K., my friend."

"Red, since we're not going to leave right away, maybe you could help me out on this soul thing."

Red nodded.

"What's all this stuff about time locks on souls? Is it like reincarnation? And when we die, does our soul randomly drift until we receive a time lock at conception somewhere else on the planet and start over?"

"Ah, the secret of life. You're very close to correct. For humans, yes it is random as you said before unless alien forces are interfering. For Greys and our people, at death the soul is under a controlled collection as you mentioned. Martians have been genetically altered over the years to allow it. Like the Greys, you see, other groups discovered while developing the manipulating process of time and space for intergalactic travel, that other related phenomena pertaining to the initiation of life itself became revealed. Like the unified field theory, all things in our universe are highly interconnected unless you've gone to hyper space outside the laws of our universe. From conception you are locked into a linear time lock. The matter and soul energy meet to form intelligent life. We can intentionally move our souls to a new body with the proper frequencies. Explained this way, all matter is nothing more than combinations of various frequencies. The technology utilized involves controlling a soul or energy frequencies which are then transferred to a different body or matter frequencies. Energy to matter through a rotating field. The secret of maintaining your soul and personality while infusing it into a new pre-made embryo was uncovered accidentally. A kind of immortality, if you will, can be achieved. It's not magic, just science on a vastly more advanced level. Souls are a quantity of wave energy on the extreme electromagnetic spectrum. This means they can be measured and manipulated like any other wave or frequency on the spectrum."

"It sounds a little too damn advanced for me," Steve complained as he tried to follow.

"That is the same conclusion the Greys and many other outside civilizations utilizing it have reached. Being able to transfer your soul into a new genetically altered body for continual life seems ideal. But if all your happiness, love, and emotions are sacrificed over time, what have you achieved? When you evolve beyond nature itself, no matter how perfectly planned, there will be fallout somewhere. It is not unlike your advancing medicines on Earth. They may work miracles in healing a particular illness, and yet there can be serious side effects associated.

Unfortunately, we Martian survivors were forced to use these methods of reproduction to remain alive since being colonized and subjugated hundreds of thousands of years ago. So, to an extent, we share in their gains but also suffer from the shortcomings. Happiness and emotions have been the cost. To a higher degree, it has affected the Greys more than my people.

"I'm sorry I asked," quipped Steve.

"The implications are mind-boggling and very scary," Carol said as her curiosity was reaching its saturation point.

"Correct," agreed Red. "This is why your leaders deem it necessary to conceal the truth. A very gradual release of these realities is the only way to avoid disrupting your society."

"Well, our society is about to be heavily disrupted if we don't get the hell out of here soon," announced Steve.

"Quite correct."

"You're right, Red," said Carol. "I can see why the debunkers working for the government are determined to muddy the waters. Information like that would shake every aspect of our civilization."

The three captives sat quietly while their minds raced through the complicated revelations that would turn humanity's preconceived notions upside-down.

The first to gain consciousness from the anesthetizing trance was Bobby. Soon afterwards, Kim and Al came to. Carol went to each one asking if they were all right.

"A little tired but O.K.," yawned Bobby.

"Where's the freakin' coffee?" moaned Al, momentarily unaware of his surroundings.

Kim looked a bit foggy when she suddenly realized where she was. She panicked. "Oh my God, we're prisoners!"

"Calm down. We'll be all right," Carol urged as she quickly began explaining that Red was working on an escape plan. Red turned in her direction to contradict her, but he decided against it as he recognized Carol's intentions.

"What's going on, Steve? What did we miss?" asked Bobby.

"Trust me, not a whole lot. And room service really sucks."

Captain Al inquired, "Those little Grey bastards who shot through the wall put us here?"

"Yep, and they're not exactly ambassadors of good will."

"Shit."

In another section of the saucer, the Grey commander, along with a few subordinates, monitored the captives' conversations through telepathic eavesdropping. Brain waves emitted by the group revealed no eminent danger to the Grey's plans of annihilation. The mention of Spaceman and the disc didn't concern them. His hasty departure with the dangerous targeting disc was observed. The speeding asteroid would be in control range in twenty minutes. Earth's eco-altering event would initiate Cro Magnon's patiently awaited extinction. Phase II of the Master plan would then be completed.

The Greys were becoming extremely overconfident. Even if the Alignment approached against them, they now felt it would never arrive before the dark asteroid's impact. It was evident these Greys needed more feelings incorporated into their race. There was a total absence of compassion shown for the criminal violation about to be perpetrated on humankind, only the singular gratification of accomplishing their long-standing, twisted, corrupt purpose. No regard or concern for the rights of another civilization were evident. They knowingly intervened in a developing planet's sovereignty which violated universal laws.

Al and Bobby aimlessly searched the walls for a seam or opening. Like trapped rats, everyone became restless.

"Steve, are they actually planning on smashing an asteroid into Earth as Red told us?" asked Bobby.

"That looks like the deal," came the reply.

"This just isn't happening," said Kim in disbelief.

Al suddenly jumped back from inspecting the wall. "Look out," he said.

The Greys' images reappeared on the wall's surface. As if in a magic show, the four Greys stepped into the room without using any smoke. Their weapons were drawn. The leader spoke first.

"Our plans for Phase II will be coming to fruition shortly. Regrettably, you'll not be here to record the historic event. We must depart right before impact and no passengers are allowed."

"Let us go," Steve said. "It doesn't matter now anyway."

"Sorry, but if we must abort the impact at the last minute, it would be foolish to leave witnesses behind who will alert Earth's military and the Alignment."

"You bastards!" Carol screamed. Her composure was beginning to collapse.

"There is no need for irrational flare ups. Humanity's fate was determined long ago. I believe your own end will arrive when a tragic fire traps everyone in one of those old structures on the surface."

"You'll be brought to justice for this!" Kim naively sobbed.

"In all probability, there won't be a soul left to bring us to your justice, even if they knew," the leader said with a smile spreading from tiny ear to tiny ear.

Al was unable to remain quiet. "Look, you little creeps. Drop those sticks and I'll be glad to, Badda Bing, give all four of you a good ass kickin'."

The leader's demeanor turned to what suspiciously resembled anger. He said to his guards, "I have not seen a better mutated specimen to validate our actions than this one."

132

"Hey, watch your mouth, you bug-eyed freak," retorted Al.

Tensions became elevated quickly but the four power sticks left the Greys possessing the winning hand.

Behind the little monsters, a large opening quickly materialized to the outside hallway. "Let's go," commanded the leader. He spoke dramatically from his mouth. It appeared as if he was gaining some perverse pleasure from acting out the entire scene in a manual face-to-face confrontation. In performing their duties it appeared they actually were enjoying the whole thing as if it were a recreational game. These insecure little goons fed off others' misery and fear. Playing the role of God had empowered them to the point of corruption. So not only had genetic engineering altered the Greys' physical bodies, but their very souls were twisted and warped by the unnatural evolution. And like any mad dog who endangers others, they had to be stopped.

One at a time the prisoners were led out into the circular hall. Two more guards showed up to help herd the lambs to slaughter. This craft was much larger than Red's small scout vehicle. Ever so gradually the curve bent the hallway which silently revealed the ship's huge dimensions. They passed a half-dozen doors with strange symbols embossed on their surface. Up ahead the procession was ushered into a spacious room. Its ceiling rose higher than others on the ship. Centered directly in the middle of the room was a ten-foot round glasslike tube or dome resembling a clear cake dish cover. It appeared to be suspended from the ceiling by a circle of bizarre looking coil structures. The purpose of this equipment it was later learned was to transport individuals to a desired location via teleportation.

At this spot the ring leader signaled his guards to halt through telepathic command. Everyone kept walking with the exception of Red, who's brain receptors' capabilities were similar to theirs. Pointing where he wished the others to stand beneath the transparent dome for the trip to the surface, the leader drew near for a final farewell. Again he spoke through his mouth.

"All of you must consider yourselves greatly honored to have been able to consciously witness the next step in your artificial evolution. At least you can rest assured that all Phase II humans did not perish in vain. Your contributions to the vastly improved Hybrid should make you proud."

"We're really impressed," Steve said sarcastically.

Turning toward Red, the Grey added, "And you shall be an example to the remaining Martian population as to what happens to colonized traitors."

Red remained silent. He only blinked his eyes at the leader knowing fully their capacity for cold, calculating cruelty.

Kim began weeping at the hopelessness of the predicament. Carol blurted out, "You bastards!"

The leader's patience wore thin. He raised the power stick slowly and selected Red as the object of his pent up aggression. He extended the power stick menacingly close to Red's human-like nose. The master's large insect-shaped almond eyes peered with intimidation into Red's blue colored corneas. The bulbous end of the weapon took on a white glow. Red bravely stood his ground and didn't flinch at the threatening gesture. A static charge similar to lightening reached across the six-inch gap and stung Red's face. He dropped to the floor instantly and shook in pain. Steve started down to help his friend, but he was cut off by the other wand-wielding guard.

The head Grey stepped back before anything could happen and the domed enclosure dropped swiftly around the party and its five guards. The leader's mouth exhibited its evil smirk as he looked over his encased lab rats. They were trapped, like a child traps insects in a mayonnaise jar. Seconds later an energizing force could be felt shooting through the entire enclosure. Bright light bathed the entire area. Then snap, they found themselves in the dimly lit farmhouse above in the swamp.

In a flash they'd all been teleported to the surface from their subterranean prison. Even though the guards planned on killing them, just being in the night air again gave everyone hope.

One Grey commanded, "Outside."

Bobby glanced over at his brother, trying to tell him he was going to make a move. Steve shook his head in acknowledgment.

The group marched outside heading for one of the old barns. Bobby and Steve lagged behind the group with only one guard behind them. Perhaps the stiff wind made it tough to hear or distracted the guard but a large gust enabled Steve to get the drop on him. He signaled to Bobby and dove, kicking the Grey's legs out from under him. This action caused the alien to fly head over heels to the ground. His power stick got tossed into the high grass. Bobby instantly broke for the swamp.

In the distracting weather, the other guards continued their march, oblivious to the uprising behind them. The wind provided a noisy cover for Steve who closed on the fallen Grey and hit him with a powerful upper cut on his scaly little jaw. All of Steve's hulking physique was launched at the outsider. It left the clammy alien lying on the damp ground in a lifeless heap. It appeared as if someone had cut the strings on this alien puppet.

Bobby neared the edge of the treelined water running full tilt. Steve thought his brother would make it until the other Greys swung around. The unconscious guard must have signaled them telepathically. Steve received a stun blast that dropped him on his stomach. He contorted in pain. Carol saw this and ran back to aid him. Bobby had almost made it to the tree line when Kim shouted loudly, "Run, Bobby. Run!"

This caught the guard's attention, and they hit him with a stun blast that knocked him into the shallow swampy water between two trees. One of the Greys quickly broke off running in an unearthly shuffle toward his location. The two remaining guards corralled the rest of the prisoners and tried to revive their fallen comrade.

Luckily for Bobby, he'd received only a glancing blow which allowed him to rise to his knees in the brackish water. Arriving at the water's edge, the Grey raised his weapon in his hand and told Bobby to come out. With his adrenaline pumping, Bobby limped out of the water but collapsed on the muddy bank.

"We can burn an unconscious body just as easily as a conscious one," his pursuer announced.

Bobby thought it was over. The Grey raised the power stick at his head. The small quantity of light given off by the alien's device had suddenly reflected two small orbs floating on the water behind his captor. Bobby tried to stall for time. He knew exactly what it was that approached from the murky waters. His enemy, however, stood totally unaware of the silent hunter drifting nearer.

"Wait," shouted Bobby raising his hands up.

The guard had his back to the water. He lowered the stick and asked, "What do you have to say before I kill you, human?"

"I don't even know your name. If you're going to kill me, you owe me that much," he demanded. Bobby silently scooped up a handful of wet mud.

The alien hesitated briefly as he pondered the Earthian's strange request in his cold, analytical brain. His mind became confused at the illogical nature of the demand.

A moment of indecisiveness was all Bobby needed. He unexpectedly tossed the handful of muck at the alien's face.

Instinctively, the alien took two steps back into the knee deep water. Realizing Bobby's actions were a ploy, he pointed the weapon at his prisoner this time meaning business. The execution was abruptly canceled due to a thunderous crash of water. A huge alligator lunged out of the darkness at the unsuspecting tasty Grey morsel. Most of the slender alien fit easily between the giant reptilian's jaws. They locked down with a vicious pressure. The attacker and his stunned prey disappeared into the abyss without a trace. Bobby crawled away from the black water and noticed the rippling undercurrents. He spoke to his vanquished foe, "I guess your name is Mud, pal."

Shaking off some of the dampness from his clothes, Bobby crawled quietly toward the old barn that the Greys planned to burn. He knew it wouldn't be long before his pursuer was missed. From his vantage point, the others were plainly visible. They huddled together right outside the barn. The guard who'd gone down was revived and giving commands to the captives. Kim and Carol stood together and consoled one another in light of the inevitable. Al and Red had helped Steve to his feet, shaking him back to consciousness. Steve recovered quickly and asked if his brother had made it.

"I think so," said Al. "The little creep chasing him never returned."

"Your brother might have made it. I say this due to the fact that there are no more telepathic signals from the Grey that went after him."

"What's that mean?" asked Al.

"It means one thing: his pursuer is dead."

Steve said, "Bobby's got to act fast. I wonder if Space ever made it to get help?"

"That freakin' nut," moaned Al. "I knew we couldn't count on that pot smoking hippie."

"Yeah, well it may be too late anyway," said Steve as he watched the four Greys fighting the wind as they approached. Red's discouraged face said it all. He knew only one chance to deter the Greys' plans existed, and that was the alignment targeting disc. In twenty minutes the Alignment's ship would fire from Deep Space, homing in on the targeting disc. Anything in the immediate vicinity would be incinerated. The disc had to be found because, come hell or high water, the deadly ion particle beam would go off on schedule.

Without Spaceman there, however, its location was a mystery. It's possible he even left it on the property as he fled. As far as Red was concerned, that scenario would be welcome since they were all to perish anyway, and at least these devils would be foiled in their diabolical attempt at erasing humanity.

Any humans surviving the induced asteroid cataclysm would certainly be at their mercy. And if you're of another species or race, there is no mercy or respect shown. Not being Grey meant automatic subjugation. At this late date having the targeting disc on site would be a bittersweet victory for Red and his Earthian friends—but a major victory for humanity.

CHAPTER TEN

Snaking along in the high grass, Bobby felt his way behind the old barn. The rear door was missing enabling him to enter the black interior. After banging into a few piles of debris, the front side of the old structure was finally reached.

He peeked out through a crack in the front doors to see the group preparing to come in. Bobby crouched down thinking of springing some kind of an ambush. Suddenly he heard one of the Greys yelling for him to surrender or they would kill the others immediately. Somehow they knew of his presence. This unsettling turn of events took him by surprise. Bobby was confused, dazed and didn't know what to do.

Steve yelled from outside, "Don't listen. Run, Bobby!"

Bobby knew he couldn't. His submission was mandatory for the others' safety. Resigned to that obvious conclusion, he reached to open the rotted door handle when a strange noise stopped him.

Over the roaring wind which rattled against the tree tops a pronounced whining could be heard. Every passing second brought the mechanical sound closer and closer. The crack in the front door revealed a bright light shooting in at tree top level. At first, he thought it was more Greys coming to assist the others. But its form finally came into view announcing a jet—a Marine Harrier hovering above. In the overgrown yard outside the barn door, Bobby heard shouts of joy.

"We're saved!" screamed Kim.

"Over here," they yelled competing against the howling wind.

Surveying the action, Bobby could see the blank expression on the Greys' faces. It was now their turn to be surprised and they didn't react well when events veered from their script.

Fearing a loss of control, they quickly made a confused retreat toward the safety of the old farm house. In their beeline to the front porch, it became clear they were quite different anatomically from humans. Their alien gait illustrated this fact as the intruders shuffled away like a pack of scurrying rats whose nest had just been discovered.

The captives were all face down on the ground not knowing what to expect. Steve looked up first at the jet's half opened canopy to see a bearded, long-haired pilot waving at him.

"Spaceman!" he yelled. The others saw it but couldn't believe who sat at the controls of the aircraft.

Rotating quickly in the direction of the retreating aliens, Spaceman squeezed off a burst from the new 25mm rapid fire cannons. It kicked up earth in a stream of muddy clumps which closed from behind on the departing Greys. The second they hit the porch, the cannon fire caught them. Smoke and wood splinters exploded as if the front of the house was in a giant meat grinder.

Al yelled at the top of his lungs, "Get 'em, Skippy, you beautiful nut!"

The dust cleared rapidly courtesy of the blustery weather to reveal three dead Greys, two of which were in pieces. This abrupt turn of events left everyone cheering on Spaceman. Only one Grey remained standing as a result of his raised power stick. It projected a purple field of body armor which preserved him from the devastation. Spaceman let out another volley of cannon fire that blew huge holes through the delapidated farm house. To no one's surprise, the shielded Grey still stood there unmarked.

Spaceman struggled to keep the Harrier level against the buffeting winds. He battled to lower the fighter closer to the ground. Its powerful vector nozzles were pressing plants flat against their roots. Red appeared to be telepathically communicating with Spaceman and ran underneath the hovering craft dangerously close to its exhaust.

Spaceman dropped the power stick he had in his possession to the awaiting Martian below. Realizing he'd have to fight fire with fire, Red immediately squeezed hold of the wand and pointed it at the purple-clad foe in the wreckage of the house. A laser-like line of light flipped on striking the purple field of armor surrounding the Grey and shortly snuffed it out. Whatever he had done, it worked.

The tip of Red's wand didn't glow as it once had, indicating a power drain. He transmitted a brief telepathic signal for Spaceman to utilize his wing-mounted rocket clusters now. "Fire quickly," he urged.

Spaceman reached for the firing controls that operated the pod of Zuni rockets beneath the wing pylons. Red shouted below for everyone to get on the ground right away, and they immediately dropped to their stomachs. The bucking jet pointed nose down, like a bird of prey locked on its target and ready to attack. White flashes erupted from the wings. It was followed by another and another until over a dozen rockets zeroed in on the presently exposed Grey.

Fourth of July shows had nothing on this exhibition. The heat alone almost singed Steve's eyebrows as he peeked out from his low lying shelter. Diminishing the storms ruckus, the explosions force hit everyone. Bright fiery mushroom clouds rose high into the night air. Sound waves echoed and reverberated throughout the water laden swamp. Large pieces of glowing cinders drifted down on top of the still burning depression where the house had stood a moment before. This little blast most assuredly alerted the incubus buried safely in their subterranean lair.

Spaceman knew of the need to leave the premises in a hurry. He bounced his jet roughly down on the ground. He left the engines running and slid off the wing steps and landed on his rear end in the mud. Steve and Al arrived first.

"You O.K.?" asked Steve.

"Yeah, baby. We got to get our asses out of here, mucho pronto."

"Skippy, where'd you get the jet, you maniac?" Al asked caustically. He had to admit, he was glad to see him.

"I like, uh, borrowed it for a while," he said as a smile crossed his bearded face.

"We'll all never fit in the cockpit with you," yelled Al.

"I got an idea flyin' over here. We need rope."

"For what?" asked Steve.

"To hang you guys from the hard points under the wing. Tie the ropes around you, and then I'll close the bomb locking mechanism down on the ends."

"We'll be killed," Al pointed out.

"Do you want to stay here and be roasted alive by those little bastards?" asked Steve.

"Badda bing, we need some rope," snapped Al seeing the immediate logic.

"In the barn," said Steve.

Bobby sprinted from the barn and rejoined the group.

"You made it!" Steve shouted as he hugged his brother.

Bobby looked at the jet and asked, "Spaceman?"

"Yeah," answered Steve. "Bob, was there any rope in that barn?"

"I think there was."

"Quick, grab Space's flashlight. Hurry, Bro."

Spaceman tossed his big pocket knife to Steve and they bolted for the barn. The girls huddled near the jet with worried expressions.

As fast as Steve, Bobby, and Al disappeared into the old building, they reappeared with a large coil of some rather suspect rope. Bobby was busy with the knife cutting off smaller individual pieces. Steve and Al exchanged glances and Steve told him this might just work.

"It better," remarked Al.

"Space, we'll signal you with the flashlight on the ground to let you know we're all hooked up," said Steve.

"Cool," he answered.

"Aye, Skippy, I know you can do this, pal." Steve noticed two five hundred pound bombs on the wings and asked, "Space, the jet won't have any problem with the extra take off weight, will it?"

"No, man," he replied. "The vertical takeoff payload capacity for the Harrier II is seven thousand pounds, dude. So if we leave Captain Al behind, we'll definitely make it." Spaceman maintained a straight face.

"You're a funny, freakin' guy, Skippy," Al retorted.

Red ran past the girls and tugged on Steve's jacket. He looked worried.

"What's up, Red?"

"It appears our fortunes are drastically changing. I must remind you that the Alignment will fire on the targeting disk in approximately 15 Earth minutes time.

Remaining here will be most unpleasant. I cannot even communicate using mind telepathy due to the field block put forth by the Greys' ship. No mind frequency will penetrate the jamming powers."

"Oh shit," said Steve. "Space, where did you leave that targeting disk?"

"Close to my heart, baby," he said as he pulled the highly polished disk from his shirt.

"All right, Space."

"I can drop it on those little ground hogs on the way out of here."

"They will finally be stopped," rejoiced Red.

Steve counted the rope sections and realized they were short one. "Hey Space, can Red ride in the cockpit with you?" he asked.

"No problemo. There's just enough room for his skinny ass behind the seat."

Kim listened to the hastily assembled plans and asked, "Can't we simply leave the way we came in?"

"No way. We'll never get out in time. I'm afraid this is it," Steve told her.

"The main thing is we've got that targeting disk now," said Carol.

"Amen," Steve agreed as he fastened a rope under her arms.

"You hold on tight, honey," Steve said as he showed her where to place the rope for it to be locked down. Steve checked everyone's knots before slipping on his own.

Red observed the hectic efforts to escape and walked in between Steve and his brother. "Hurry. We only have a mere ten minutes before everything in the vicinity of the disc is annihilated."

"We're almost ready," announced Steve. He tied a section of rope about his waist. The thick line was old but still strong as proven by its toughness while cutting. With everyone standing beneath their designated spot, Spaceman ran along verifying the rope ends' positions. The lifelines appeared to be aligned properly for a hook up with the closing bomb clips. Hopefully the rope wouldn't be cut when squeezed tightly by the hydraulic mechanism. Bobby, Kim, and Carol stood under the left wing while Steve and Al held their rope ends in position below the right wing's hard points.

"O.K., man. Next stop, the beach," shouted Spaceman. He gave the dwarf-like Red a boost onto the wing foot holds. Having no one to assist him, Spaceman strained his out of shape torso, finally joining his Martian ally on top of the wing. Red slid in behind the ejection seat. Any tighter a fit would have required a rather large shoe horn.

A few more moments of struggling earned Spaceman entry to the cockpit as he flopped in.

Down on the ground five people stood scared but anxious to depart. Each pressed overhead their lifeline into the slots to be pinched closed. Steve was to signal with the flashlight once all the non-paying passengers umbilical cords were hooked up. He yelled for everyone to watch their hands as his flashlight blinked on the ground signaling a go.

Space wasted no time. He hit the switches controlling the bomb locking mechanisms. It worked. Each clip hydraulically pinched the ropes in place suspending a payload of human yo-yos instead of the normal stack of high explosive weapons. Spaceman watched for the second flashlight signaling their take-off. Steve yelled to Carol and Kim to lift their feet and test the slings which would soon keep them alive.

"Good," responded Carol with her feet dangling above the ground.

Illumination given off by the jet's red tinted landing lights, enabled Steve to see Carol mouthing out the words, "I love you." He returned the gesture and added a small hand wave. Steve had only just met her, but there was a bond already. Her caring nature and guts in a crisis were greatly admired by him. If they got out of this mess, he felt they would develop a lasting relationship.

Looking further over, Steve saw Kim more than ready to go. He flashed the light again in the grass.

This crazy escape scheme appeared to be coming to fruition although a rough and dangerous ride to freedom still remained.

Everyone held on for dear life as the Pegasus engines revved up, lifting the jump jet straight up in the air. The sight was an odd one indeed, a giant mechanized marionette dangling its puppets over the swamp. Al's cuss words could almost be heard above the powerful vector nozzles that performed the vertical takeoffs and landings. The canopy remained wide open which allowed room for the disc to be thrown out. Space wrestled with the controls against the buffeting turbulence outside. Red now held the disc and prepared to toss it as they flew over the burning wreckage below.

"Go for it, little buddy."

Red, not a powerful individual by any means, summoned all of his strength and released the disc like a frisbee from the coiled grip he had on it. A heavy gust of wind caught him off balance and drove him back down behind the seat to the floor. Unfortunately he missed seeing the same gust of wind push the frisbee-like disc back into the front cockpit between Spaceman's legs. The smoking pilot was occupied searching for it out the wrong side of the plane. He hadn't noticed the unscheduled re-entry which now rested by his feet.

"Did you throw it?"

"Yes."

"O.K. Hold on little buddy."

The Harrier hovered in a slow progression eastward toward the river. All the yo-yos dangling beneath the wings' composite skin, wore faces of sheer terror. Their newly attained peril-laden perspective was not comforted by the knowledge of who sat behind the controls. Both hands firmly clutched the questionable rope sling by which each person was suspended.

The canopy was lowered as Red leaned forward. He asked, "Did you see it fall, Mr. Spaceman? It will not be long now."

"No man. I must have been looking out the wrong side." Spaceman complained, "Ah damn," as he dropped the hot end of his smoke onto his lap. He slapped at the glowing ash when a bright flash of reflective light caught his eye on the floor. "What the hell? Red, climb up here pronto, dude."

"What are you alarmed about?" Then he also saw the targeting disc reflecting light down by Spaceman's feet.

"I can't reach it without crashing the plane. You've got to get it, man."

"We only have minutes until they fire on the disc."

Red scaled over the top of Spaceman's fuzzy head while the jet slowly did an about face. The silver-suited Martian dove for the disc and hit a couple of control levers by accident. One of the five hundred pound bombs attached to Al and Steve's wing let loose and dropped to the forest below. The forthcoming concussion shook everyone on the low flying jet. Captain Al, who was almost hit by the discharging bomb, started cussing and yelling, "That freakin' maniac."

Back in the cockpit, chaos reigned. Spaceman struggled to keep the ship aloft. "Hey, be careful, man."

Red's legs kicked wildly and hit Spaceman in the face. The ride was rough enough but now the flight plan was experiencing some scary deviations. Red stretched his small body and finally reached the round device. Squirming uncomfortably he made his way again to the small perch behind Spaceman. They were headed back for the glowing fire in the jungle canopy plainly visible on the dark surface ahead.

Steve swung on his short leash and caught sight of Carol's expression of bewilderment as to why they were heading back. The unsettling course change worried him. Everyone seemed to be securely fastened to their ropes in spite of the tremendous discomfort of its noose-tight grip under their arms.

"Hurry, Mr. Spaceman, time is running out," pleaded Red.

"I've got people on the wings, man. I can't go too fast. Get ready. It's coming up."

The clear canopy went up and Red hung partially out of the jet. He threw the disc out. Clearing the two engine intake ducts just under them he watched it tumble onto the center of the burning farm house rubble.

As the canopy lowered, Red turned to Spaceman, "In order for this vehicle to survive, you must, as you humans say, 'haul ass'."

"Hold on, baby."

He took off much faster than their previous departure. The decision to fly slowly so as not to lose anyone no longer applied. It was crunch time. If the jet didn't accrue some distance from ground zero, the entire craft and all lives would be lost. Space pulled back on the throttle without hesitation. He increased the air speed from 150 knots to 200. Its effects under the wings forced everyone into a horizontal position. Intense best described the wild ride they were on.

Steve wondered if the erratic journey would ever conclude. At that juncture, Red was able to reach him by telepathy. The message explained what had occurred and recommended they all hold on tightly due to the expected shock waves to come. Steve replied in his thoughts that, despite the beating they were taking, they would be able to stand more speed if necessary. He realized the urgency in getting as far away from the target area as possible. Red went on to warn the others using his telepathic powers. The calming effects of his communications helped console each of the five human weather vanes blowing beneath the plane.

Red pressed his nose up against the back of the bubble canopy attempting to gain a glimpse of the incoming beam.

"Hey little buddy, are you familiar with this weapon that's going to go off?"

"Yes."

"Will we clear the blast?"

"It's not the blast as much as the debris from the impact with the ground."

"Man, you mean like a meteor impact?"

"Correct. Any second now."

Out of the stormy skies a brilliant flash illuminated the countryside. Red's allies in the Alignment were right on schedule. The powerful beam reacted as lightning would, except it was brighter and lasted considerably longer. Maybe ten seconds in all.

A plume of earth rocketed into the atmosphere and immediately snuffed out the ground behind them. There must have been an unbelievable energy force released at the point of impact on the old farm. The recent meteor impact on the planet Jupiter was similar to this action-reaction blast sending a well-defined jet plume of debris straight up and on into space. Albeit on a much larger scale than the beams debris field.

Rumblings reverberated in the distance. Everyone braced to receive the shock waves. In anticipation, Spaceman let off the throttle somewhat as the jolt hit the plane. Even though the jet was a couple miles from the zone of destruction, heavy air turbulence shook the plane. Spaceman's concern wasn't as much for the air craft which seemed to hold together as it was for his friends outside.

Red still focused on his mission and let out a victory shout. At last, he witnessed success against his people's sworn enemy. The Greys' mother ship had been destroyed. He hoped this lesson would curb future meddling. Maybe now they will abide by universal laws regarding planetary sovereignty and non-intervention of evolving species. More importantly the Earthians would now be able to continue on living and naturally developing—unlike the Martians' fate.

"We've stopped them, Mr. Spaceman."

"We'll drink to that later, little buddy. Right now we need to get our cargo down."

Dust particles from the pulverizing beam became suspended in the air as Red had predicted. It was a thin ash-like cloud that blackened the visibility in the surrounding area. A large wiper blade popped up and cleaned the forward windshield. The light coating of dust grew steadily thicker. Out on the hard points, everyone took on the appearance of coal miners. Red advised Spaceman to monitor his instruments for signs of too much suspended ground particles entering the engine intakes.

"Don't worry, baby, I'm puttin' down at the gas-mart another quarter mile ahead."

"This would be very wise," retorted Red. "Steve thinks five baths are in order upon landing. I've read Steve's mind and he said everyone is black with soot."

"Hey, that gives me an idea, man. I mean the bath thing," Spaceman said revealing a devilish smile.

As he crossed to the river's eastern shore just before the barrier island, he slowed to a hover at twenty feet in altitude. Opening the bomb controls, he switched on and off hard point number three's locking mechanism which held Captain Al's rope. Al quickly plummeted into the water, emerging seconds later and shaking his fist at the plane.

"He's going to be extremely unhappy," commented Red.

Spaceman tried to hide his expression of uncontrollable hilarity. He spoke in an indiscernible voice, "Yeah, his rope must have finally given out." His laughter forced tears from his eyes. Laughter was an emotion that had been unused by Spaceman for quite some time. This release was long overdue.

Red joined in the merriment, "Give me five, dude."

Al waded ashore through the chest high water and dropped on the bank. He was pissed off but damn glad to be alive and free. The others who were still hanging were extremely anxious to get safely on the ground. Weather conditions had improved and the squall that had threatened earlier had totally disappeared leaving a quiet calm. Only the bizarre fog-like dust hung in the air. The streets and homes on the beach were lightly coated by the dark blizzard. Red seemed to feel the worst of it was over. He told Spaceman it wouldn't get any worse. It amounted to a clean up inconvenience for the residents.

The Harrier began to descend after clearing some power lines along Highway A1A. Their destination lay right below. Lights from the gas-mart were clearly illuminating its boundaries. Half of the oversized parking lot was claimed by the large aircraft. Spaceman had opened the canopy all the way and could see his small Hindi friend out actually trying to sweep the dark colored fallout into a dust pan. He'd recently finished cleaning all the sand off his premises as a result of the group's last visit to his establishment.

Two neat, little piles of ash meticulously spaced were blown in total disarray by the hovering Harrier. The small proprietor looked up in disbelief. He spied Steve and Carol hanging from the wing. Spaceman waved from the cockpit, mouthing the words, "Hey, baby."

Hodgi threw his broom down and screamed in his Indian accent, "No. No. You can not park here. Go away!" The dark dust blew into the air and created a smoke screen that camouflaged the jet's presence on the pavement temporarily. Once the landing gear hit, Spaceman immediately cut all power and released the bomb locks which freed his passengers.

Steve pulled down the ropes from his armpits and ran over to assist Carol. They all complained of chafe burns under their arms.

Kim blurted out, "Thank God we made it."

Steve didn't hesitate, "Carol, quick. Call your dad. There's a phone over there."

"I've never used the number. I hope I remember it," she answered.

"You've got to remember it or we're dead," he said as their stiff bodies ran towards the pay phone.

Bobby hugged Kim tightly. They both looked exhausted, sore, and covered with ash dust. The satisfaction of escaping and watching the Greys get what they deserved made up for their discomfort.

Hodgi ran to the plane and started climbing up toward the cockpit, "You can't stay here. No, no, no. This is very bad."

Spaceman looked him in the eye and said, "I'm going to buy something, man. How much for those giant cokes?"

"No, no, no. You don't understand. I can not have - - -"

Just then, Red's oversized head poked out from behind the pilot's seat. His large eyes stared right into the shopkeeper's face.

Hodgi's mouth dropped open in shock. He almost went head over heels backward in fear. He muttered, "What? What is dot?" Not waiting for an answer, he jumped to the pavement. Landing on all fours, Hodgi scrambled for the safety of his store.

Carol and Steve got to the pay phone only to realize neither one had any change in their pockets. Steve ran to the store's check out counter. A jar full of coin donations for charity became the solution to their problem. Reaching over the counter, Steve lifted the hard can and promptly slammed the tightly sealed container to the floor. Coins cascaded across the floor, rolling down every aisle. At that point, Hodgi entered the front door and observed Steve picking quarters out of the crushed container.

Hodgi put his hands in the air as he ran from the scene, "Help! I'm being robbed!"

Five seconds later, Steve pushed quarters into the phone and said, "C'mon, Carol. You've got to hurry."

She slowly dialed the number nervously talking to herself. "I know the code is either two or three," she said. Finally taking a guess, she pushed a three. At the other end, a Pentagon operator said, "Please hold. Your call is being immediately forwarded."

A man answered, "Preston Cole."

"Daddy?"

"Carol, are you in some kind of trouble?"

Carol's courage finally broke down at hearing her father's voice. "Yes, I'm scared and I need your help."

"What is it? Are you still on vacation in Florida?"

"I'm in Satellite Beach, Florida, with my friend Kim. We've gotten involved with a flying saucer recovery and we were taken captive, escaped, and now the military is after us."

A look of total shock and disbelief registered on the face of the Chairman of the Joint Chiefs. Not from the fact that aliens were mentioned, but because his own daughter was implicated in this National Security matter. A matter the Pentagon was currently trying to straighten out.

Despite the initial shock, the Chairman maintained his cool, well-disciplined demeanor. Calmly he said, "Carol, listen to me very carefully. You and your friends can not speak to anyone about this. It is a National Security issue of the highest possible classification. Where are you exactly?"

"In a small gas mart on Highway A1A." Carol looked around for a distinguishing address, "Number 2501."

"O.K., do not move from there, and do not speak to anyone. Everything will be fine, honey."

"Thanks, daddy. I love you."

"I love you, too." After hanging up, the general grabbed another phone which connected him to a subordinate. "I want my plane ready ASAP," and hung up. The next call went to Fort Meade, Maryland, and the Office of the National Security Agency's director.

"Hi, Bob. It's Preston. Yeah, listen. I need your assistance right away. It concerns that IAC downed off the Florida coast. I may be personally involved..." He went on to discuss his situation.

Outside the gas mart, Carol hugged Steve as tears formed in her eyes. Although they'd interrupted the Greys' plans and escaped, certain covert government agencies would still be hunting them. In particular, the group who visited the Wilcox farm earlier. Patrick Air Force Base was also looking for their missing aircraft. Spaceman's incursion there probably touched off an extensive search effort. If that wasn't enough, the massive explosion at the abandoned alligator farm, which sent dust particles in a ten mile radius, most definitely had everyone on alert. In spite of the urge to high tail it out of there, the group kept their mouths shut and remained together under the jet as Carol's father had advised.

Spaceman climbed down from the cockpit after telling Red it might be a good idea for him to remain inside hidden from view. Steve and Bobby greeted him and expressed their gratitude with pats on the back. Spaceman seemed to enjoy basking in his monumental achievement.

"You saved our butts, buddy," Steve said shaking his hand.

"Yeah, way to go," added Bobby. "You're a genuine hero."

Becoming embarrassed, Spaceman responded, "It was nothing special, man."

"What happened to Al?" asked Steve.

"Don't know. His rope must have given way," responded Spaceman nervously.

"I saw him walk to shore out of the water. He looked all right," Steve said.

Spaceman changed the subject. "Like, the main thing is those creepy little double crossers won't be screwing with humans anytime soon."

"That bunch won't be," Steve agreed. "Now we have to deal with our own military."

After all they'd been through, their situation continued to remain unresolved. Kim ceased crying long enough to tell Carol how sorry she was. "I don't know how we got involved in this tangled web."

Carol responded, "If we hadn't become involved, just think of the terrible consequences."

"I guess so," she sobbed.

"Don't worry. My dad can straighten out this mess." Carol looked around. "Where's Red?"

Spaceman moved toward the girls as he lit a smoke. "Keeping a low profile inside the plane. Like, I think your father needs to be informed as to just who our allies really are, baby."

"It sure seems that way," she said. "And you better believe he will be told the truth."

A small crowd of people had formed around the gas mart gaulking at the big jets unannounced presence. Their ranks were broken suddenly when two military vehicles raced into the parking lot. Spaceman instantly recognized the large Hummer 4 X 4 as belonging to Patrick Air Force Base Security. "Oh shit," he muffled.

Four MPs dressed in camouflage fatigues and blue berets spilled out flashing their M16s at the small group sitting together under the plane. A picket line of ten security men circled the Harrier. Their captain shouted at the two dozen bystanders to leave the area immediately. He told them there were live bombs which could explode at any minute. That little lie worked well and sent the curious mob jogging in the opposite direction. He told his sergeant to radio the base for backup and then made a direct path to the huddled heroes.

He announced loudly on approach, "I don't know what the hell you are up to or which one of you stole this government property, but someone's ass is really in a sling."

Kim broke out shouting, "There's an alien spacecraft in the swamps off Rt. 192 and…"

Bobby's hand caused her words to stop in mid-sentence. He casually whispered in her ear, "Remember what Carol's father said, dear." She shook her head in acknowledgment.

"O.K. Everyone stays right where they are," barked the captain. He climbed into the Harrier's cockpit with his sergeant in tow. A brief inspection of the equipment turned up nothing out of the ordinary. Only the lingering smell of cannabis remained which testified to the unauthorized flight. Red huddled behind the pilot's seat and tried not to move to avoid detection. The reflection off Red's silver suit caught the eye of the officer.

He ordered, "All right. Let's go. Out of there."

When Red popped his large head up, the captain jumped back into the sergeant who had been standing behind him. "Damn. Sergeant, cover him with your pistol and give me that damn radio."

"Yes, sir," answered the stunned subordinate who fumbled to pull his 45 caliber pistol out of its holster.

The captain grabbed the hand-held radio to call headquarters. "This is Captain Barnes. We've secured the missing Harrier, but I've got a Code Aquarius here. You better get the base UFO Officer out here on the double. There's a visitor in the recovered aircraft." No answer came over the airwaves. "Yes. You heard me correctly. On the double. Roger and out."

As protectors of the entire Cape Canaveral area, some of the base personnel are no strangers to alien interaction. They play a certain game of cat and mouse with these stealthy visitors. Our sophisticated surveillance aircraft and ground equipment are aware of their presence. But of course it is at the pinnacle of secrecy classification. It will never be relayed to the public's attention.

The guards that encircled the plane were not fooling around. Their M16s carried live rounds and they pointed them liberally at anyone willing to move. Captain Barnes climbed down, leaving the sergeant to cover Red. He was preparing to order his men to search the group when Spaceman stepped forward.

"Hold on there, dude. These people had nothing to do with borrowing your little airplane, man."

"And who the hell are you?"

"Well, I don't have any I.D. on me, but my name is Commander Whitson. Naval Intelligence, counter-intelligence with Astro I clearance, and test pilot with Project Snowbird."

The captain surveyed him up and down and began laughing, "Yeah, and I'm Franklin Roosevelt."

148

"He's like, dead, man."

"And so are you," said the captain who was no longer laughing.

Steve noticed a stream of bright lights rapidly approaching from the western sky. The pounding helicopter rotors filled the night air. Steve nodded at Spaceman in their direction. Black colored helicopters hovered overhead and stirred up more of the dust as they surrounded the gas mart.

The captain turned and said, "Now we'll get to the bottom of this."

Spaceman also watched the new arrivals and commented, "Those aren't your boys, Captain."

"What are you talking about?" he laughed.

Just then, two separate loud speakers announced to the Air Force Security team to drop their weapons at once. The instruction emanated from two Apache gun ships. These beauties both possessed an ungodly amount of firepower, all of which was aimed down on the parking lot. Three other large Blackhawks had dispensed their commandos to the ground via repelling ropes. An outer circle of scary machine gun toting commandos ringed the ten Air Force men. Identification insignias and patches were absent from their camouflaged uniforms.

Space whispered to Steve, "I thought we were in trouble before, but Stevie, man, the shit's just getting deeper."

A small Bell helicopter with the same black color dropped to the ground. Out of its door emerged Spaceman's worst nightmare. The two shadows he'd evaded a couple of times earlier in the day were back. To say they appeared pissed off would be a gross understatement. Spaceman slid down behind Carol and Kim as if he'd go undetected. Steve watched the agents draw nearer and grew concerned. The senior commando joined in their procession.

Steve yelled, "Not you guys again!"

The agent in charge missed the humor in the statement. "Where is he?"

Before Steve could say anything, they pushed through the girls and seized their prisoner. "Commander, how nice to see you again."

The Air Force captain interrupted and demanded an explanation.

Agent Number One flipped out his National Security Agency identification and said, "Take your men and go back to your base, Captain. This is a high level National Security matter being handled by our group. I've spoken with your C.O. General William's and we need your men out of here now."

"Who do you guys think you are?" he asked indignantly. He was highly agitated and resented his men being bullied.

"We're people you don't want to screw with. Now move!"

The captain considered holding his ground until the top commando handed him the radio. "Yes General. Right away, sir." He saluted the new arrivals and recalled his men to the Hummers. As the Air Force officer departed, he turned and said, "Oh, by the way. There's someone in the cockpit you might be looking to interrogate."

"Thank you, Captain." The agent nodded to the commando who sent two men scampering up the plane. They escorted Red quickly down to an awaiting helicopter after securing a large rain poncho over him.

Standing before everyone in an intimidating fashion, the vengeful agent spoke directly to Spaceman. "I don't know what you used on my partner and me outside the base fence, but paybacks will be a bitch. I think your luck is running out." Clearly he didn't like Spaceman and any chance to attack him was greatly relished. He got right over his face and ripped the joint from his lips, crushing it with a boot heel on the ground. "You see, you and your accomplices are all going away to our special sleepover camp. I've got some treats in store for you there."

Spaceman didn't offer any explanations at all to the agent.

"You leave him alone! The only thing he's guilty of is doing your job and protecting this country," argued Carol.

"Oh really?" responded the agent who was amused at Spaceman's defenders.

"We did nothing," protested Kim in tears.

Bobby added, "You can't talk to these mindless mercenaries."

"I can see you folks are going to need a lot of attitude adjustment. Load them up," he barked out to the commandos.

The prisoners were herded into the large Blackhawk helicopter Red had entered minutes before.

The elite troops who were dispensed to the scene were definitely members of Blue teams used for crash retrievals. These specialized individuals are stationed around the country at different military bases awaiting for their talents to be called upon should the rare incident or crash occur. On this occasion, the alien craft didn't need to be secretly transported. The saucer which had been stored at the Wilcox farm was already secured and removed elsewhere. No diversionary tactics were needed to shield the truth from the public's preying eyes. Outside of hiding Red, it was a simple operation.

Differences did exist between an accidental crash, and a premeditated weapons attack as on Red's ship. Our brilliant SDI Defense Systems were misused due to forced alliances, faulty intelligence, and the Greys' effective deceptions. The end result was the downing of a benevolent group's craft. The truth pertaining to Grey treachery needed to be exposed definitively and laid bare for our leaders to witness before mankind is led into the abyss. Because their subtle manipulation does occur at the highest levels of power.

CHAPTER ELEVEN

Their flight from the beach to the highly sensitive base consumed a half hour's time. The chopper's landing lights lit up two small buildings below inside a large rectangular bob-wire fence. The installation sat on the outskirts of the Ocala National Forest in Central Florida. It lay adjacent to the Navy's Pine Castle Electronic Warfare Range. Terrain outside the tiny covert base was most inhospitable to anyone save the local Seminole Indian peoples.

The Blackhawk carrying the prisoners touched down on a circular concrete pad within the fence line. An Apache gunship which had escorted their craft peeled off and headed east again. In the rear of the Blackhawk were rows of bench-style seats that held the military's precious live cargo. Each captive had their hands handcuffed behind their backs with a half dozen commandos present to keep them from becoming too lonely. Two soldiers watched over Red particularly closely keeping their gun barrels very near to his head.

Steve could hear Red communicating with him via telepathy once again. His Martian friend told him they planned to use brainwashing techniques to erase the alien experiences from everyone's conscious memory. This base was a top secret deprogramming station. Steve inquired by brain waves if Red thought these guys would listen to reason about the Greys.

The non-audible answer arrived right away. "You can try but they're probably too low level. We need to speak with people in Washington. Our captors definitely won't listen to anything I've got to say. I also believe the two NSA men are going to exact some personal revenge on Mr. Spaceman. Unfortunately we are perceived as the enemy, and there in lies our dilemma."

"What do you think they'll do with you?" questioned Steve.

"Let us say, my fate will not be as pleasant as yours. Especially if their Grey friends have anything to do with it."

The main door on the helicopter slid open allowing the night air to rush in.

"All right. Let's move it," commanded the rude agent while motioning for the troops to escort the small parade. Halogen type lights on fifty foot support poles lit up the small compound area. Not much was on the surface except two small blockhouse-style structures. Roadways were also absent save one small dirt road leading from the blockhouse out through the only gate and on into solitude of the forest.

The agent ordered everyone to halt while he borrowed a soldier's weapon and proceeded to smack the stock's butt against Spaceman's stomach.

"That's just to welcome you, Commander."

Space doubled over in pain.

"Hey Psycho!" Steve shouted at the aggravated operative. "Take these cuffs off and I'll let you try that with me."

"You own the farm where the saucer was hidden. That's aiding and abetting an enemy of the United States which is punishable by death."

"Prove it. I'll see you in court."

"There's no need for courts or proof here in our little reality my friend. My word is quite final."

"Another government agency out of control," said Steve.

"I can see we have some major attitude adjustments to be made. All right, move them inside."

"Adjust this, you mental ward reject," snapped Steve.

He promptly received a gun butt to the head. Carol let out a scream, and the entire party was pushed by the soldiers into the building.

One level below the surface a much larger complex flourished. Corridors extended out in different directions from the elevator lobby. In the style of Area 51 and other covert subterranean facilities, this operation goes on where even satellites can't detect it. However, this complex didn't go very deep due to the native Floridian soil. At one end of a long hallway was a high security chamber which awaited the first three customers off the helicopter. The large steel door and bomb- proof walls testified to its impenetrability. All the dirty deeds required to run an effective Intelligence operation occur in the shadowy underworld. On occasion, small visitors working with our military offer their expertise assisting in the base's primary function, controlling minds and the outsiders advanced methods produce extremely effective results.

Steve awoke to find himself in the vault-like room. He couldn't move because of straps holding him down to a heavy reclining chair. Both Spaceman and Carol were also tightly secured to these dental chairs. A tray table resting to one side contained syringes and vials of unknown contents. Normal brainwashing techniques implemented now are fifty years ahead of where people think they are. It's due in part to alien technological assistance. As part of the program to keep the public in the dark, any high profile abductees, talkative government aerospace workers or military people in the loop who've witnessed or worked with alien related events are dealt with quickly. On occasion, military intelligence works with their small advisors, if necessary, to erase any memory of any uncooperative individuals' experiences. Powerful combinations of exotic drugs blended with telepathic hypnotic suggestion is used to induce memory loss. The aliens have it down to a fine art after thousands of years of tampering with humans. This method ensures total secrecy for our government and the aliens without any messy killing.

The government, primarily MJ12, keeps the alien presence a secret until they feel the revelation won't disturb civilization too severely, and we're prepared technologically to defend ourselves. On the other side of the coin, the aliens, in particular the Greys, can continue to work undercover on their nasty little genetic programs undeterred. Unfortunately the government and military may have to reassess just who it's in bed with. That is, of course, if they can do anything about it. The Greys' sophisticated treachery was well-planned many, many years ago. Their cunning and deceit were implemented on a regular basis.

In recent years, no obvious visible threats have existed. As far back as 1948, the Pentagon and newly formed MJ12 determined there to be no immediate military threat. It wasn't until twenty years later while working closely with these beings in ultra-secret underground bases that this opinion fell into question.

Presently, however, the deadly serious plans of one group almost executed at the abandoned alligator farm sounded a major wake up call. Without the adventurous saucer hunters' intervention, a complete shift in planned human evolution would have occurred as it has at times in the past. Steve and Carol knew Washington had to be warned, and they knew their only mechanism to achieve this was Carol's father. She possessed a direct line to the source.

The door opened and both agents, along with two fatigue-clad military men, marched in straight for the three restrained prisoners. Carol immediately tried to reason with them from her position of vulnerability. She wanted to impress upon the military men the importance of her information. Her hair almost stood on end at spying two Greys trailing the men into the room.

"We're not the enemy. They are!" she shouted. "Don't you realize what's going on here? They're using you. The Greys want to eliminate humanity as we know it!"

"Save your breath, Carol. These low-level schmucks are too ignorant to understand the big picture here," said Steve.

Their agent friend turned to one of the military men and said, "You see our problem?"

"This might take some extensive washing," the soldier responded.

The small Grey nodded in agreement.

Carol was shocked by the close cooperation between the two aliens and the military people. She just closed her eyes in disbelief. It left her extremely upset and somewhat betrayed. Maybe the military had no choice in maintaining this uneasy alliance, and yet the irony of our defenders assisting humanity's ultimate threat turned her stomach. Even though she hadn't all the facts, the scene was particularly offensive since her father most assuredly had knowledge of this deal with the devil. But as has been seen many times in our own past, politics makes strange bedfellows.

The head counter-intelligence agent pointed at Spaceman and said to one Grey, "This one here has probably been talking to the others. He once held a 'need to know' clearance and was deprogrammed for security reasons, apparently unsuccessfully."

The Grey just nodded again. Only one alternative existed if brainwashing failed: termination. Reasons for such a severe penalty were simple. Leaks are totally unacceptable both for our national security and because it would ruin alien plans which would make them quite unhappy. Plans that our leaders had no knowledge of.

When President Eisenhower hastily signed the treaty at Edward Air Force Base in 1954, promises were made on both sides. It is said we were in no position to dictate terms. Even an ignoramus knows what happens when a more advanced evolved civilization comes in contact with one less developed. The end result isn't good for the latter.

One of our terms in the agreement was to help keep the general population from having any knowledge of these aliens here on Earth. Through the years, any method needed to maintain the deal and insure secrecy has been employed against anyone unlucky enough to discover the truth and stubborn enough to want to talk about it. No one, regardless of station or rank, is exempt. President Kennedy and Secretary of Defense Forestall learned that the hard way.

Most threats of various degrees are not carried out. It's the old game of the carrot or the stick. Everybody usually plays ball because of the National Security implications involved, whether you receive the carrot as a reward for silence or you tell them to go to hell and receive a wide range of sticks. Most people involved choose the carrot such as military personnel who are promoted in rank, transferred to more pleasant bases, etc. Civilians like Mac Brazzell, the rancher at the Roswell crash, was given money and a new truck to recant his story of the events. It can be easy or hard, but either way, it will be suppressed until the boys in Washington figure the whole thing out and feel society is prepared to deal with all the challenges. Secrecy may be necessary now, and yet, the right of human beings to know intelligent life not only exists but has been here for thousands of years is crucial. Especially when you consider the danger involved from not realizing a potential threat exists within an arms length. The current situation is good for the aliens, but bad for humans.

Even if the Defense Department couldn't prevent the Greys' plans, they certainly needed to be aware of their ominous, hidden intentions. The two Grey advisors whose job was to administer the drugs to the detainees and supervise the special hypnotic procedure, were acutely aware of a potential leak from one of the restrained captives. The information they had could alert the military to their true motives and break an already shaky alliance. Totally unacceptable.

Unknown to their present military accomplices, the two Greys were prepared to perform much more than a brainwashing. None of the prisoners would ever leave this facility alive. By killing all the captives not only would their deadly schemes die with them, but a measure of revenge would be exacted for the loss of their ship in the swamp.

Almost directly above the secured chamber on a higher level, Bobby, Kim, and Red sat in a cell containing only four small beds, a sink, and a toilet. Kim's tear ducts had just about run dry from persistent crying. She was becoming slightly delusional after the last twenty-four hours of non-ceasing tensions.

After some silent thought, Kim asked, "Bob, do you think they're going to kill us all?"

"No. We'll probably be interrogated and let go," he answered in an attempt to defuse her alarm.

"This is all your fault!" she blurted to Red as she searched for a scapegoat.

Red announced briefly, "That is an incorrect assessment."

"Don't blame him, Kim," said Bobby. "He risked his life coming here to save us all. What we need is a way to escape."

Kim grew quiet and started weeping in Bobby's arms.

Red showed a strained expression. "I may have an escape solution." He then grimaced and both his handcuffs slid off onto the floor.

Bobby and Kim turned in amazement to see Red stretching his shackleless limbs. "How'd you do that?"

"My skeletal muscles are far more flexible than yours. I have a plan. The two Grey advisors' quarters are right next to this room. I've picked up their telepathic conversations. There could be equipment in there to aid in our escape. Their communications revealed they intend to inject all of us with a deadly toxin instead of the normal memory-altering drug."

"Carol, Steve, and Spaceman are down there right now!" screamed Kim.

"Relax Kim, relax. The soldiers won't let that happen," insisted Bobby as he tried once again to put her at ease. This unconventional operation left him with some serious doubts as to what was possible.

"Your military people down there are unaware," Red proclaimed. "Before we help the others in the vault room, we must eliminate the two guards outside our cell in the hallway."

Without hesitation, Red transmitted a distress call by telepathy to the patrolling guards on the other side of the door. He sent the panic ridden brain waves pouring out emotional pleas for immediate help. On cue, the two commandos rushed in with automatic weapons at the ready. Red concealed his free hands to one side appearing to still be restrained to the bed. Another mind blast reached the confused guards which this time translated to a warning, "look out behind you." It reverberated in their heads causing them to spin around leaving their backs exposed. Red showed some nimble dexterity and quickly pulled out the unwitting sentry's pistol from its holster.

"Drop those weapons right away," he firmly told them. This time he communicated the old-fashioned way, using oral sound waves.

"Ah shit," one of the guards mumbled and dropped his sub-machine gun.

"On the floor and back in here, please."

"You know, you'll never leave this compound alive," one of the guards informed Red.

"Incorrect. Your keys please."

He freed Bobby and Kim and handed the gun to Bobby. "Please remain here with them. One of these keys opens the advisors' quarters next door."

"Will those open the vault room below?" asked Bobby.

"No. We need technological assistance urgently, and I believe it could be found next door. I should returned shortly."

"O.K., I've got these guys covered."

"Good luck," Kim whispered in an appreciative voice.

Red peeked out the crack in the open door and left seeing no one present. He shuffled down the hall to the unguarded advisors' quarters. The first key selected opened the steel door. Inside was a sparsely furnished room. It appeared as if the spartan interior was hurriedly assembled for its temporary visitors. This place was definitely not a permanent residence. Red didn't notice anything indicating the Greys' presence except a large container of the nutrient-rich liquid both he and the Greys digestive systems required instead of food sitting on a small table. Being unsure when his next meal might come along, Red guzzled down a sustainable quantity of the high energy liquid. He let out a loud burp after sucking down a good quart of the fluid. His energy level rose immediately.

Outside of the table and two cots with blankets on the them, there wasn't much to search. Red sat on one of the cots wondering if escape really was possible. As he leaned back, one of his supporting hands slipped under a blanket and felt something hard. Flipping off the top blanket, he discovered a small black box with symbols on it. Bingo. It wasn't a power stick, but he knew this Grey Transposer would allow him free access through any structure. This small device permitted the operator to pass through any barrier or material. It utilizes the space between atomic particles in your body and the barriers particles to be traversed. It's a controlled field effect. The same field effect was exhibited in 1943 when the sailors participating in the Navy's Project Rainbow a.k.a. the Philadelphia Experiment were locked into the steel walls of their ship, the Eldridge, during Einstein's infamous experiment. In that incident, the men's particles co-mingled with the ship's steel structure trapping and killing them. Not having much control over the process proved unfortunate for the sailors involved.

This device, however, is far superior technologically and is highly controllable. The end result is that you appear to be walking through the walls, and in fact you are. In the living room of the old farm house in the swamp, the Greys demonstrated the devices devilish effectiveness at traveling though solid structures undetected. A transposer redefines the term sneak attack. Red was familiar with its operation, but needed a quick test before venturing a rescue attempt in the vault room. He decided to re-enter the holding cell next door where Bobby and Kim waited. By energizing the instrument, which converted him to pulse wave energy thus affecting the gyroscopic spin on the subatomic particles in his body and the wall, he was able to casually move forward and intersect with the wall.

In the next room, Bobby and Kim held the guards at bay, their bodies pressed face down on the floor. Nervously they stood watch over the two soldiers. Doubt arose as to whether Red would ever return.

Kim said, "Maybe we should try to get out of here, Bob. I don't think Red is coming back."

Bobby didn't answer. He knew the chances of breaking out of this facility were zero. As he pondered this fact, an image of their small friend projected itself noiselessly on the wall and then Red stepped out as if by osmosis. His two friends had their attentions focused on the guards and failed to see him enter from behind. Red calmly walked up and pulled on Bobby's shirt. "She is incorrect once again."

Their surprise was complete and vaulted them a foot in the air.

"Jeez," shouted Bobby. Kim simultaneously gasped, "Oh my God. Where did you come from?"

"Next door. I retrieved this transposer."

"Are we all going downstairs?" asked an anxious Bobby reeling from the sudden ambush.

"No," was the response. "I must go alone and survey our chances. Carol, Steve, and Mr. Spaceman are going to be terminated by the Grey advisors if I do not hurry."

"Won't there be guards outside the vault room door," advised Bobby.

"That will not be a concern. My penetration won't originate from that direction. Please watch these men. I will return."

"Hurry Red," urged Kim extremely concerned.

Inside the secure vault room one of the Grey advisors had created a technical excuse for the other men to wait outside. The two Greys wanted no witnesses to the prisoners "accidental" deaths. Their human partners looked at one another and reluctantly followed their instructions leaving. They had orders from their superiors to cooperate and help the ally advisors even though an undercurrent of mistrust existed.

One floor above the ominous plans, Red lay face down on the cell floor grasping the small black box tightly.

Kim observed his actions. "This is no time to rest. You need to hurry, Red."

Bobby, Kim, and the two guards looked on as Red took on a slight glow and began to sink into the floor. Below in the vault room, Red's image shown against the ten foot high ceiling like a figure painted on the Sistine Chapel at the Vatican. And it was evident that angels were never more desperately needed to defeat the forces of evil than right now. The Martian's body did not totally emerge from the ceiling's surface. Only his head was lowered down to peer into the underworld below. Both Greys were all alone with their prisoners. They worked feverishly preparing the doses of lethal injections to be administered. Once given the Greys' problems would be over. Steve, startled by the initial sight above him, saw his friend and remained silent. Spaceman and Carol eventually caught sight of the familiar ceiling fresco which calmed them somewhat. Red wanted to speak to them via telepathy but didn't dare since he might be intercepted by the Greys and found out.

One of the advisors spoke to the captives as he held a loaded syringe in the air.

"Your interference has cost us much. This accidental dose of the wrong drug I'm holding will end your meddling into our evolutionary plans for Earth."

Carol shouted, "You'll never get away with this."

"Leave her alone!" yelled Steve.

The Greys looked at one another with an slightly detectable grin of emotion and went to inject Carol's arm.

Red didn't know what to do. In his confusion, he leaned too far out of the molecular bond with the two-foot thick ceiling when gravity took over. He tumbled down head over heels, using one of the aliens beneath him as a mattress.

Red's fall was broken nicely by the unconscious Grey pillow he sat on. The victim's partner still clinching the needle, lunged at Red who still held the black box. By controlling the transposer box, Red watched while the Grey swiped at him seemingly scoring a direct hit on his chest. But no, the syringe and attackers arm passed right through his torso. Working the device with great precision, the Martian's body returned to solid matter. Red immediately shoved the Grey who landed hard against Spaceman's restraining chair. Unable to free himself, Spaceman helped himself to the small Greys arm which had landed by his head. He opened his mouth and bit down like a pit bull on the thin alien's limb. For his efforts, Space received a taste of black colored alien blood. He spat the foul taste from his mouth and for a moment had second thoughts about the desperate move. The alien's arm went into spasms which sent the needle harmlessly to the floor.

Red had made his way to Steve's restraining straps and frantically tried to loosen them. At that second, the vengeful Grey performed a running lunge, tackling Red to the ground. The collision forced the transposer box out of his hand. Red, still shaken from his entrance fall, was knocked against the wall. He slid down into a helpless heap. His attacker pursued him and slapped him viciously. Choking his victim, the Grey began to display rather primitive qualities of brutality that contradicted behavior expected of such a highly intelligent race. It demonstrated just how far their advanced race had really advanced. The frustrated Grey kicked Red for what he considered the rebellious act of a subservient race.

Red was taking a beating when his attacker received a gentle tap on his shoulder. He turned away from the merciless punishment he was dolling out long enough to see Steve's large fist arrive in front of a tremendous upper cut.

The crack could be heard on the other side of the room's thick walls. Literally, the vindictive alien's light body rose off the ground. If he wasn't dead, he'd definitely be asleep for awhile. Steve leaped over his body and scooped up Red in his arms. Space and Carol were loose and unstrapped. They joined Steve in a concerned attempt to revive their Martian ally and friend.

Everyone was huddled around Red as he came to. "Are you all right?" asked Carol.

Red struggled to sit up. "Yes, I believe so."

"How'd you get in here?" questioned Steve.

He pointed at the black box.

Spaceman shouldered a M16 rifle. "Hey look what I found over there."

"Anymore?" inquired Steve.

"Nope."

"How are we going to get to Bobby and Kim?" asked Carol.

Just then the steel door swung open, and the agents yelled in, "C'mon out with your hands over your heads!"

A control room had apparently been watching the whole affair on a surveillance camera mounted on the wall. The commandos outside were poised to commence firing. Spaceman stumbled and fell forward crouching low beneath a chair. His miscue accidentally sent off a burst of fire from the M16 he held. Steve and Carol looked on in terror-filled amazement as their clumsy friend raised his hands as if to say, "Whoops."

Outside a response came right away. Automatic gunfire riddled the large room. All four detainees realized they'd gotten in over their heads now. They were becoming desperate and yet, did not trust their captors enough to surrender.

Red laid face down trying to avoid being hit and suddenly got an idea. He yelled to Spaceman and asked him to get the black box lying just out of his reach. Spaceman bent over and stretched for the transposer. At that moment a hail of bullets bounced off the floor and caused an immediate retraction of his hand. Spaceman gasped for air. "Stevie, do me a favor, man? Grab that box for me, will you?"

Steve crawled closer while Spaceman remained behind the cabinet table that provided cover for the group.

"I'm not sticking my hand out there. Hey, give me your gun. I think I can hook it using the M16 as an extension."

Before moving, Steve spied the camera up in the corner. He said, "Get ready." He squeezed off a burst which shattered the camera and drew a heavy return fire from the troops.

"O.K.," he said and stretched out to hook the M16's tall gun sight around the box. The black box slid toward them through a light storm of ricocheting bullets. "Got it!" He tossed it over to Red.

Red's large mind was scheming away as he prepared to rise with his security blanket. Before standing he told Steve to remove the bullets from his weapon. A befuddled stare appeared at the strange request.

Carol asked, "What are you going to do, Red?"

"Did that fall affect your head?" questioned Steve.

"I sustained no serious injuries. You see, when I energize this transposer, the surrounding wave energy will ignite the chemicals in the shells. Please toss the bullets over by the door."

"I don't know, Red. This is our only defense."

"Incorrect. Do you trust me, Steve?"

Steve looked at his rifle and confidently said, "Absolutely."

"Good. I plan to disrupt our pursuers outside, then make my way to the power room and cut off all electrical power to this facility."

"Go for it, dude," Spaceman said.

"If you can pull that off, we've got a shot," reasoned Steve.

Carol suggested that Steve throw the bullets by the doorway as far from their position as possible. He disconnected the clip from the weapon and, along with an extra clip Spaceman had, lobbed them at the open door. It evoked another volley of fire in their direction.

Red pushed something on the box. There was no big reaction, only a waviness around the Martian. It was similar to what is seen when heat rises off hot pavement in the summer.

"Are you on?" asked Carol.

"Yes."

She reached over curiously to touch him and watched her hand slide right into his shoulder. He was there, but he wasn't there. A manipulation of space at the atomic level was taking place.

"Wow," Carol said in total amazement.

"I must hurry while the power supply lasts in the transposer."

Steve asked, "What do you want us to do?"

"Remain here until I cut the power."

"Good luck, Red."

The crowd that gathered outside the vault room door was armed to the teeth. Alarms rang out through the entire complex, putting everyone on alert. Red knew the power source in the black box was getting low. He made a direct path for the doorway. A murderous hail of lead passed through his image hitting the opposite walls behind him. The brave little alien stopped ten feet from the assault group and raised his hand.

"Please drop your weapons and ammunition before you depart."

An agent shouted back, "We're not going anywhere, you are."

"An unwise decision," concluded Red as he slowly approached them. The two bullet magazines Steve had thrown over were in close proximity to Red and began exploding loudly. Only seconds afterwards the soldiers prepared to open fire and were completely caught off guard by their own guns and ammunition belts randomly igniting.

The field effect caused by the transposer box had indeed set off the ammunition's powder exactly as Red had predicted. Bullets ripped everywhere instigating a chain reaction of panic among the soldiers. They dropped their guns before scrambling in retreat to evade the exploding cartridges. Two minutes of smoke and flash was preceded by an amazing sight. No one lay dead. All the attackers had crawled away save one wounded NSA man. Spaceman's buddy laid on the floor with two holes in his arm.

Red hardly noticed him as he worked the small black box and proceeded down the hall to find the electric power room. The first door he passed was marked "Arsenal." Considering what he carried in his hands, passing quickly by this room seemed like a good idea. If he got too close, he'd risk a major explosion that would destroy the entire base. Fifty feet away lay his destination: a door marked "Power Station."

He immediately turned and passed from the hall into the cramped equipment-laden room courtesy of the black box. Once inside the Transposer lost all power and went dead. His advantage had suddenly evaporated into thin air. Red made for the power breakers but was unable to shut them off. They would not budge due to large padlocks on all three lines. There seemed to be no way to cut the power. He'd come this far only to be stopped by three simple locks.

His sharp Martian mind went to work. Out of nowhere it came to him. A primitive plan. But it meant leaving himself vulnerable to attack. He had no choice.

Switching off the black box, Red opened the door that led to the hallway. He silently tiptoed to the arsenal and pulled out the guard's keys he had taken earlier. Once inside, Red searched for a specific item. Luck was with him. In a box marked "Grenades," he'd found what he'd come for. Three of the explosive balls were needed, one for each large circuit breaker. He would simply blow up the power lines feeding the base.

As Red proceeded with his plan, the whole base was being locked down tighter than a drum. The escape attempt had caused every exit to be sealed and guarded. Troops retreating from the vault room reported just how dangerous the prisoners were. In their hasty departure, however, they'd left the NSA agent to fend for himself. He sat quietly on the floor attempting to operate a small cellular phone with one hand. Steve and Carol had made their way nearby after hearing his rustling outside. They peeked out of the doorway and spied only the lone injured agent. Steve instantaneously leaped on top of him and slapped the phone from his hand. As Steve rose above him, Carol yelled, "Look out!"

The agent was trying to draw a knife with his good hand. Again Steve landed on him and got right in his face. "Not today, pal."

"We're not your enemy!" cried Carol.

The switchblade was extracted forcefully by the muscular surfer as the struggling operative spat on him in frustration.

Spaceman, watching the brawl, asked the government man, "Hey dude, was that a long distance call? If so, you need to dial 10-10-321 first, baby."

This only served to infuriate the new age mercenary. "You bastards think you're actually going to leave here alive?"

Steve answered, "Yeah and guess who's going with us?" He lifted the man to his feet. As he did, Steve noticed the government man wore a bright yellow neck tie. Steve grabbed it and commented, "I thought you Men in Black were allowed to wear only dark colors."

"Screw you."

Carol said, "I saw some handcuffs in the other room."

"Great. Go get them, honey." He turned to the agent. "You know, you're not a very nice man, Psycho."

"Screw you. I'm going to personally take care of you and your hippie friend over there."

Steve squeezed him by his injured arm and yelled, "Move it."

The procession cautiously traversed the empty hallway to find Red. Steve unexpectedly raised Psycho's knife when a door swung open ahead only to see their friend exiting the power room in a big hurry.

"Get to the ground!" Red yelled.

Everyone dove to the floor. A second later, Red landed on top of them. An ear shattering blast bounced off the walls followed closely by two more. The hall lights went out instantly. It was darker than a tomb with not a speck of light from any direction entering except for a few sparks popping under the Power room door.

"This is our opportunity," exclaimed Red.

"Who's got a light?" asked Steve.

Flick. A flame lit up the disoriented group's path. Spaceman's face was visible. One of his cigarettes he'd hid in his beard started to draw flame and give off its unmistakable aroma.

"Where'd you get that lighter?" asked Carol.

"Out of Psycho's pocket, man."

Red told everyone to follow his lead because his eyes could see better in low light. They formed a chain by holding hands. First Red, then Carol holding Steve who pulled the agent by his bad arm, and finally Spaceman bringing up the rear. He held the lighter which gave off just enough light for Red to lead the way. At the end of the dark corridor, they noticed the large steel exit door was now oddly open.

"That's curious. It's open," said Red.

"Be careful," cautioned Steve. "Go slowly and put Psycho up front."

Steve placed the knife at Psycho's back before they moved out in the direction of the elevator lobby. Four different corridors intersected at that location. Someone yelled, "Now!" which set off a startled reaction through the escapees. Portable lights flashed on revealing at least a half dozen troops stationed in each corridor. Their rifle barrels all converged at one point. Them. Bobby and Kim were also present. They stood gagged and bound, silently watching events develop. It was evident that their presence was required expressly as a bargaining chip.

Steve was told straight away to drop his weapons and to release the prisoner if he wished to live. The commando leader pointed at Bobby and Kim and said, "These two will die first." A lump formed in Steve's throat.

Carol assessed the overwhelming odds. "They'll kill them, Steve."

Reluctantly, he lowered the knife from Psycho's back. The commandos rushed them and relieved Steve of his weapon .

The head commando reported to Psycho, "The building is totally secured. What are your orders?"

"Hand me your pistol." Psycho started laughing but winced momentarily as a result of his wound. "Are you ready for payback?" Steve found the pistol cocked and pointed right at his temple. "Any last requests, wise guy?"

The top commando said, "Don't do it, sir." Most of the other soldiers looked on as if they questioned the counter-intelligence man's sanity.

"Stay out of this, Colonel."

Everyone expected to hear a bang as he tortuously delayed pulling the trigger.

The silence in the subterranean lobby was broken by the loud stampede of clattering footsteps. Both stairwells on either side of the powerless elevators spilled forth troops. One side emptied its cargo of high ranking military types, the other troops.

A voice rang out, "Put that gun down, now!"

The agent in charge turned around to discover who dared oppose him. His face grew white with shock. Before him stood the man he was accountable to— the Director of the NSA. Next to him was the Chairman of the Joint Chiefs.

NSA Director Johnson asked, "What the hell is going on down here, Ryker?"

"Prisoner interrogation, sir," responded the nervous agent. He knew he was in big trouble. Especially when Carol jumped up with tears streaming down her face.

"Daddy!"

"Honey, are you all right?"

"We are now."

"Are these your friends?"

Carol looked around and nodded.

"I brought Director Johnson with me. We're going to personally get to the bottom of this one." He glanced at Agent Ryker who hesitantly said, "Yes sir."

The commandos' leader stood down as what appeared to be Navy Seal teams moved in. They began assisting with the captives' departure. A Seal captain asked General Cole about Red.

Carol intervened right away. "You've got to listen to him, Dad. He came here to help us and to speak with you."

Her father told the captain to camouflage him and that he would be traveling with everyone else to Eglin. The whole group was moving to Eglin Air Force Base located on the Florida panhandle. Things could be much better sorted out there at its large facilities.

CHAPTER TWELVE

After a brief helicopter ride to an air strip, Preston Cole, Director Johnson, Carol, and Steve all boarded a military Lear jet for the ride to Eglin Air Force Base. Red, Spaceman, Bobby, Kim and the Seal teams would make the trip to the air force base in slower helicopters. On board the plush jet, Carol hugged her father genuinely and formally introduced him to Steve. She went on to explain how the Greys planned to eliminate humans utilizing an asteroid deliberately guided into the Earth. Carol's father, a man who always maintained a calm demeanor, raised his eyebrows as she described their efforts to foil these plans. Carol brought up her friends' bravery and determination in stopping the diabolical schemes. She told him of Red, a true friend and ally to his earthly neighbors, and how he came here to warn humans of the Greys' treachery. Along with his sponsors from the Alignment group, they had set out to terminate all meddling in Earth's natural evolution.

Preston Cole simply sat alertly with his mouth open, listening in disbelief to his little girl's story of personal survival and heroic deeds. He shook his head. "My God, Carol. Do you know how lucky you are to be alive?"

"Yes. But I did what I thought was right."

"I know, honey, and I'm very proud of you."

Director Johnson questioned Steve. "You mean the Greys are advising our SDI personnel to shoot down benevolent groups approaching this planet?"

"Yes sir. They told us directly before they thought we were to be killed."

"Hmmm, this information will be very valuable."

Chairman Cole was now listening. "Were you both very near the explosion occurring in that swamp outside Melbourne?"

Steve answered, "A Grey ship was hiding there. Its mission was to direct a small asteroid in its final approach to impact Earth. Fortunately the alien alignment group fired a beam weapon destroying the ship and causing the explosion. Our friend, Red, targeted the craft for destruction just in time."

"Incredible," commented the chairman.

"Apparently there are other outside groups trying to prevent Grey intervention in our civilization," formulated Steve.

"Yes son, we are aware of their existence," admitted Carol's father.

The two military men got quiet as they thought over the implications of the recent news just revealed to them. Director Johnson made eye contact with Chairman Cole whom met his stare and exhibited the same deep concerns.

"This only verifies suspicions we've had, Preston. The other members must hear the evidence for themselves."

"You're right."

A small room containing a table and phone was located toward the front of the cabin. Carol's father departed to it and got on the phone. Once Director Johnson entered, the door was closed. One of the three armed sentries at the rear of the plane came forward to guard the door.

Carol slid across the empty seat closing the gap between her and Steve. She rested her head on his chest and they embraced.

Steve said, "I've got to wonder if we're not better off being in the dark when it comes to these things. Some of the reasons for secrecy are now abundantly clear."

"I know having this knowledge can be very disruptive and upsetting."

"Carol, I give your father a lot of credit. Having to deal with this ongoing problem ."

"Yeah, he's great."

"Carol, when this is over, I wish you'd think about finishing up school down here in Florida."

She lifted her head, "You do?"

"Yes."

"But where would I live?"

"Oh, I know of an inexpensive place right on the beach."

She smiled at him, and they kissed passionately. Carol flipped out the overhead light and they pretended the two sentries posted in the rear of the cabin didn't exist. They could feel the jet slowly descending after a short westerly flight across the Florida peninsula.

Once the air craft landed on the ground at Eglin Air Force Base, a long black limousine arrived to greet the travelers. Government leaders of the caliber aboard the Lear jet seldom ventured out into the field for these incidents. However, the very personal involvement forced Chairman Cole and his friend, Director Johnson, to climb down into the trenches. Discovering the truth first hand would be a positive experience for both policy makers. The wakeup call was necessary, although what steps could be implemented to remedy this sensitive situation remained elusive. After all they were dealing with a very powerful and highly advanced race.

In any event, the two defense minded leaders knew the other members of MJ12 needed the same dose of reality they'd received. The compelling proof relayed by the saucer salvers, especially their rescued friend Red, left no doubt. Red's very presence spoke volumes. Both men knew there remained members unconvinced the Greys were not trustworthy. Chairman Cole pondered a way to leave no doubt in other members' minds as to the actual intentions of their so-called allies, the Greys. A precedent setting idea came to him. It involved presenting reliable witnesses face to face with the ultra-secret MJ12 at their meeting facility in the Naval Observatory in Washington, DC. No one had ever been permitted to witness the Jason Scholars, as they refer to each other, in operation. The recent near devastating threat well warranted the unusual breach of security.

Everyone was taken to eat, shower, and grab some sleep. The following day after breakfast, guards escorted the entire group to a meeting room. Kim kept asking when they'd be released, but no answer was forthcoming, even though Carol's father was there. The entire trip had left everyone unsettled. The constant presence of the guards never allowed them to relax.

Upon entering the large conference room, the group saw Carol's father talking with four officers and the base commander. All detainees, including Carol, were guided to their seats in front of the military men. Most of the officers departed, and the exits were locked down by the Seal teams. Preston Cole leaned forward and surveyed the anxious group. Pointing at Bobby and Kim, he said, "You two are free to go. Our security people will have you sign the necessary National Security oaths and inform you of the dire consequences of not complying with them. A helicopter will return you to the East Coast today."

"What about the others?" questioned Kim.

"They'll be joining you later. And on behalf of our country, I thank you for your efforts in a most difficult situation."

Two security guards quickly materialized and escorted Bobby and Kim from the room. Some brief hugs and good-byes ensued before Chairman Cole left his desk and stood right before the remaining patriots.

"Now, I need to ask you all a favor. Would you all accompany Director Johnson and myself to Washington for the purpose of explaining your accounts of this incident to an authority capable of acting on its vital information?"

Spaceman spoke first. "No problemo."

"I'd be glad to, sir," seconded Steve.

"They'll all help you, Daddy," uttered Carol.

Her father stared at the quiet member sitting silently fidgeting with his new clothes and golf hat covering his head.

"Red, will you go?" asked Carol.

"Yes."

"Good," said the chairman. "Your testimony above all others is crucial to understanding the threat."

"How could I not go. This is why I've come," Red softly told him.

Something was bothering Carol's father. He began studying Spaceman as if he recognized him. There was a familiarity he felt with the tattered, grungy bearded beach bum. Finally the words came out. "You, sir, look very familiar to me. Was it Vietnam?"

"No baby. My step-father was an original member of MJ12."

"Of course, Commander Whitson."

"Correctamundo."

Carol intervened, "Daddy, without his assistance, we'd never have stopped the Greys. He borrowed one of your airplanes and saved us all."

"So you're the one who stole the Harrier."

A nervous Spaceman replied, "I, like, had no time to do anything but act."

"Relax, your actions meet the highest standards of bravery. You're a national hero. You and the others will receive the Medal of Honor. Of course no one outside of this room can possibly ever know the reason why."

Steve stood up. "Sir, perhaps you could look into Commander Whitson's file. The commander had some damaging injustices perpetrated on him in the past and should be compensated."

Chairman Cole signaled an aide over who pulled pad and pen from his pocket. He said, "Captain, get to the bottom of this for me, will you please?"

"Yes sir."

Steve was satisfied by the response. He smiled at Spaceman who was preparing to show some emotion. They both sat down.

"All right people. We will leave for Washington immediately aboard my plane. The only responsibility you have is to retell any pertinent information as it occurred.

(Washington, DC)

At eight o'clock in the morning two black limousines with darkened windows pulled under the portico at the back entrance to the Naval Observatory. Plain clothes agents closely chaperoned all four witnesses inside. They were escorted to an elevator which descended underground.

Spaceman became very nervous. This was a homecoming of sorts for him. He had been on this very elevator at times in the past. Those memories, for the most part, he preferred to leave buried.

When they had dropped a number of levels below the street, the elevator opened to a small hallway. At the end or it, lay two large metallic doors. Two highly decorated Marine guards blocked the entrance. The massive doors opened electronically as soon as one of the escorting agents slid a card in its security slot. At this, both sentries saluted and stood aside.

As the witnesses entered, Steve took notice of the heavy oak paneling lining the spacious chamber. It would put to shame many a corporate board room. Twelve high back mahogany chairs encircled a lavishly carved horseshoe-shaped table, awaiting their owners' arrival. Off to the side of the room were computer terminal along with tables and desks for support staff which also lined the walls of the huge room. Four men who outwardly appeared to be dressed as janitors were just finishing up passing some strange electronic gear over the furniture. They definitely were not the types of individuals to be working as custodians.

As they departed, one of the agents assigned to the visitors asked, "Are we clean?"

"Totally clean for the meeting, sir."

"Thank you."

Steve was extremely curious and whispered to Space, "What was that all about?"

"They're sweeping for alien bugs, Stevie."

"In here?"

"Oh yeah."

Red stood up from his seat, barely visible under the oversized golf hat which concealed his head. He walked toward Steve. Two chaperoning agents carefully followed staying right on top of his every move. Red halted by Steve and peered at the chair supporting him.

"Excuse me, but there is another type of listening device present."

"Where?" Steve asked.

"Beneath your chair."

Spaceman said, "The technicians cleared the area, little buddy."

The agent who had spoken to the phony janitors joined the conversation, "Something wrong?"

"Our friend says there's a bug under that chair," exclaimed Carol.

"That's impossible. It's been cleared."

Red turned toward the agent and said, "Your devices are very sensitive, but they measure on the electromagnetic spectrum. The device I refer to contains no electronic material. Its components are made of carbon-based human materials such as collagen, calcium carbonate, and other non-detectable substances. It broadcasts via telepathy not electromagnetic waves. Hence, undetectable."

The doubting agent demanded, "So, how do you know it's here?"

"Simple, I'm also picking up the broadcast in my telepathically receptive mind."

Red reached under Steve's chair and extracted a small beige-colored round wafer. The flat object only measured the diameter of an aspirin. It slid around in the palm of Red's hand under its own power as if it were alive or remotely controlled.

Closing his hand on the device, Red continued his explanation. "This bio-device is similar to BTL implants used by Greys in human bodies. Except this transmitter is much more powerful. The crystalline structures in my brain tissue allow me to receive its transmissions."

The agent stood motionless as did everyone else, awestruck by the depth of espionage capabilities revealed.

"That's a new one on me, man," Spaceman proclaimed.

"God...," said Carol.

"Get me a tech team on the double!" ordered the agent to his men.

The small object became restless and skittered back and forth on Red's palm. It tried to secure a hiding place but was unable. Two of the phony janitors rushed in to examine Red's find. They quickly produced a tweezer-like instrument and placed the object in a container only to be put inside another. When it became evident that the bug was secured, they scurried off.

"Is anything safe from their technological intrusions?" asked Carol.

"Not much," responded Spaceman. "When my step-dad was a member of this body he had to endure a battery of test once a month to check for implants."

"You mean, my father goes through that?" Carol wondered.

"Like, I don't know what they're doing nowadays, but I'm sure it's some kind of high-tech scanning."

"This is insanity," she concluded.

"No, baby. Actually, it's reality."

The guards circumvented the chamber and kept a close watch over their unusual guests. After all, this was truly a major precedent-setting event. Actual witnesses were taking part in the most secretive organization in the annals of human history. Under Project Aquarius, this group's mission is to study and learn everything possible pertaining to the alien cultures who are here studying us. They also are the policy-making arm of the government and military in these matters. It was expressly established in 1947 to shield the public and deal with the clear and present danger. A highly skeptical and controlled public doesn't have a clue to the truth. The fifty years the government has been aware of their presence pales in comparison to the length of time some of these alien groups have been visiting our planet. Some for research, some for experimentation, and most for discovery. All activities are carried on in secret which is why people only see glimpses of fleeting aerial discs. The secrecy is in adherence with long standing treaties for the non-intervention of evolving cultures and planets.

Carol's father entered the room and stopped to ask his guests if they needed anything. Then he explained that the other members would be arriving shortly. Each one had received a complete report on the entire affair last night. Chairman Cole tapped Red from behind and thanked him for discovering the eavesdropping device.

Red warned the chairman that MJ12 must remain on constant vigil when battling this type of problem. He said, "This place was to be my second destination upon eliminating the threat to Earthians. I have important messages for you."

"You'll get your chance in a minute, my friend."

Members of the Jason Scholars began arriving. Officers, attaches, and secretaries escorted their bosses inside. A large, sound-proof plexi-glass wall was about to move. Its purpose was to shroud the staff in privacy so highly classified topics could be discussed by the need-to-know members. Steve noticed some of members were powerful people he'd seen on TV or in newspapers. The directors of the FBI and CIA entered sitting at the grand horseshoe-shaped table. The Secretary of Defense joined them, nodding to the unorthodox visitors. It was like a "Who's Who" of the Department of Defense and government agencies. But members from outside organizations also showed up. A noted astronomer appeared along with two egghead characters exuding an air of scientific prominence. Then a five-star admiral, no doubt in charge of Navel Operations arrived. The presence of this high-caliber leadership from every arena was impressive. Carol's father and Director Johnson took their places to start the meeting. All the Jason Scholars were present. Due to the unusual guests in attendance they refrained from addressing one another in their J code names.

Guards moved to close the exits and secure the room from the outside world. Chairman Cole rose to his feet. "Gentlemen, this emergency meeting was called in light of recent information indicating a direct threat to our National Security along with an even greater danger to the very survival of humans on this planet. As you have read in last night's reports on the incident, this threat originates with a so-called U.S. ally. It has long been known that this forced alliance with the Grey race has been suspect at best. The recent incident has validated many members' suspicions. As incredible as it sounds, my own daughter, while vacationing in Florida, was caught up in the plot. Due to the near cataclysmic event almost set in motion by the Greys, I've asked my daughter and her friends involved to speak before this council. Especially an EBE they rescued named Red sent here to warn our military of the impending treachery. With that said, I'd like Steve Wilcox to step forward and extrapolate on the incident in Florida."

Steve rose and strode between the intimidating panel of members. "Gentlemen, I am no expert on the subject of alien races. I do have a better than average knowledge, though, because of information leaks in recent years and my association with the former Naval Intelligence Officer sitting over there. In fact, he's an extremely brave and patriotic man. Without his experience and efforts, none of us would be alive today.

"The alien plan to impact an asteroid into Earth thereby killing its human inhabitants was brought to our attention by another hero. This individual, known as Red, was saved by our friends when his spacecraft was mistakenly shot down by our SDI satellites. His story was instrumental in our success. Unlike other outside groups he is indeed an ally and true friend to humanity. No one would be sitting here today if he hadn't journeyed here to help.

The only real point I'd personally like to make is that the need for vigilance has never been higher. Man's very survival may depend on not becoming complacent and placing too much trust in these outsiders. From what I've witnessed in the last few days, it appears no security measure is too severe when dealing with these more highly evolved cultures. It occurs to me that if a threat does materialize, it won't come in conventional battle strategies we are accustomed to. The assault will consist of a far more sophisticated and deceptive conquest. I certainly don't envy your responsibilities, due to the extreme difficulty and confusion involved in your tasks. One last thing I would say is people must be told of the danger so they aren't totally blind to the threat. I believe that to be the greatest peril to mankind. Not knowing."

Steve looked down and said, "That's all I've got to say." He walked back to his seat. Not a sound could be heard at the members' table.

After a moment Preston Cole exclaimed, "Thank you, Mr. Wilcox for you input. Carol?" he said waving her up.

She confidently proceeded toward her father, kissed him, and began her testimony. "Some of the information and knowledge I've acquired recently is quite mind-boggling. I've learned the public's reality of human life and the universe is for the most part inaccurate. I've also discovered we most definitely are not alone in the cosmos. Just as in humanity, there are some good individuals, so to does this phenomena exists in other intelligent life. The two types of aliens I personally experienced may have had similar body shapes, but that's where the likeness ends. Our friend, Red, is caring, has integrity, and respect for different cultures. As Steve said, he was sent here by the benevolent Alignment group to assist in our defense against the Greys' destructive agenda.

"They are the others I've met. This group maintains a secret treaty with us. These creatures are arrogant, deceptive, and violate universal laws with regularity. I only wish I could ask them right now why we all can't simply be more tolerant and live together in peace. After all the Hubbell Telescope has recently shown the universe to be a very big place. There's enough room for everyone to live and thrive. I fail to understand how these highly intelligent beings can totally disregard the rights of other civilizations who are still developing and no threat to them. This destructive meddling attitude exhibited by the Greys doesn't show me a high level of intelligence. On the contrary, aggressive destruction denotes a more primitive ignorance found in lower life forms or worse, a premeditated evil disregard. I have nothing else to say."

This testimony had upset Carol a bit and she wiped tears from her face. She hugged her father before sitting down.

He whispered, "Good job. I love you."

She returned to her seat and was comforted by Steve.

Next to be called to speak was Spaceman. "Commander Whitson?" announced the chairman.

Spaceman had been fighting off a tremendous urge to light up one of his cigarettes. Although his mind seemed unusually clear. Some of the older members of the distinguished panel strained to recognize Commander Whitson beneath the unshaven long haired beach comber disguise.

"Ahhh Gentlemen, excuse me, man. I'm trying to control my emotions. I've been in this building many times years ago. A few of you, I'm sure, remember my step-father who was an original member of this body. Things were different back then. When I served under your policies through various related agencies, there was no real cooperation and close dealings with the outsiders. But now it seems we not only communicate regularly but also consider certain groups allies. However, even years ago I witnessed disturbing activities perpetrated by the group known as Greys.

"For the most part our side does an excellent job managing a truly overwhelming problem. But man, there are rotten apples present whose motives are more greed oriented than protecting our National Security. They need to be weeded out. The fact is, baby, any organization without open accountability can easily spiral out of control and fall susceptible to greed and corruption. The crooks should be called on the carpet. Deals made with aliens for personal gain, harassment of citizens instead of protecting them, are all unaddressed problems. An internal policing unit would help ensure these covert agencies operate at least sometimes within the framework of the law.

"Beyond that little snafu, the threat of alien infiltration into our military high command is a very real one. We just like saw it earlier in this very room after your security team declared the room clean. An alien bug was removed from that chair over there. The sophisticated techniques employed from human implants to totally genetically engineered human beings with alien orientation are a constant danger, man.

"At times while in the service I would wonder just who was shaping policy at the top, us or them. Their level of technological advancement could allow for one of them to be sitting quite comfortably among us in this very room. But you all know that.

"Finally, I believe, as I have in the past, the people need to be told the truth. Man, everyone has a right to know and just be aware that we are not alone. For my belief in this idea years ago, I was eventually discredited, severely brain washed and dishonorably discharged. I harbor no ill feelings, man. My belief in the absolute importance of disclosure to the public is still stronger than ever. I'm a patriot and will always believe in this country. Like I know about the emergency plans existing since 1948 to alert the public if it became absolutely necessary. Frankly it didn't work or wouldn't have if the Greys' plans had been successful yesterday. People are not even aware of this threat to their survival and that alarms me, man. It's time to deal with reality and let the chips fall where they may."

Spaceman took a deep breath, "That's all for me."

Commander Whitson went back to his seat appearing to have lifted a tremendous weight off his chest. The members he'd addressed sat in deep thought quietly glancing at one another while exhibiting an uneasiness not there before.

The blunt, unscented observations pulled no punches and had them squirming in their seats. A large dose of reality had been served up by Spaceman and it wasn't pleasant. This was a different view that was presented by someone willing to see things as they truly are and not conveniently assume all is under control.

Chairman Cole's pace quickened as a result of Spaceman's comments. Red was summoned next to speak before the gathering. Unlike the two previous speakers, two guards rushed over to escort the tiny alien to the forefront. The small Martian removed his extra-large golf hat and exposed his oversized cranium. None of the members were shocked or even surprised by the oddity. Due in part to having seen and even negotiated with various alien groups in the past. Especially the dominant Grey race.

"Honored leaders," Red began. "I have come here representing the Alignment, the group with which many of you are familiar. This organization is attempting to stop any interference and disregard for universal laws regarding planets being perpetrated by the Grey culture. The Greys covert alliance with your military is a false and hollow agreement. Their intentions are far from honorable.

"Many of you have never seen a Martian for the simple fact that we are held prisoners beneath the surface of our own planet by the Greys. My people's saga of capitulation and subjugation needs to be told to Earthians as a warning. You would do well to heed the words of Mr. Spaceman for he speaks the truth. History very nearly repeated itself in the last few days. Greys tried to stop me from reaching you. However, these brave individuals sitting behind me made it possible to achieve my mission. The Alignment group that sent me is very powerful and believes in the sovereignty of developing civilizations. It was their decision to terminate the Greys' ship in Florida—punishment for continual violations.

"My personal message to Earthians is a warning. A warning not to allow Earth to succumb to the same fate as Mars did hundreds of thousands of years ago. A fate suffered at the hands of the Greys' genetic experimentation and eventual conquest. The Martians who were not killed in the asteroid blast were genetically altered and to this day serve our oppressors. I'm a hybrid myself. Although we have some Grey traits as Earthians do, we are by no means pure, and therefore subservient. We are mear slaves.

"The Alignment will be visiting this body soon to assist you in anyway necessary in deterring any future threats. They will signal your Nevada listening station with the normal pulsed wave signals in exactly one month.

"In closing, I would like to reiterate my deep-felt gratitude to the courageous friends I've made in the last two days. If your people all possess their qualities, the human race will no doubt survive and prosper. This is all I can say to you now."

"Thank you, Red," uttered Chairman Cole. "You speak English quite well. On behalf of all humans, I thank you for your crucial help in preventing this near cataclysm. We will always be indebted to you and the Alignment. The warning you've delivered has arrived at the proper destination and will be acted upon immediately."

Carol's father announced the next speaker. He was a member of the Jason Scholars. Dr. Watson, the senior policy maker, desired to present a brief explanation of the subject to their honored guests. He felt it necessary to clarify policy upon hearing these incredible stories.

"Courageous guests. You must understand the importance of such a high level of security involving Project Aquarius, or as you know it, the Alien issue. The fact that intelligent life not only exists but has visited Earth countless times and are here currently, was determined to be too devastating to our culture if divulged back in 1947. It was thought this information would rip apart our society at the seams. That is why such a determined effort of debunking and discrediting anyone bringing attention to it is ongoing to this day.

"Also, it is believed that a disclosure of this nature would turn man's belief system upside down. Disclosure can not occur abruptly. A scheduled plan of gradual desensitization is in effect because we hope to eventually fit into the galactic community out there one day. Your disturbing incident with the Greys was not totally unexpected. We didn't know their exact methods and times. They've bullied us from the beginning in the late forties. Ours is a very uneasy alliance. The promise of assistance from the Alignment is very welcomed news indeed. It will allow us more autonomy in decisions related to sensitive defense issues.

"You must consider there are many different races of intelligent life traveling the cosmos. Most bend time and space to arrive here and secretly study us. It is crucial that humans are not influenced by these future beings, some of which are decendants of Earth itself. We must live and develop in our natural time flow. But presently there are, and have been, plans to accelerate our evolution as seen in recent technological leaps. These leaps are needed, not only to make life easier, but to defend ourselves against the possibility of non-benevolent intervention, such as you witnessed first-hand in Florida.

"Although we members are still learning to comprehend and deal with this very complicated problem, there is great promise and hope amidst the gloom. It was brought here by future descendants of Earth, as I mentioned previously. Just as we differ from the bi-pedal apes of a half million years ago, so too do they contrast with our present evolutionary forms. The primary message is one of hope. Mankind will survive well into the future. You see, the very existence of the group I speak of, guarantees man's longevity." Dr. Watson paused and looked into the faces of the guests. They were convinced that what he said was true.

"Thank you, Doctor," commented the chairman. "I would like to add to Dr. Watson's words by addressing the security concerns you've made.

175

"Our budget for Security is in the many billions of dollars on these projects. The security is excellent but always can be better, especially when confronting a superior, technologically advanced threat. We must also guard against corruption in our ranks. Operatives in our covert services have little accountability and sometimes too much power. Those actions we can try to control with stricter supervision. Treachery by so-called benevolent alien groups is another matter. In our dealings with them, closer inspections and verifications of actions will be increased where possible. Benevolent friends have warned us in the past concerning similar incidents of outside interference. And now with the Alignment's help, our security nightmare will be somewhat diminished."

"Everyone here has done a tremendous job not only in protecting this country's National Security, but the well-being of the entire globe. Again, your country thanks you."

Carol's father walked past her and whispered, "I'll see you at home this evening, honey," and motioned for the guards to escort the group out. Each visitor was to be given three separate National Security oaths to sign and had to sit through a brief series of explanations about consequences. These consequences were extremely severe and would only be initiated if they broke their oaths and spoke to anyone about the matter.

The group finished with their promises of allegiance and filed toward the exits. Carol noticed Red had been detained by four large MPs.

She asked Steve and Spaceman, "Where are they taking Red?"

"Not with us, man," uttered Space.

Carol yelled to her father who was standing just across the room. He left the other Jason Scholars who were still seated and made his way to his daughter. Carol asked, "Dad, why are they holding Red? Can't he go with us?"

"I'm afraid not, honey. That's standard procedure with any EBEs taken in a crash. Especially if they originate from an unknown destination. He could never be allowed to be free among the general population. At least, not presently."

"It's not fair. It's just not fair."

"Don't worry. He'll be well taken care of in our specially maintained underground environments we operate. He'll be fine."

The three friends moved to bid farewell to their fourth partner, knowing they'd never see him again. Carol's tears rested high on her cheek bones as she hugged her friend good-bye.

"Do not worry," Red said. If he had less emotions than humans, it certainly wasn't evident in his farewell to Carol. Steve shook his hand and then hugged him while trying not to squish his fragile body.

"Thanks for everything, Red."

"Thank you."

Spaceman came over and pulled the smaller Red up against his fuzzy beard, evoking a small sneeze out of the Martian. "Be cool, baby!"

"I'm always aware of local temperature gradients."

"O.K. man, we love ya."

"Goodbye my friends, I will not forget you."

With that, the room was emptied of its visitors allowing MJ12 the normal security conditions for its policy makers to proceed with the work at hand.

Spaceman, Steve, and Carol were spirited out of the building to a black Suburban which had its windows darkened. Outside the sky grew very dark due to an approaching thunderstorm. Behind their vehicle, a second SUV sat awaiting a well camouflaged Red completely encircled by MPs and agents.

Upon moving to the second vehicle, a very bright light came on, illuminating the entire side of the building. Panicked voices of MPs and security men rang out as a result. A beam of blue light extended down from the overcast skies. Carol and Steve could see the burst of light through their darkened windows. They lowered the glass in time to witness Red being drawn up off the ground. The surrounding guards seemed incapable of movement while their prisoner rose effortlessly into the air. Red caught sight of his friends in the first truck and smiled at them with his right hand waving good-bye. He rose higher and higher in the tube of blue light getting ever closer to its source.

The large outline of a ship approximately three hundred feet across was barely visible in the fog-like air. Rows of bright colored lights lining its exterior edges materialized suddenly in plain view of the terrestrial observers. Their small Martian comrade disappeared along with the blue light traveling directly through the craft's metal underbelly.

On the ground alarms sounded everywhere. Scurrying security people and MPs looked up in frustration realizing they were powerless against such technology.

Apparently Red's taxi ride home had arrived and the meter wasn't running long before the Alignment's ship's gravitational amplifiers kicked on. Without as much as a pin dropping, the huge object was sling-shotted away from the Earth. Our planet's gravity rendered no affect whatsoever on its instantaneously achieved flight speed.

"Wow," said Carol.

"You're not kidding," seconded Steve.

"We'll be doing that in a hundred years or so," commented Spaceman.

"It's inevitable," said Steve.

"I'm glad Red got away. He'll be much happier with his own kind," professed Carol.

"Yeah, he's a pretty good friend, Carol. I've got a lot of respect for that little guy."

"And that's the key to co-existing among all the intelligent life," she added.

Spaceman looked at his two friends next to him and said, "Right on, baby."

177

(One month later. Port Canaveral Pier Florida)
The beautiful sailboat sat at the marina with engines idling in a smooth low hum. Its captain arose from below decks, his fuzzy beard blowing in the breeze. On the stern deck, Steve, Carol, Bobby, and Kim reclined comfortably in their loungers.

"Beautiful, Space," complimented Steve.

"Yeah, it's a real beauty," added Bobby.

"Thanks, man. It sure beats my old place under the boardwalk."

"So they gave you a nice settlement?" added Carol.

"Yeah, man. Thank your dad again for me. He's cool."

"They owed it to you," she replied.

Spaceman pulled out the ribbon-like material just under his shirt which held a medal at the end. "I thought you guys would, like, be wearing yours, too!"

"Mine's hanging over my mantle at home," answered Steve. They referred to the Metal of Honor which was presented to everyone involved by the Pentagon. Along with the honor came the sworn oath of never revealing the why and how of its presentation. Each person had signed enough National Security documents promising silence to fill a large notebook.

Carol just finished pouring Pina Coladas for everyone to toast their success when a late arriving voice echoed from the dock.

"Aye, Steverino."

It was Captain Al with his medal draped around his neck. He waved to everyone and then caught sight of Spaceman. He yelled, "Aye, I got a score to settle with you, Skippy, for the dunking you gave me in the river."

Carol reached over and threw the stern line onto the dock. Without the engine engaged the sleek vessel continued drifting slowly away from its berth.

Al jogged down and grabbed the end of the line. He wrapped it around his forearm in an attempt to prevent the craft's premature departure. "Don't you ignore me, Skippy," Al shouted while momentarily halting the boat's drift.

Spaceman pretended he didn't see the irate Captain and gently leaned on the throttle. A short burst of thrust was initiated. Al immediately found himself in mid-air, parallel to the water and about to water-ski on his belly. Everyone shouted for Spaceman to cut the engine.

In a state of surprise, he pulled back on the throttle. An inquisitive expression came across his face. The others were doubled over with laughter.

"Like, what happened back there?" Space asked innocently.

Steve smirked, "He's going to be awfully pissed."

"That's cool, baby."

ABOUT THE AUTHOR

A graduate of Hofstra University, Rocky was a top insurance salesman in New York until moving to the Cape Canaveral area of Florida in the early nineties. At that time he developed a deep interest in ufology, in particular the military and government connection. Acquaintances in the area related many similar recollections of military operations involving experiences dealing with ultra-secret alien encounters. The research he conducted, spurred on by personal sightings, turned up mountains of information that in turn formed the basis of his stories. He currently lives with his wife in Satellite Beach, Florida.

Printed in the United States
19043LVS00002B/283-366